A GOD OF WAR

By

Enn Kae

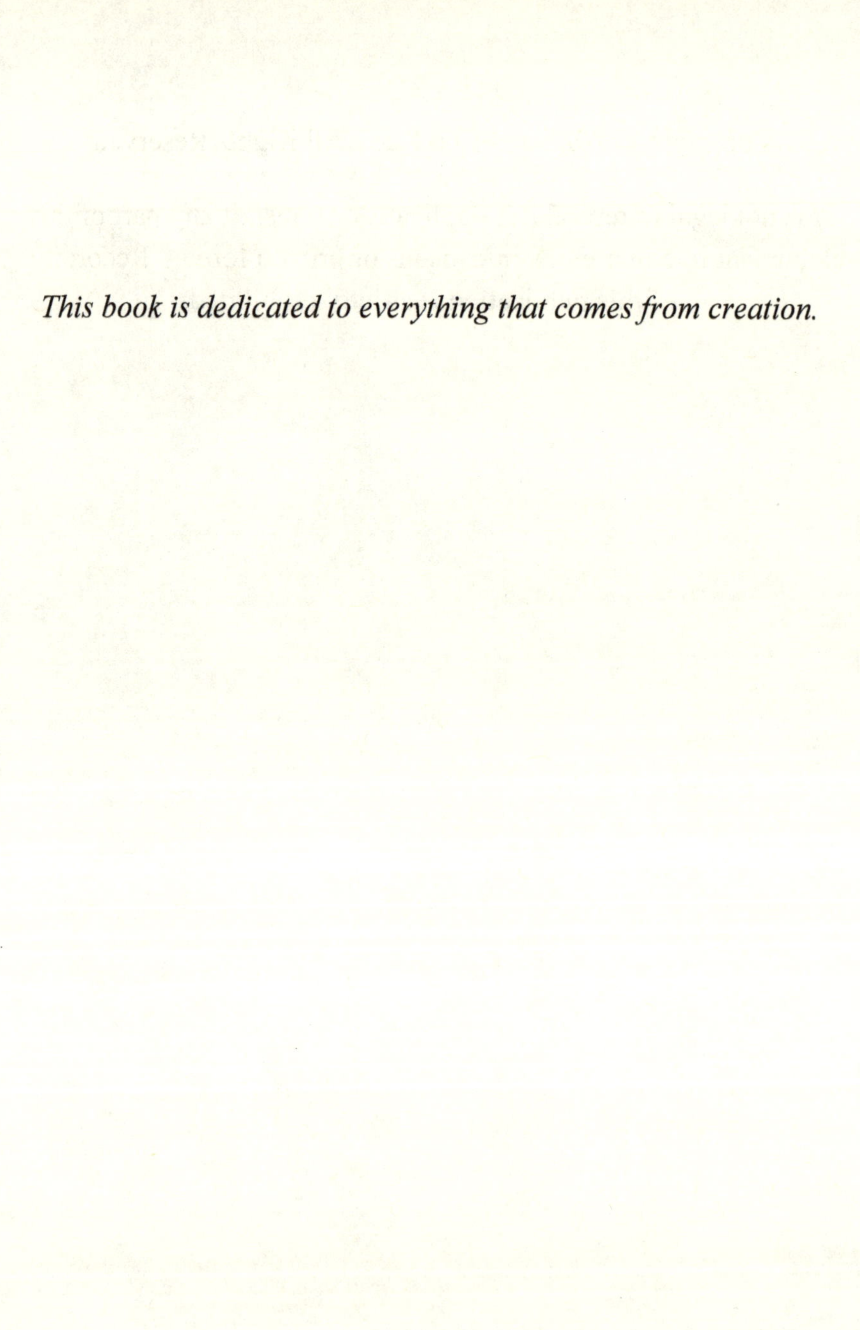

This book is dedicated to everything that comes from creation.

Acknowledgment

The immense amount of work that Zachariah Sitchin did in translating the Ancient Sumerian cuneiform data, breathed life into this story. I would also like to acknowledge the work of Linda Moulton Howe, for paving the way to an understanding of the existence of our galactic family.

About the Author

Enn Kae is a seer, a visionary. He writes to free humanity from their shackles. His writings resonate with the struggle between the human spirit and the fabrications of this world and technology.

Contents

"Beware, the military industrial complex"

President Eisenhower's Farewell Speech, January 1961.

Foreward

Two step-brothers landed on Earth, from Planet Niburu millenia ago. One was called En.Lil and the other was called En.Ki. They were the Annunaki. The character by the name of En.Ki in this story is not to be confused with my author's name - Enn Kae - which is the phonetic sound of my initials N K. I am not a God, nor an alien. Just a writer. Now that's out of the way, I hope you enjoy the ride. Buckle up!

Chapter 1

You can't get to the truth if you aren't awake to the lies that are being told around you. We spend most of our lives asleep, walking through it, idly watching the time go by, some of us alone, some with our families. If we do wake up, we can start to change the world, using only our imagination. Because that's all this world is made up of: our imagination, my imagination and your imagination. All working simultaneously. When our imaginations don't match, we get conflict. Waking up is like being able to see all the different realities around you. Having the ability to project your imagination, regardless of what is being projected around you, onto you, is what differentiates us from the rest. The winners are the ones who can create their own reality.

I look at the fellas around me and I sometimes wonder how they got there. How did they get to be their age and not question what they're being told? Maybe they did, when they were my age, but even kids in high school just want to fit in, blend in with the crowd. But, under the surface, they long to say or do what they want. Eventually, they'll end up rebelling, doing things they shouldn't be doing. Indulging in misguided rebellion. But true rebellion involves questioning. When kids get to school, they learn that they must toe the line, in order to become successful. I don't know anyone who doesn't toe the line, if they want to fit in. Only the bums reject everything they are taught. That's why they're bums. They just can't fit in. And that's why nobody questions things but, instead, they choose to walk through life asleep.

As we go through life, we come across the snakes, baboons and chameleons. Snakes are at the top of the food chain. They keep everyone in check, to make sure everyone toes the line. They poison your spirit or try to destroy you for having one. The baboons are the jokers. They make people laugh about the way the world is, but they are utterly depressed because they don't have nor ever will have the level of power that the snakes possess, nor the power to affect any change. Lastly, the chameleons. They will change like the wind to simply fit in because their biggest fear is not being able to fit in. Chameleons have no identity but a lot of spirit. Both the snakes and the baboons hate and mock them for being disingenuous.

School is like that. I see it every day. Not only with the kids but with the teachers. They hate each other, hiding behind a façade of fake smiles and posturing. We all know they hate each other as much as they hate us. The teachers that still have a spark get hounded out of their jobs. We've had a few teachers leave our high school here in Sandy Springs over the years. The kids are alright and we're in an okay area. Mostly white kids, some Hispanics and just enough blacks that the area and district will permit. We have to maintain our world the way it is. This is our reality.

We're pretty safe here, in Sandy Springs. Life ticks by slowly but safely. There isn't a real threat to who we are. Our identity is at least intact, safe from intrusion. We salute the flag every morning and sing in church every Sunday. And, as long as the foreigners follow our rules, we consider them a fine bunch of people. We don't like too much mixing here. We don't want to change the world that we imagine it to be. We like what we like and that's that. It's just who we are. It's sad that a lot of folks, particularly them up north, in DC, don't understand that. Always trying to push their agenda upon us. Guess God made some of us different and that's all there is to it.

That's what my Dad says. And my Mom agrees. In actual fact, you'll seldom see them disagree. Dad used to be a General in the Air Force, serving our Great Nation. They met after college, when they both returned home from their studies, away from Sandy Springs. Mom studied out West in California and Dad studied over in Boston. Dad joined the service whilst he was in school. Mom didn't pursue her career in journalism. She opted to become a homemaker, after they met in Sandy Springs and got married to my father. I often wonder if Mom didn't want to stick out, here in Sandy Springs. Being a mother and having a career isn't exactly what would make a woman fit in around here.

Mom is the real glue though, she's the one who keeps us all three together: Me, Mom and Dad. Dad does best to provide us all with a good life. He works hard for us and he's a decorated war hero. Recently Dad has started to do some recruitment at our school, which he started a few summers ago. Every summer, he will try to recruit for the Air Force, trying to catch some of the seniors who are leaving school with no direction, hoping to catch them and to use their potential in a structured environment, where they might flourish.

I wasn't too far off from leaving school when I had to make a decision. I wasn't sure at first. I told myself that, if I did decide to join up, I would make damn sure that I was ready to serve. It always was a big thing, seeing Dad at school before school was out for the summer. Everyone always came up to me and asked if that's my Dad. And I was always quick off the bat: "sure is". He always showed up in his fatigues, even though he works for the NSA now.

He'd easily sign up at least 25 recruits. That's a big number from a graduating class of 200. He said he did it because he loved his country and we could all see how proud he was of the time he spent in the Air Force. He did the recruiting voluntarily. Guess it was just his way of showing everyone how happy he was to do it. Can't say I didn't like it. I got to shine too. It felt like Cunningham Day in our high school; with all the attention on me, by way of my father. Kinda like the Bushes have come to town.

Dad recruited all four of us that summer of 2000. Josh was the first to suggest it. I think he was trying to impress my father. He wanted to look like the man, trying to show Dad that he was a leader like him. I stood by with my mouth open, when Dad hugged him, thanked him and called him "son". They both looked at me and it was a foregone conclusion. I can't say I was mad at Josh cuz Josh had lost his father and Josh wanted to impress Dad.

So, what was I going to do after that? Say no? How would that have looked? Justin and Brandon signed up after me. They weren't going to take much convincing anyway. It's not as if they had a future to look forward to: both from broken homes and living in Section 8 housing. Josh and I took them under our wing as pals in High School and it ultimately made Dad proud of me, and proud of Josh - that we were doing our bit for the less fortunate. Sandy Springs has its fair share of the underprivileged and we did our bit.

That was that. We were all set to join up after graduation. Justin and Brandon just about made it to graduation, scraping just enough grades, despite all the tuition that Josh and I gave them. Only Brandon's mother showed up to graduation. We didn't speak about Justin's mother on the day and Mom made sure that there was enough love to go around later at ours, at the party. She offered Justin to stay the night, but he felt awkward about it and left early to go home to his mother.

Not long after graduation, we all were sent to Fort Benning, to start our Basic Training. Fort Benning was a good start to the military. It wasn't too far from home and we were allowed to return home at the weekends, at least in the beginning. Everything was familiar to us and we were all together. We settled in quickly and I enjoyed catching-up with Mom and Dad at the weekend. Just like Josh did, with his Mom. Justin and Brandon would sometimes stay the weekend at Fort Benning instead of going back to their moms. I can't say that surprised me.

Josh came up to me one day and told me that the planes hit the Twin Towers and I should come and check it out. We weren't even supposed to be watching TV cuz we were meant to be prepping for our basic training. We were done cleaning our barracks and Josh heard it from the fellas down the hall: "a plane went into the towers" then "the towers are falling". Shortly after, some of the fellas were shouting "the towel-heads did it, the towel-heads did it!"

A crowd gathered in the mess hall where there was a small TV. The rabble was beginning to get louder, the fellas were starting to cuss, and the sheer sense of anger was coursing through the room, travelling through each and every one of us. A new recruit became overwhelmed and started to bang his tray against the table. He was led out by an officer. We all looked at each other, like *what the fuck is going on?*

Another recruit sat by the table and covered his face with his hands and started screaming, then crying an anguished cry. "Not our country, not our country". The officer told him to hush up and get a grip. Just as the shock was about to wear off, the second plane hit the second building. It looked like a military plane and I called it. "Is that a military plane?", I asked. With everyone's hands on their heads and covering their mouths, the collective shock was too great for a response.

I asked again. But there was still no response. The officer cut me a look so I stopped asking. Nobody spoke, still in shock. Then the first building came down. "Is that building exploding?" The newscasters commentary was clear: "the buildings are coming down". But I could only see one building coming down. Then, as if the newscaster's presumption caught up with the second tower, down came the second tower. "What the fuck is causing that?" asked another recruit when the shock wore over a bit. "What the fuck did that?"

The officer silenced them and all of their questions, telling them to keep order. We all looked at each other, all of the dozen or so recruits in that mess hall at Fort Benning. So many questions, some unanswered and the rest we tried to figure out ourselves, with varying responses: who did it? - *the news will tell us*; what did it? - *it looked like a military plane but the news was telling us something different*; why are we being hit? - *the terrorists…* the questions kept coming but we really didn't have answers. We were instructed to watch the news, which we were already doing, for further information.

The next day, there was a definite buzz in the air. We were at war, with an unknown terrorist, hiding in a cave. The preparations had begun and we were loading up our gear. We were called for a briefing. They had declared a state of war and the perpetrators had been identified, along with their leader, Osama Bin Laden. He sounded menacing, with an annoying foreign, Arab name that just got under your skin. That afternoon, Donald Rumsfeld put out a call, saying that he wanted to find out if Iraq had also been involved in the attacks.

It wasn't long before Secretary Rumsfeld stepped up his case for ties with Iraq, as well as Afghanistan. Not long after operations had started in Afghanistan, our division was deployed temporarily to support other divisions in our state of Georgia, to get them ready. It was coming, we all knew it. We'd be out there soon, kicking some towel-head ass. Either in Iraq or Afghanistan.

Chapter 2

Justin and Brandon were in the barracks one day when Josh told me that he was having doubts about it all. I think the fear had set in at that point. Now that shit was getting real, he couldn't handle it. It was all just a show for Dad. I don't think he really thought about the consequences. I think he just thought it was glamorous and got caught, trying to impress Dad. Maybe Dad made it seem glamorous, when he was out there, on School Day for his recruitment program.

Justin and Brandon were like ducklings without a parent. They would have blindly followed any leader who came their way. Their fathers were gone or absent and Mom could only mother them as much as she could. The only alternative to what Dad was able to offer them was a lifetime of welfare and Section 8 Housing, probably with girls who would run around on them and treat them like dirt like their mothers did. They would have done just as well in the real world as they would have done in military service - they needed a lot of guidance because they were clueless.

Josh and I went way back, further than we did with Justin and Brandon, whom we both met in High School. Josh's father died when we were a year away from finishing middle school. His parents had been over at ours for dinner and we had waved them goodbye. My Dad blamed himself for encouraging Josh's father to drink more than he should have that evening. His mother was barely touched in the accident but Josh's father hit the bender, as the car swirled round, and he was squashed on his side. He died instantly. His mother had to crawl out and she managed to flag down help in the dark country lane, at night. The trucker and his truck were left unharmed. Everything changed then. There was so much tension between my parents and his mom. We didn't know what to do or say so we just continued to hang out together, after school and on the weekends. Mom didn't want to talk about it, neither did his. It was a long time before she came to visit with Josh, which was her choice, by all accounts. One Sunday, she appeared with Josh on our doorstep after church and Mom and Dad welcomed her in.

We became a blended family for a while. Mom would do her best to make Josh's Mom have all that she needed, especially since money became tight for them. We spent holidays together and they would sleep over a lot whenever Dad had to be called away for work. Mom said that it was the mark of a good woman to help another in distress. Though I couldn't help but think that, despite the best intentions, there was plenty of opportunity for Josh's mom to take advantage of my mother's kindness.

I didn't pay it too much mind, though, because I had a brother, at last. Mom and Dad were happy to have them over and Dad began joking about his "two wives", which Mom tried not to respond to, but Josh's mom always found that bit uncomfortable. Then Mom decided that it was time for Josh and his Mom to go back to their own lives and to stop living with us so much. I remember Josh's mom crying, with Mom's hand over her shoulder: "it'll be okay, just call on us whenever you need to. You do know your own life has to carry on, don't you?" said Mom and Josh's mom nodded in agreement. They left our home but they weren't gone completely from our lives.

I missed Josh being around but I didn't miss the tension that it brought between Mom and Dad. Dad appeared distant and Mom did her best to keep our home ticking over, with the daily routine. I'd tell Josh what was happening between Mom and Dad but he didn't seem to care. He'd shrug his shoulders and pretend like he didn't have anything to say but there was something that bothered him. I kept bugging him with it until he told me that he had walked in on Dad kissing his mom.

Life carried on for a while after that. We started High School, with new faces, new people and new problems to deal with. Meeting Justin and Brandon was a welcome relief to what had been going on up until that point and their problems were a welcomed distraction. I took Justin under my wing and Brandon took to Josh. We all hung out together, mostly at Josh's. His mother welcomed the company and appreciated the full house on the weekends. Neither of us got to know Justin and Brandon's mothers and their fathers were not in the picture. Justin and Brandon's mothers both sounded and looked like dragons and we were never invited to their homes.

We got to know Justin and Brandon more over time. Justin was somewhat more self-disciplined and cautious, averse to risky behavior, unlike Brandon. Brandon was a handful to have as a kid brother - no respect for authority and wanted to try everything and anything. He was impossible to control. He was the wild one of us all. He didn't care what people thought of him. Always angry. Dad kept his distance with him because he was such a jerk and a showdown wouldn't have ended well for Brandon.

So, for a couple of years at high school, we all hung out, most weekends and holidays. Mom and Dad were keen to have Justin and Brandon's moms over but they would never come so they never got to learn much about them. Aside from the time when Justin's mother came to pick him up once and I chatted with her for a while and the time when Brandon's mother once called my Dad an asshole for trying to steal her son away from her. After that episode, Brandon began to behave a bit better, started to tighten up a little, probably cuz seeing his mother like that shocked him into changing.

Brandon finally turned a corner a year before graduation. I think he was beginning to feel like he was being left behind. He saw Justin grow a bit, despite his difficulties at home. But Brandon's grades were still low and Justin was beginning to talk about life after school. We all looked out for each other and we had kept Brandon in line and he kinda knew that he was a loose cannon on his own. He needed us to ground him a bit. Brandon began splitting his time between all of our homes - at Josh's and our home but never at Justin's - I think Justin's mom reminded him too much of his own.

Then Brandon changed, quick as a flash. It was one weekend when I went away with Mom, to visit her sister in Atlanta. Dad said he'd be working at home most of that weekend so he invited Brandon to stay over and help him with the Christmas decorations on the outside of the house, and keep him company. Well, it was around that time when I noticed the change in Brandon. He wasn't his usual self when we returned on that Sunday morning.

He just sat at the table, staring into space. I asked him what was wrong but he didn't answer. Mom and I both probed further, to find out how he'd found working with Dad. He appeared subdued. He wasn't his usual loud and jumpy self. He was a different person with a glazed look in his eyes. It was as if the spark had been removed from him. It didn't make sense to me. Mom and Dad said I was imagining it but I knew Brandon like a brother and something was definitely wrong.

After dinner, we went down to the basement to put back the boxes which were left over from the weekend of decorating. "Hey, Brandon, are you sure you're okay? I'm worried about you man," I said. He didn't respond. He sat on the couch there and stared at the wall. "Man, what the fuck? Did something happen between you and Dad? I know you both don't get along but you can tell me", I said, probing further. He looked at me as if he didn't know what I was talking about and he simply replied, in a flat tone: "I don't know what happened. I can't remember what I did over the weekend"

He sat in a trance for a while. I didn't know what to do with him. I gave him something to drink - some water. He kept staring at the armchair, there in the centre of the room. "What's wrong?" I kept asking, until he moved towards it. He placed his hands tentatively on the armrest and he looked at me. I kept asking him, questioning him, but he didn't change, and he slowly moved towards the chair and sat on it. "I remember sitting here", he said. "And then?" I asked? "And then?" He returned his gaze, first to me and then to the wall.

The next day, I rang up Josh and I told him what was happening with Brandon and that we should keep an eye on him. At school, Brandon appeared a different student - studious and diligent, no longer a jerk. He stayed in class, he wasn't a bother to the teachers and he began Bible studies on Sunday with me and Josh. Then Justin joined our studies, because of Brandon. We were stunned. We didn't know what to make of it. Months went by, like that, until we forgot what the old Brandon was like.

Josh wanted me to get Brandon back in the basement to see what he wanted to say. The trouble is that we couldn't get him back in the basement for love nor money. He would do everything to avoid the bait, like he knew what we were trying to do. Even getting Mom to try and get him down there didn't work - she said we were being silly and we should just leave him be. Perhaps Brandon changed because he knew it was time to grow up. Perhaps he was just mimicking our behavior. But whatever had happened worked.

Brandon graduated with a GPA a little above Justin's. I reckon he would have made it to Valedictorian and stolen my title, if he had another year and a half on him. He was smart, all of a sudden. Not just streetsmart as he used to be but also booksmart. Did less of the talking and more of the listening and grew and learned and got wise and got some respect. It was a remarkable transformation.

I still wanted to know what happened that weekend, in the basement, in that chair. Maybe we'll never know or maybe he'll come up to me, one day, after a dinner with his wife and kids in the future one day and he will tell me what changed in him that weekend when Mom and I went away, and we came back to a whole different Brandon, after he spent a weekend with my Dad.

That final year at school was strange. It seemed as though we got serious about life just as soon as we got to enjoy being seniors. A year of being in some twilight zone - all that play and messing around gave way to a horrible feeling in the pit of my stomach that life would change. I began to think about Justin and Brandon's future - living with their moms after we graduated, possibly well into their 20s.

Brandon and Justin got jobs at the local grocery store for the weekends but, of course, they never got to enjoy their money - their moms saw to that. Justin's mom would sometimes tell her son to enjoy it for himself - he'd save up and buy himself some new clothes. But Brandon's mom was a real bitch about it - kept threatening to kick him out the house unless he paid his rent, as she called it, which we all thought was pretty wild. The poor boy was barely old enough to buy cigarettes but was old enough to be responsible for himself, in her book.

I told Mom about that and she put together some funds for a birthday gift for Brandon and Justin that year, a sort of reward for their growth over the years and a graduation present all in one. Brandon got a whole bunch of clothes and Justin got some money for concert tickets to see Pink with his girlfriend. Justin broke down in tears when he got his gift and said he would do anything for me as a brother, which he said we had all become.

I asked Mom if we could take in Brandon, if he could come and live with us. Justin's mom had mellowed out a little since her son wasn't so much of a financial burden on her but Brandon's mom was a real demon and I just felt so bad for him. I think we all did but that wasn't enough. Mom said that it wouldn't do him any good staying with us cuz it wouldn't change the situation with his mom and taking him in might make it worse. She promised she would talk to Dad about it and come back to me.

A few days later, Mom suggested that I take Justin and Brandon to the recruitment booth when Dad attended school for his annual recruitment fair. She suggested that Justin and Brandon would definitely sign up if Josh did it so I guess it was left to me to get Josh riled up about it. I spent the following weeks dropping hints to Josh but he wasn't biting.

Along came recruitment day at school and the mass of seniors, mostly jocks, some nerds, gathered round to hear Dad give his speech, along with alumni. They were all kitted out in their uniform, with the flag behind them, the sun bursting through the blue skies, making their white teeth sparkle against their weathered skin. They had been in the thick of it and they were proud to tell their tale, share their stories, and be called heroes, by boys, girls and parents alike. It didn't take long for Josh to get swallowed up in the glory of it all and that was that. That's how Josh signed himself up. And the rest followed.

In the days that followed registration, we all swung between excitement and worry, from extremes of bonding as brothers to drunken get-togethers, with ceremonious hugging and proclamations of brotherly love. When the dust settled, the feeling returned in the pit of my stomach. That dread. It returned, like a faithful dog you just wished would go away and give you a break.

That summer together after graduation was like being in the final throes of adolescence. I met Jessica and had sex for the first time in the basement of our home. We had seen each other a lot in High School but it wasn't until after graduation, in the summer, when we clicked and started hanging out. She didn't have any plans to leave

Sandy Springs soon and wanted to settle. I told her she was too young but she kept shrugging her shoulders until I slept with her, then I realized that she would make the ideal housewife if I ever went on a tour of duty.

I soon introduced Jessica to my bros and Mom and Dad. They took to her right away and doted on her. Mom insisted that it would be wrong to lead her on, have sex with her and then dump her before moving to service. Jessica was easy going and that's what made it work between us. She brought me down to earth whenever I was getting hyped up about something. We spent a good summer, amongst the fireflies at night, learning about each other and seeing our future together. We both had our own things going on but we couldn't stop wanting to see each other. The bros were getting impatient with me giving up my time with them in the summer for her, but I reminded them we'd see more of each other in service anyway.

Mom and Dad soon started to pass the idea of marriage around. Mom said that Jessica reminded her of herself and that she would cope well with me. In any case, Mom said, I'd still be based in Sandy Springs for the first few years unless I was called away but we both agreed that there wouldn't be any immediate threat to our country that would require a long period of absence. But you never knew. Mom told me to think about it. In the meantime, I passed the idea to Dad, to see what he thought and he agreed: "Boy, get yourself settled now and you won't regret it like your dear old man," he said.

Mom and Dad soon invited her parents to join us for dinner as the weeks progressed. Dad was the first to hint at Jessica's Dad about the possibilities of joining families. They simply responded by allowing Jessica to decide. Jessica was easy going in many ways. Easy for sex and easy for any attention I gave her. It was as if she was made for the role of a serviceman's wife. She soon embraced it, soon making sure all my needs were met.

The wedding took place in August, three months after we had officially started dating. We didn't have to convince anyone, though my bros started to question the pace of everything. "But you're going to be in training soon?" and "are you not worried that the pressure might be too much for her?" were the types of questions I got. They were only worried for both of us, I understood that. They weren't acting out of jealousy, or anything. "Look, guys, we're still young, I get that, but it's not like I will be away a lot," I said.

We were married in the Baptist church in Sandy Springs. The Reverend, Tom Jeffry, gave a good service. Josh was the best man, there was no question about it. Justin and Brandon didn't question my decision, though I think Justin may have talked about it in a discussion with Brandon at some point. They were both told to visit the hire shop to get measured for their suits and they went together. Josh and I were fitted separately.

The day went smoothly, without any real hiccups. Josh, Justin and Brandon gave fantastic speeches and we all danced in Mom and Dad's 10 acre garden. Mom and Dad paid for the reception at their home and Jessica's parents paid for the wedding service. It was more or less an even split. Justin and Brandon cried that day. I think they realized for the first time just how quickly life was beginning to progress and just how far behind they were in the game. I told them that it would be alright, that they had us and the military and everything else would take care of itself.

September came around and we were at Fort Benning, starting out boot training. Some kids would have started their own lives, moved out of home or gone to the city. It felt weird to be together but not in school anymore. It seemed like the 4 years that we spent together, prior to starting Basic Training were, in a way, preparation for that moment itself. We had come together as friends and now we were brothers, in the military. We took an oath to look after each other, as a fraternity. Why not, since we would never get to experience one at college!

Chapter 3

The basic training was intense but it only gave us enough to learn the ropes. A lot of physical, mental and emotional endurance. Stripping you down to the bare bones of your soul and rebuilding your character again. I went in, expecting to be treated like a son of a hero but came out barely a man. We were nobodies that had to earn our respect and nobody felt that more strongly than me. I had to earn that respect twice: once for the military and once for Dad.

Josh changed the first, the most and the fastest. He listened less and challenged me more. I guess he was trying to show me that he wasn't going to be the underdog anymore. But he never was, in my eyes, at least. That must have been how he felt and now he was going to prove himself otherwise, I guess. I gave him the space to be who he wanted to be, despite the ugly version he had become. I was reminded constantly of his father's death and, in fits of rage, he would lay on the guilt: "I wouldn't be here, trying to become my best, if I still had a father to guide me," he'd say.

Justin and Brandon distanced themselves from Josh and I, turning almost into one person. They then began to reject us as big brothers. They were only out for each other, in their own little unit. They made that clear by sitting to eat with a new crew in the mess hall. Our weekly card games turned into monthly meets and then bi-monthly until, by the end of the first year, we were not the same people anymore. At that stage, I was just grateful to see them in the unit, doing what they needed to do.

I began questioning my own self. Why was I isolated by my brothers? Why were they angry with me? What was I even doing there myself? I was beginning to sink into myself and I felt out of my depth. Josh, Justin and Brandon were now so far removed from what I remembered them as being, before they enlisted. They were becoming strangers to me and strangers to themselves. Pangs of anxiety and dread began to return and become more frequent, growing in intensity.

The only break I had from obsessing over our broken brotherhood was the birth of my child. I welcomed the distraction, though the news was received apathetically by my brothers. They made time for me, we all got drunk together but it wasn't the same. The old feeling wasn't there. "Hey, you're gonna be a great father" and "I guess we'll be seeing even less of each other" were comments which added to the air of growing distance between us. After a night of illicit card games and drinking, they would return to their dorms with all the self-discipline of strangers. Soon after, I was on home leave for a few weeks, back with Jessica and Mom and Dad, glad to see the back of the first year of life as a soldier.

Chapter 4

They told us they would give us a month's notice but it didn't work out like that, not least cuz our unit had a high state of readiness. I kissed my family - Jessica and our baby - goodbye and that was the last time I saw their faces. They waved me goodbye from the porch of my parents' house in Sandy Springs.

The call came one day in late September, when we had just finished eating. It was early evening when they rang. The heat tried to bite all day long. It was soft, you know, like you know summer's going to end. I remember the breeze of those last days there. We were sitting outside as we always did – like half the year. The weather in Sandy Springs always pulled us outdoors. Mom was inside, cleaning. Jessica was helping out and the baby was asleep in her crib.

Dad was telling me about the first war. He was there in 1990 for about nine months. He said he could never be more proud of me for going because I was following a long line of military men. I was doing my duty to protect our freedoms. That was important for us. I wanted my daughter to live in a world that was free from psychos like Saddam and Osama.

I went indoors to make a cup of coffee. I had quit the smoking I started in high school so I liked having coffee after dinner. It perked me up right away, after eating mom's cookin'. We had honey-mustard chicken, sweet potatoes, corn, biscuits and gravy. Mom always cooked fresh, never out of a packet and fixed it with a lot of love. She used to say her hands were an extension of her heart.

I could still remember the light that shone through the kitchen window and covered Jessica's neck. I can still remember the way she looked. She was wearing a yellow dress and a white apron. I remember thinking how that happy color matched the kitchen paint. I kissed her neck and poured myself some coffee. That's when the phone rang and, when it did, the butterflies in my stomach went, stirring a shudder.

Mom looked at me and I saw the worried look on her face. She had that woman's intuition – you know, like she sure as hell knew if anyone was lying to her and like she knew some bad news was gonna come our way. My Mom was – is – the best mom in the world. Kind, you know. Never judged no-one and always had a good word to say about everybody. If she didn't like someone, she didn't say it. She just didn't keep their company and that's how you knew.

I never really knew what Mom thought about it all. She stood by her man when he went to fight for us but I know she would be happier without all of that war talk because she just wasn't comfortable with it. She didn't like it when I talked about Saddam or Osama. She always reminded me to be understanding. I wish I had taken her advice before I enlisted. I guess I really just did it for my Dad.

I saw Mom's face drop as she took the call. Jessica was stood by her in the kitchen. I saw Mom's nervous face so I took the phone from her. I was given just a day's notice; anything longer would have been too much. Mom and Jessica were upset, of course. They talked some 'bout having to change plans and cancel the food for the party and that I should have been given more time. Their complaints barely hid the lost and disappointed look on their faces.

I had just enough time to pack and say goodbye. My heart felt heavy and torn out. A wave of emotions began washing over me, like a high tide of fear; but you have to fight it because you're a guy and you can't let it show. I buried my feelings that day, hid them well so nobody could tell and nobody was let down. It was important for them, especially Dad, that I went.

I remember Jessica's long, golden hair flowing down her body and my mother holding back her tears as she smiled and blew kisses in the air, on the porch. Mom's big blue eyes and the whites of her eyes were like the blue polka dots on her white dress. She was crying and smiling. Jessica held back her tears though – she just smiled all the way as I loaded up the truck with my gear.

Dad was waiting for me by the car door. I looked at him – he had that sort of "I'm proud of you son" look about him. I could tell he didn't wanna show what he was really thinking or feeling. He just wanted me to get in the car so that we could drive on off to base. He didn't want me to hug him…he just sort of grimaced as he opened the door for me to get in. The sun was setting and the street was empty – everyone in the neighborhood was indoors having dinner, spending time with their families like we should have been doing.

I saw Dad's face change when he looked over my shoulder. A little old lady appeared out of nowhere. She was a little old thing, with a kind face. She asked me where I was going. I didn't wanna tell her but I thought – yeah – she's old and who knows when she's gonna drop dead, right? So I told her. Then, she said: "oh son, I hope you're going to be ok. Just remember you're doing God's work, son" and she kinda went on like that for a while. She gave me a white lily from a bunch she was holding and she told me that she was on her way back from church when she noticed me in my gear and wanted to wish me well. So, I asked her where she lived cuz she looked familiar but she just said "oh, you know, in the neighborhood."

She was wearing all black, like one of those widows that you see in New Orleans – and she had that sort of voodoo vibe going on about her. Then, her face changed. It went from looking like a sweet old lady to some old hag. She started saying all this stuff that I had only ever heard at church. She said: "he that killeth with the sword must be killed by the sword." I was like - "okay!" Dad walked forward, to lead me to the car but she grabbed my hand and she said: "watch out for the great deceiver."

Dad pulled her away from me but her grip got tighter and she kept going with all that church-stuff. I remember some parts of what she said really well 'cause the pastor had been saying a lot of the same stuff in church: "beware of the false prophets who will have the power to perform miracles." We finally got into the car and Dad ordered me to roll the window up but it got stuck. Then, she leaned over and gripped the car door with her long, wrinkly fingers. She looked me straight in the eye and I felt my skin crawl. Her eyes locked mine and she said: "he will speak like a dragon to you."

On the way to the base, Dad told me she had been quoting from the Book of Revelations. I'm sure I would have known that too, if I had kept up with my Bible studies but I stopped going when I joined the army. Just didn't have time, you know. Some of the fellas got together at the base to form a group but they never really kept it up. Being told how to think was a full time job and adding religion just added to the pressure.

It was a quiet drive to our base, Fort Benning. Dad said nothing during the whole ride. He hugged me at the gate and told me to go and be a hero. I shuffled through, along with the others, who were being dropped off by their families or arriving on military buses. A real rent-a-crowd. I saw Josh first, when I arrived inside the housing complex.

We had a chat and I found out we were bunking together that night. He told me that Justin and Brandon were going to be joining us later. We were all going to be part of the Armored Brigade Combat Team of the 3rd Infantry Division, responsible for foot and air defense. Josh welcomed me like the old Josh I knew, telling me jokes as soon as we started chatting with that wicked sense of humor of his. Maybe he wanted to get serious in training in the year prior to the call to war, cuz the Josh that stood before me was the old Josh that I knew. Maybe he was happy that we were all shipping out together. I hoped to feel the same when I saw Justin and Brandon.

We were at the base for one night before we flew out. It was nice to catch up with the crew and get back into the vibe after our leave. Joshua was sitting in his room, listening to some music. The sun was beginning to set and the sky was that warm, orange color. It was coming through the windows, still a bit strong. Josh was laying on his bed and he was telling me about how he was looking forward to kicking some ass.

We had breakfast together. The mess hall was really busy and that's where we met up with Justin and Brandon. We knew this was going to be a really big tour. Everyone was pumped. Josh was rocking his head back and forth over breakfast and some of the others around us were asking if he was okay. He said he had been playing music all night and it was still fresh in his mind but some of us knew what was really going on in there. I remember thinking, my God, everyone is really pumped except me. The energy of that mess hall was intense. Everyone just wanted to get on that plane and shuttle out.

We got ready by noon and started boarding shortly after. After getting strapped in and as the plane started taxiing, I noticed Josh started thumbing the beats of the tunes against the arms of the seats. I turned around to look at Justin and Brandon, to see if they noticed Joshua too, but they didn't see and I decided to ignore it. I sat back and thought about why I was going.

My family expected me to go cuz my Dad had been on tour in Operation Desert Storm and because I wanted to prove that I could do it too. When I was growing up, I saw the honor and respect he received for having been there. Buddies in high-school started coming to me for advice about the war on the terrorists cuz they knew what my Dad had been through. My Dad was a decorated war hero and, after 9/11, our house was suddenly busy again. People came from all over to hang out with Dad just for some sort of advice and reassurance.

Those towel-heads were coming at us again and America wasn't gonna back down that easy, he'd say. He told us that we had to show them who was in charge, once and for all. Everyone in our living room would look at me and I could feel the expectation come off them. That's when I decided that I wasn't going to let my country down. Besides, I didn't wanna go to college, like a pussy. My dad needed me. My country needed me. Anyway, how could those dirty fucks attack us like that and not expect retaliation?

Dad was busy with our visitors when I told Mom. Dad and I both agreed that I would be the one to tell her that I had enlisted. It was on a Friday, early evening, and Dad had just finished with the BBQ and Mom was getting ready to prepare the buffet for our hordes of visitors for their garden party. Dad was busy chatting with some of his friends from where he worked, the NSA, the place he ended up after his successful tours. I came home at around 4pm and Mom was going around, like Mom always did, fussing over everything she was fixin'. I went upstairs to take the day off, hit the shower and change. From my bedroom window, I could see more visitors starting to trickle in.

I saw Jessica's parents walk down the road towards the house. Her dad and mine went back a long way at work but they never really used to hang out but, of course, that all changed in time. They were standing at the front gate and her dad opened the door for his wife. I ran downstairs, to make sure I got there before the bell rang but I never made it down in time. I arrived at the front door, panting. With a deep breath, I opened the door. I shook their hands and walked them through into the living room as I had done so many times when I was growing up, whenever we had visitors. Dad nodded at me to sort of say that it was okay, I could leave the room, but I waited for them to take a seat on the sofa. They could sense I was nervous and it was hard not to hide it. Jessica joined them later, at which point Dad pointed me to sort out the drinks.

Jessica sat on the sofa, staring at me, as I was preparing myself to tell everyone that I had enlisted. I thought it would be a good time, since everyone was together, but Dad just looked at me again with that cold look of a military man probably because he saw I looked nervous. So, I went into the kitchen to give the drinks order but I looked shaken 'cause I was nervous. Mom told me to calm down and to tell her what was going on, so I did. She jumped and gave me a huge hug and tears started rolling down her eyes. I heard Dad's voice coming into the kitchen and we both turned around to see him walk in. Mom then told him and his face lit up, in spite of already knowing.

Dad rushed forward to hug me and he patted my hair down. He led me and Mom into the living room where Jessica and the other guests were standing, to announce the news and his buddies huddled around me to shake my hand. Through the shakes and the pats and the smiles, I remember Jessica's face the most. I was concerned about how she would take the news. I could see her through the spaces in the crowd.

When I finally got to see her expression, she looked calm and I remember thinking - wow, she is the sweetest thing ever! She comforted me with a smile that blew me away and I forgot all about where I was and what I was doing. She stood up and walked towards me, arms stretched out. She was like a doll and her eyes sparkled when she smiled. Her dad stared at me with daggers and I did my darndest to shrug it off. Later that night, we spoke some more about my decision and I never left her side until she said she was happy with it but she was tired and wanted to leave with her dad.

Soon after, we started drawing up plans for our future together and we were married in a couple of months and it wasn't long before she was pregnant. It all seemed to happen at once. I left school, I joined the army, I got married, we had a baby, Jessica moved in with us and then I was getting ready to leave for Iraq. Dad made sure that everyone in the neighborhood knew. He threw another party, then came another, then another. After the engagement party, an enlisting party, then the wedding, then the christening… it all happened in under a year. From the day I left school and enlisted to the day I left for Iraq – it was just over 12 months. We were caught in the middle of a whirlwind of celebrations, presents and well-wishers. Then came the call to battle. Before I could blink, the parties were over and I was boarding a plane with my bros.

So, there we were – waiting to leave. We all sat together. Josh and I were together and Justin and Brandon sat in front of us. The four horsemen of the apocalypse, that was the name Josh gave us. We were all like brothers again and it felt good to be tight with Josh again despite Justin and Brandon having their own click going on - and it didn't look as though that wedge was going to change anytime fast. But we were together in the military and that's all that mattered.

Coming from messed up backgrounds might have made Justin and Brandon even more messed up as they got older but it didn't. I felt that they both kinda envied the life I had even though I made sure they were treated right. My family wasn't mega-rich but, for Sandy Springs, we were doing pretty well. Dad had a real good job at the NSA and Mom never had to work even though she sometimes talked about it. I wasn't spoiled either, like you might think. Mom always made sure I did my duties and went to church and we were always doing things for the poor.

Justin and Brandon were always treated like our own but that wasn't enough to stop the distance from growing. Maybe Josh and I shouldn't have clicked so hard but that's how it went down, with Josh eventually becoming the best man at my wedding. We all still cracked jokes and we were all still good friends but life began to get in the way of tight bonds.

Josh's mom took the news of our enrollment the worst. Had her crying all week with the news of war. "Still, it's a tough time America's going through", she said later. She didn't wanna make Josh feel worse so she stopped with all the crying. Soon after, she became more withdrawn than her usual self. Justin and Brandon – well, their mother's didn't give two hoots about them enlisting. All they said was they were pleased that there was one less mouth to feed and they barely battered an eyelid when they were called to Iraq. That didn't come as a surprise. I can't begin to imagine what they said to their sons on the day they left. Probably something heartless. It was different for Josh and I. I did it cuz I was caught up in the mix and Josh just wanted to get away from his mom for a while, and impress Dad. We both knew why Justin and Brandon signed up for the army – cuz they needed it, you know – boot camp, discipline, reward and all that. Josh and I both doubted if they would be able to survive in Iraq though.

We were all laughing down our nerves in the plane and I felt my stomach rumble as it was moving off. The rest of the combat team were probably all as nervous as we were. Josh was pumped. I was quiet, thinking, and Justin and Brandon – they were foolin' around and joking and the sergeant yelled at them a couple of times. We were all meant to be serious.

They gave us our itineraries when we were on board. As soon as we touched down, we all knew where we were going, what was happening, who we were reporting to and where to find our units.

There wasn't any time to think about it – we just had to do it. The sergeant shouted out the orders of what we were expected to do and what was required of us on the flight. Mostly, it was paperwork and eating. The flight lasted 36 hours including a layover in Turkey. As we approached our destination, the briefings on board got more and more intense. I saw Justin and Brandon's demeanor change. Josh got more attentive to the mission. I began to feel a bit lost.

When we landed in Turkey all we did was offload and spend a few hours waiting in the hangar for our ongoing carrier to get prepared. We reloaded with all our gear and flew straight into the north of Baghdad in the military carrier, the KC-130, to proceed with our mission. They called it Operation Iraqi Liberation. We were there to kick some ass and that's what we had to remember. We were gonna fuck up Saddam and Al-Qaeda and Osama for nine-eleven.

When we landed in Turkey, I turned around to Josh after we had been briefed on Operation Iraqi Liberation, and I asked him if he thought it was weird that the name of the operation spelled out OIL. He told me to shut up and take the mission seriously, which came as a shock. He seemed to change again but I just put that down to his nerves. We stepped off the plane in Baghdad and things automatically changed for us. The first thing that hit us was the heat – it was dry and it stung us. By the time we were walking on the land there, we were sweating through all our gear. Never mind all of that other stuff about war is all about, that heat's gotta be right up there with the worst.

Justin and Brandon were deployed into their units – the 3-3 Special Troops Battalion, where they mostly took care of administration and communications - and that was the last I saw of them during our tour. Josh and I were deployed to the same unit – the 3rd Squadron, the Blackhawks. We reported for duty then off we went for our recce mission in downtown Baghdad.

Chapter 5

"I am standing here outside the International Airport of Baghdad and I am being told that the Iraqi Army are fighting day and night to attack the American and Allied forces. I have been told that there is a definite operation to try and get Saddam because he needs to be brought to justice for his involvement in the September the 11th attacks on our country. Some say that this war is about oil but, let me tell you, that is further from the truth. The truth is that Saddam has Weapons of Mass Destruction which he can fire into the USA using long-range missiles and we need to take him out before he does our country any more damage. He is linked to Osama Bin Laden and the Al-Qaeda network and it is a proven fact that the terrorists like nothing but to work together to try and destroy our great nation, America, because they hate us so much. The terrorists need to be stopped because they hate us. This is not a war for oil but this is a war against the terrorists. The terrorists are the greatest threat to world peace right now and it has been coming from the Middle-East region for a long time now and we have a God-given right, just as our brave President Bush said, to protect our great nation here on Earth."

"Well, Dan, can you tell us or give us some insight into the mood of the allied forces on the ground there?"

"Let me tell you one thing, Sean. Our troops are the best in the world. They are the most highly trained and the most equipped and they are, at this moment, the most charged. I see the average age to be around 20, of those that are here to fight for our great nation against the terrorists, to protect us, and whether you agree with this war nobody can disagree that we have the best heroes of the free world here to take down the dictator Saddam."

"Do you know if there are any signs about how long this will take or what the long term plans are?"

"Who knows Sean, who knows. This is probably going to take a while - we don't know how long we are going to be here for. It all depends, I guess, on whether Saddam goes with or without a fight and if his army is going to stay and fight for him because, by all accounts, he has fled Baghdad. His statue has been brought to the ground and the crowds are jeering and that can only be a positive sign."

"Yes it looks that way, Dan. Thank you for that report there Dan."

"Well, joining us in the studio today is Vice President Dick Cheney."

'"Thank you for joining us Mr. Vice President. Sir, you gave a speech where you said that we will be 'greeted as liberators' and regime change in Iraq and that you have clear evidence that Mohammed Atta, the guy who flew the plane into the twin towers, had met a senior member of the Iraqi intelligence in Prague. This, you say, is fundamental proof that Saddam Hussein and is indeed linked to the terrorist attacks and Al-Qaeda. Do you still stand by that, despite what the CIA are saying?"

"You know that we are at a time when Americans are sending their sons and daughters to war and I have to be absolutely clear before any decisions are made. These decisions are not made lightly. There are evil forces out there that are seeking to destroy us. We need to go in with an clear direction and this administration has had clear support around the world especially from our strongest ally Tony Blair in the sense that he is being like Churchill and history will show us that this dictator, Saddam Hussein, will be put to bed and we will find the WMDs and uncover his brutalities and we will send a message out to the Middle-East that democracy can take hold and that will silence our critics."

"Well, Mr. Cheney, you are certainly right there and I see that you do indeed have the best interest of Americans at heart in these troubled times. What do you say to your critics who say you are only interested in the oil?"

"You know Sean, again, this is not going to surprise me because I guess the critics will be silenced when they see that Haliburton will be involved in the reconstruction of Iraq but no money will leave the Iraqi economy. We were threatened on 9/11 and we put in place policies to deal with the threat of terror. Look, nobody is saying that this is going to be easy. The confusion out there and the criticisms are doing nothing but arming the threat to the American way of life. Everything will be put into perspective after Operation Iraqi Liberation will be successful."

"So, there you have it folks. Operation Iraqi Liberation from our Vice President, Mr. Cheney here on Hannity - you heard it first. Sir, I would just like to say that you definitely have the confidence of the American people behind you but, before we go, please have a word with your people because erm…Operation Iraqi Liberation…well, you don't want to go ahead with that name because it sounds like it could be shortened for something a bit sorta well…I'll let you be the judge of that."

"Oh….ha…well…I'll certainly get onto that Sean but thank you for having me on your show."

Chapter 6

I was there, in the thick of it. The heat, the noise, the chaos, the Iraqis, the women, the children and those fucking Al-Qaeda going at us. Our first reconnaissance mission was in Baghdad and we had to figure out where the insurgents were hiding. When we arrived there, we were given a lot of AKs and were told to keep 'em just in case anything happened. And a lot happened.

The first thing that hit me was how hard the soldiers were going – they would shoot at anything or anyone. I remember the main road leading into the center of Baghdad and one of the soldiers in the tank in front of us took out someone on the right side of the boulevard. All the guy did was turn the corner onto the main road but the soldier took him out anyways. That was the first time I knew this was gonna be a whole lot different to what they expected of us and were trained to do and how to conduct ourselves.

We were in the tank, driving down the boulevard that led to the center of Baghdad. Up ahead was the mosque and there were civilians everywhere going about their business like it was just another day. It wasn't like the civilians were not at home in their own country. They had jobs to go to just like everyone else. That's what made it difficult to weed out the insurgents and that's why some of the soldiers started firing indiscriminately. If we were not careful, we could have all gotten trigger happy at those towel-heads and then we'd be left with no ammo.

The rules of engagement were simple: do a recce and only take out insurgents. But we probably weren't the best people for the job. We were too young to hold those powerful weapons. We didn't care, we just wanted to take those fuckers out any which way we could. Josh was up on top of the tank when he was hit. It didn't matter to him. He came back down, wrapped himself up and went back up again, all the while complaining about his hillbilly armor.

Pretty soon we were acting out of fear for our lives. We also began shooting indiscriminately, causing complete and utter destruction, in every split second decision to shoot a perceived threat from an unknown enemy. After we finished our mission in central Baghdad, we moved onto a post overlooking the Tigris River.

We were told to form a 50-meter perimeter and to shoot at whoever came within it. It was for our own protection but, within days, we were firing at innocent civilians driving down their own streets. It became increasingly difficult to weed out the insurgents from the civilians. Over time, one questionable shot became more frequent, turning into another questionable shot, then another, as the bodies piled up. We started swapping stories on who had the best hit, such as who got the most amounts of dirty towel-heads, irrespective of whether they were insurgents or not.

I saw Josh chatting to a man who approached us one day when we were on patrol. Josh started talking to the man and his wife came out on the street. I was sitting on top of the tank, watching. I heard Josh talking normally then I heard the woman's voice grow, louder and louder, then Josh walked back to the tank and opened fire on the couple before getting in. My heart stopped before it sank. They dropped dead on the streets and the driver rolled on with the tank. Inside the tank, Josh couldn't look at me when I yelled at him: "what the fuck did you do that for?" He stared straight into the periscope, his hands grasped tight around the handles. Something clicked in him and he was a stranger to me again.

Josh put every action down to the intelligence we were getting and that happened on a daily basis. After about a month, we got to thinking that we could do anything we wanted cuz we knew that nobody was monitoring our actions so nothing was gonna get reported and nobody would check up on what we were doing, as long as we kept ourselves alive and that's all that mattered. I contemplated reporting Josh after the first incident but, by the third, I hadn't and, after that, I just never could muster the courage to do it. And Josh knew it. And that gave him free reign to become who he did.

A couple of weeks carried on like that and we still hadn't identified, captured or killed any insurgents. Nothing of anything of what was really going on was being reported. We were told by our company commander that, if we got our first kill by stabbing an insurgent to death, we would be given a 7-day pass. The trouble was that Josh didn't want to fess up to how many he was killing, nor who or how for that matter. We were getting confused ourselves. We didn't even know who "they" were anymore. We were meant to look out for the civilians and insurgents but "they" all became the same to us.

We were at a bridge over the Tigris River and there was a house over on the other side, on a little hill. We saw fire coming out of the window. We couldn't get over to see what was happening cuz we were on the other end of the bridge. We saw some people coming out so we decided to throw an 84-mm rocket at the house. Josh loved seeing it blow up and laughed it off, saying: "that's one way of putting out the fire!".

It went on like this for days until I ended up with my first kill. We were still in Baghdad, by the Tigris River, in a rich folks' area where we thought there wouldn't be many insurgents, so we did a recon-by-fire. We waited until dusk and there was no response and nobody on the streets. Our squad then did a recon-by-foot of that neighborhood which meant that we just knocked on, kicked in the doors and terrorized the families and questioned them about any insurgents in the vicinity. Information was a valuable commodity and it was important to get it out of them.

In that neighborhood, we came across a house which we were informed by an informer was hiding an operative. He was a father and husband with his wife and his young daughter. They were all trembling and crying when we stormed through. I began to question him before detaining him. Josh kept yelling at me to follow the orders cuz he was an insurgent. We had to get some information from him then detain him. Or kill him, if he came for us. I detained him and tied him up with the intention of questioning him outside, away from his family. We shut the door and stood him against the wall.

Josh was having none of it - telling me that we needed to take him out. I kept yelling at him to back the fuck off. As soon as I untied him, with Josh yelling at me from a few feet away, the captive took out a knife from a holder hidden under his shirt. Josh pointed the gun and fired at the captive, grazing his arm, and he fell to the ground. I turned around to watch him fall and a fire of rage within me grew in an instant. I grabbed Josh's gun and I pointed it at the man's chest, burying it deep in. He squealed for mercy and that made me rage more. I yelled at him: "are you fucking kidding me?" over and over and over, until I couldn't contain the rage any longer and I pulled the trigger, spraying a shower of bullets all over him.

They all said it but I didn't want to listen: "once you get your first kill, everything will change". I didn't want to listen. I thought that, by ignoring it, I'll avoid it somehow. It's crazy, if you think about it. How could I possibly ignore it? It just was never going to be that easy. The sight of his bullet-laden body and the blood bursting out of his veins. The thud of his flesh being torn apart and the echoes of screams from his home. That's the terror that stays with you. Josh gave me some pills as soon as we were in the tank: "here, these pills will help you forget". He gave me downers for the surge in adrenaline, with a ready stash of uppers when the time came. I didn't question him, taking a swig of my water bottle as I took the pill from his hand without so much as glancing at him.

In the craziness that followed in the weeks to come, I did my best to do what was required and to follow the directives as I possibly could, without needless casualties. The thought of having to go through that every time became more and more intense. That intense feeling of guilt was masked or eroded by the camaraderie and praise from my field crew but it lingered. We were only trained to think with our impulsive instincts. Our hearts and minds were not up for discussion.

The only time I can remember when we acted responsibly was when we were handed a reporter from CNN. All of our company changed, quick as a flash. We had to make sure we were on point with everything. We did as we were told. We sat by the river and scaled our perimeter like we were told to. We got out of our tanks, listened to the whining civilians and we did our best to please them. When the reporter went back the next day, we went back to our old selves. We did the same with the reporter from the BBC.

All the dog-fucking around with our duties became a general attitude which infected us all. We thought it was just our company that was like that but I don't think it was. We were told to shape up around reporters but, besides that, we mostly did anything we wanted. Our next recon started at Maghreb but we didn't stay there long. We were ordered to keep moving down-river if our post was replaced or we had to replace the other post further down.

One of the things that we loved to do was blow up minarets, taking down as many as we could without arousing too much interest from other battalions, who might decide to arrive as back up. There were only so many excuses we could give for our indiscretions before they ran dry - just like running the risk of reporting more insurgents than there actually were, because they would send more tanks and more troops and our game would be up.

About a month into our tour, and about a week after Maghreb, we were ordered to move down river. We were in the Al-Safena area where the river Tigris snakes to the west. That's where we were clocked by Al-Jazeera. Josh and I had been stationed and listening to the commander, on the radio. The tank driver had it on real loud. We were inside the tank when we felt something hit it. We dropped down our hatch and the driver locked onto the target and fired. He told us the coast was clear and we got out to check.

When we walked down the street to check where we had fired, we saw crowds gathering round the streets. Most of what we could see were city folk, some students and medical staff because they weren't too far from the University and the General Hospital. The crowd seemed to triangulate from the two buildings and from the streets that rang along the river promenade.

At that moment, we felt we might be screwed. Josh and I walked to the place where the weapon that we had fired from our tank had burned a whole in the ground. Around the hole were displaced bodies and little shoes and jackets and legs. I'm guessing, from the size of the body parts, they couldn't have been any more than the age of 11 or 12.

When we saw the crowd that had gathered, we noticed a TV crew and they were all Arab and I saw that logo that we were told in our brief to be especially aware of. It was the Al-Jazeera news crew, with that golden Arabic writing scrawled on their cameras. I whistled over to the crew member to stop filming and we saw him back off and make for the streets so we began running after him. They ran off and we didn't fire in time cuz we couldn't get through the crowd. After that, more reporters started swarming in from the side streets.

So, we headed back to the tank where we got a radio call from our company commander. He asked us for a report so we told him what had happened. He immediately ordered us to drive the tank down the street and go on a recon to hunt down the reporters and find their offices. So we drove out, through the streets off Corniche Street, which is a main road that runs along the riverbank. It was me and Josh and a couple of others who did the stake out though I stayed largely behind. We walked across the streets and passed an elementary school. Up to the left was a tower block and we all had a suspicion that's where the reporters might be. We basically had it confirmed to us by asking a couple of civilians and talking to some kids who identified Al-Jazeera's logo. They pointed up the tower block and shouted "Al-Jazeera, Al-Jazeera".

When we radioed in, we were told that we had to take out their power supply. That was when I made the fatal mistake and asked the commander why we were taking out Al-Jazeera, making me ping on his radar. Josh got real mad and started yelling at me to shut the fuck up so I did as I was told, after he backed me into a corner in front of the crew. I started feeling like I was gonna start losing it. We all regrouped and Josh came out convincing everyone that we should just fire a rocket at the building and be done with it. After we left a hole in the building, we went back to our tanks and moved on. We informed our commander over the radio what we had done, and we were told to move on with our duty. Things were beginning to get more dirty and I didn't like the feeling it was giving me, in the pit of my stomach.

Chapter 7

MY GREAT LORD, ANU. EN.KI IS THIS. TO TIAMAT COME I BUT EARTH I FIND. THE EARTH MONTH OF MARCH. EARTH YEAR 2003. ARRIVED IN ERIDU, EARTH. DESTROYED MY SHIP IS. INCORRECT TIMELINE INITIATED. YOUR ASSISTANCE NEEDED. SEND A SHIP.

A GREAT CATACLYSM BEFALLEN A NATION IN THE WEST OF EARTH HAS . TWO TOWERS DESTROYED. PREPARES FOR WAR DOES THEIR LEADER. IN THE GREAT CITY OF BABYLON HAVE I ARRIVED. DESTROYED THE SHIP IS. LORD ANU. NOT TIAMAT BUT EARTH IS THIS. YEAR 2003. INCORRECT TIMELINE INITIATED. ERROR IN CALCULATION. LANDED IN EARTH HAVE I.

LORD ANU. SEND FOR HELP. IN ERIDU. NOW IRAQ. ON EARTH. 2003 A.D.

LORD ANU. RISK OF BEING SEEN AM I. INTERDIMENSIONAL SHIELD FAILING. VISIBILITY POSSIBLE.

MUST RETURN TO NIBIRU.

SEND STARGATE CODES.

SEND STARGATE CODES.

Chapter 8

"Hello, come in, this is 3rd Squadron Blackhawk, do you copy? Hello, this is Private Joshua Nolan. We have a report on a hit from downtown Baghdad in Al-Safena. Target locked and taken out. Over."

"This is Baghdad base. Over. Copy, Officer Nolan. Over."

"We are heading south, over. Most targets are successfully taken. Over. We have some concerns of a crew member. Over."

"What appears to be the problem? Over"

"Private Chris Cunningham is not engaging in duty. Over. Reporting concern for state of mind. Over."

"Can you give more details? Over"

"Chris Cunningham cannot follow orders and is struggling to make a decision. Potential risk to the rest of the unit. Recently, challenging command and not able to use powers of discernment effectively. Appears to be in shock and withdrawing from engagement."

"Thanks for letting us know, Private Nolan. Please send your co-ordinates and we will send a team down immediately."

"Is he going to be okay?" asked Josh.

"That depends on him, Private Nolan. He will be returned to base for an assessment. Possibly re-assigned," was the answer.

Chapter 9

"I am here in response to your call, Private Nolan. Thank you for your report and I look forward to working with you. If you work through and follow my orders, you will be promoted sooner than you think. This is also a test for you. We are in battle, in war, it is hard, it is ugly. We have no space for pussies. Either you're in or you're out. Thanks for letting me know about Private Cunningham and, for that, you will be rewarded with a 7-day pass. See to it that you are fit for your return to duty," asserted Sergeant Grisham, who had been sent by the commanding officer, to the small unit who were in need of a leader.

"Yes, Sir," said Josh, trying his best not to express his joy with his reward.

"Before you go, what exactly happened?" asked Sergeant Grisham.

"Well, Sir, I saw that Private Cunningham did not really appear to be following the orders correctly, Sir, or to the best of his ability," said Josh, with his chin up but with eyes on the ground.

"Tell me more," said Sergeant Grisham, calmly.

"Well, he stayed behind us mostly and he kept questioning everything we were told to do. He was like some whining pussy in our ears all the time. It was something we could have done without, to be honest with you," said Josh, in the same non-expressive demeanor.

"Don't you both go back a long way?" probed Sergeant Grisham, with a slight tone of curiosity.

"Yes, we do but this is different, Sir. We're not kids at school anymore. We just have to do what we're told and all he's done is whine and question everything. It's throwing the rest of the crew off, Sir." asserted Josh with a tone of annoyance.

"Do you think he's ready for this?" asked Sergeant Grisham. Noticing Josh's tense demeanor, Sergeant Grisham proceeded with: "It's okay, private Nolan. At ease. You can say how you feel."

"I got to say, Sir, in my honest opinion, I think he's surprised us all with his attitude. We all think he should be back home. He's pretty much useless to us all here. He's better off at home. If not, then he'll probably end up dead," stated Josh, with a deep sigh at being put at ease, whilst trying his hardest not to let his concern for Christopher show.

"Well, thanks for letting me know. Make sure you keep me updated. Now go and get some rest at base and we'll see you back in a week," replied Sergeant Grisham, sounding satisfied with the response he received from his new subordinate - Private Joshua Nolan, Christopher's childhood buddy.

"Thank you, Sir," said Josh, sounding extremely grateful for the opportunity.

Chapter 10

We hadn't been sleeping too well. We were getting, on average, three hours of sleep every night and we were running on adrenaline, protein bars and energy drinks. Just after that incident with Al-Jazeera, a Sergeant arrived to join our team. He was a huge guy from Texas and he wasn't going to fuck around. He gave us all a real hard time, me especially, making it clear to me that I was being pushed out of the crew.

The Sergeant that was sent to watch our company was Sergeant A. J. Grisham, a real cunt son-of-a-bitch, the devil incarnate. When he arrived, he made it clear that I was going to be singled out for harassment. One the first day, he ordered me to visit a house in Al-Safena, without back-up, and interrogate the family. I did it but not without getting my first war wounds – I was ambushed in the house by my first insurgent who slashed me on the arm and leg. I got out and I was sent to the cache for treatment before being sent back out within a couple of hours after getting bandaged up. I was still leaking blood.

When I went back to hook up with the crew, I was approached by the Sergeant who immediately told me that I was in danger of being court-martialed for not following his orders. I objected and he took me to the ground. He placed his boot on my face, pressing the entire weight of his body on my back as I lay on the ground. He was 250 pounds of pure muscle. The bastard kicked me twice before he walked away.

I got up and walked over to the tank that was parked by the promenade, in Al-Safena. I was expecting to find Josh but he wasn't there. I was told he had been sent on a mission and, after pressing further about Josh's whereabouts, they just looked at each other in silence and continued with their duties. I began to suspect Josh had something to do with what happened and I wanted to confront him about it.

Josh had been gone a couple of days before a crew member finally told me the truth that he had been sent back to base for a week. I asked them why but I was met with a wall of silence again. When Josh returned, he had changed completely. His whole persona changed. He wasn't just blowing hold and cold again, like he did when we were back in training in Fort Benning. He couldn't look me in the eye and, when he did, the light in his eyes was gone. He spoke to me worse than the Sergeant did, like he was disgusted with me. Well, that's how it seemed. It tore me up inside, like I had just lost my only brother and he was still walking around in front of me, sort of like the living dead - with a glazed look in his eyes, distant and cold.

Sergeant Grisham became a real bane of my life from thereon out. At first, it was the sneaky and underhanded things he was doing, like sending me off to fend for myself. Then it became a game to him. He would send me off to find liquor, money and drugs and storm lots of houses to do it. Then I started to drink a little, then a lot, to bring down my nerves. I was all strung out. Every mission became a white knuckle ride. I was sent down streets in Al-Safena, mostly without back-up so I fired at anyone who even looked like a threat.

What Sergeant Grisham loved to do was buy and sell liquor and drugs with the locals and in between units so there was a lot of money changing hands. He told me that, if I didn't do as I was told, then I was going to be court-martialed. As long as I did as he told me, and as long as I did it, then he would leave me alone. Though that didn't stop him. We were in Al-Safena, a day before we were ordered to head downriver to Maghreb and I was ordered to storm a house, to gather a stash of drugs of money. At that point, it became part of the routine with Sergeant Grisham so it wasn't a shock but I didn't expect I was going to be ambushed by three insurgents equipped with a bomb. After I left the house, I was walking back to the tank, which was situated about 500 metres down the road, when I passed a white car to the left of me, on the other side of the road I was on. Just as I turned, I clocked a couple of Iraqis walking away from the car and the car blew up. I landed against the wall of a building, on the opposite side of the street I was walking down.

I lay there for about an hour with nothing but the ringing in my ears, before I drifted off. When I came to, the sun was setting and I had been stripped of everything that was on me, including the drugs. A few kids began to crowd around me and began playing with my gear. I tried getting up and I looked down to see a whole lot of blood coming out of my leg. I had been stripped of my radio and the only thing I had left was my helmet. I remember pointing to the kids to the right of me, to point them to the end of the road to where Corniche Street crossed it, where I could see the riverside and the tank.

The kids just copied everything I did and laughed. I could feel my mouth open but nothing, no words, came out. I heard nothing of anything around me. I felt my face to see if it was still intact and if there was any blood. I was still in one piece, thank God. I rolled to my side and I crawled along the street to get to the end of it. I thought that, if I did that, then the kids would be able to understand what I was trying to do. Then, a car pulled up and three men got out.

They dragged and dumped me into the back of their car and drove off, whilst stripping me to find anything but they couldn't. I kept fighting them off in the back seat, the guy who was in the back with me went through every pocket, to get what he could but there was nothing for him. He yelled at the driver when he realized I was empty then, just as soon as I was in the car, I was thrown back out again, dumped at the end of the road. I managed to crawl to Corniche

Street, got up and staggered to the riverbank, where I could see the tanks and trucks.

Trying to keep myself upright, I pushed myself against the wall of a building on the opposite side of the road to the riverside, and waved my arms to get the attention of my company at the other end of the road. I managed to stay up for about a minute before I collapsed again. When I woke up, I was in the cache, where I was treated and allowed to stay for 3 whole days before being sent back out again. They said all I had was some cuts and bruises. They said that nothing had been broken, that all I had a very slight concussion, and that I was fine to continue with field duty.

But I was totally disoriented and it wasn't long after that, when I started to get flashbacks. Strong memories were beginning to cross my mind. First, the memories were fairly innocuous and they left me feeling off-center. I couldn't understand why I was getting them. They were incredibly vivid. Outside the medical unit, I stopped to take a rest and bury my head between my legs, struggling to get my brain into thinking about what I needed to be doing. Soon after, more memories of my childhood returned, with feelings of anxiety that got so intense that I started having trouble breathing. Soon after that, more memories filled my head. They just came flooding through and I crouched down, outside the medical unit, in a high state of anxiety.

I paused for a moment, taking deep breaths, silently praying to myself that Sergeant Grisham wouldn't be there when I got back to the unit. When I got back, the nightmare continued, when we were ordered by him to move downriver to the Dora region of the southern-west point of the Tigris River, that runs through Baghdad. The rules of engagement were completely out at that point and the team was completely effed up under Grisham's leadership. It seemed like I was the only one in the company following the rules of engagement. They began to completely disregard everything, even more so than before, when we were up-river in Al-Safena and in Maghreb. The Sergeant told us that anybody that we saw was evil and didn't have a right to be there. The unit had turned into street-thugs and we were being led by a monster.

Dora was a neighborhood that I knew, from briefing, had no insurgents or militias. It was a peaceful neighborhood that belonged to the Christians, Shias and Mandeans. The Mandeans were a funny bunch who wore funny white outfits. They were peaceful and you could tell that from the neighborhood, that those people didn't want anything to do with Saddam or his army. When we first rolled into the neighborhood, there was nobody on the streets and the civilians did their best to not be seen by us. There were churches in the neighborhood so I thought Sergeant Grisham would go easy but that didn't stop me from feeling that sickly feeling, like this was gonna be one of Sergeant Grisham's free-for all.

It's perverse, and having to remember it all doesn't help, because I was a part of that and that makes it difficult to live with. Who the fuck put us in charge of the world anyway? Where the fuck were Saddam and Osama? Nobody knew. We were being told that we had to take out as many insurgents as we could cuz it was them or us. But it didn't matter how much or whose blood was being spilled. Old, young, rich, poor, Christian, Moslem, men, women, children. They were all game. It was like being in a never ending video game, such as Max Payne. Nothing began to matter anymore. We were losing sleep and we were broken. We either joined in to survive or got out and died.

In Dora, we stopped at the houses and knocked on, to question and scope out the people. It was the Sergeant's way of gaining the trust of the residents before he unleashed his hell. Josh, at that point, was doing his best to impress Sergeant Grisham. Josh had been doing that a lot since he returned from leave. He was doing anything short of sucking the Sergeant's dick to get his attention. They all knew, at that point, two months into our tour, that I didn't want to be there. I remember thinking that, if I didn't make it out alive, I would have died because I took a hit, either voluntarily or accidentally.

We were told that Dora, Al-Dora, housed a secret command post that was buried somewhere in the neighborhood and that it housed Saddam's sons – Udday and Qusay. Our mission was to recon where they potentially could be hiding and to report back or to take out the targets. Sergeant Grisham completely ignored the rules of engagement. At that point, I stopped talking to everyone around me. The rest of the team were completely afraid of the consequences of challenging Grisham and Josh was so far gone that I couldn't even look into his eyes anymore.

We were in the middle of the neighborhood and Sergeant and Josh went to the nearby gas station. The gas station seemed to be functioning quite well, it seemed like it was completely untouched by everything that was going on elsewhere, like it was in an oasis. It was very still there, in downtown Dora. It was dusk and we had just finished a day of patrolling and doing some recon, by foot and fire. We were just shooting up in the air to try and draw out any insurgents. There were none. The residents were scurrying indoors and the streets were empty. Nobody was to be seen. I stood at the end of the street and to the right of me was the gas station.

The street to the left of me led all the way down some 4 kilometers to Dora Expressway – which was the freeway that led out of Baghdad. I thought "fuck, I would love to just get the fuck out of here." I turned to my right and I could see the Sergeant and Josh leaving the gas station, carrying two sacks. I thought – "what the fuck? They just took the cash from the gas station!"

We got into the truck and moved down the street and turned left down the first block. We were told that we had to cut through and go to the Assyrian part of the neighborhood cuz that's where the underground command post of Saddam's army might be. The neighborhood was dead quite. It was like something was going to happen. It wasn't like before, where the people weren't afraid to come out. Sergeant Grisham said it had everything to do with the fact that everyone in the neighborhood was linked to Al-Qaeda so we had every right to take out anyone we perceived as a threat.

Just before we got to our destination, we passed a mosque and several churches. We didn't trouble the churches but, naturally, we fired several rounds at the mosque. We took out the speakers at the top of the minaret so they couldn't say their prayers. We turned right and down a big road called Tuma Street. Along that road were just rows of shops and most of them were still open, even at dusk, in the middle of a war zone, as though they were trying to maintain normality. The shopkeepers and customers didn't approach us and they didn't make eye contact either.

Sergeant Grisham ordered us to stop and we went into a cafe cuz he wanted to presumably spend the money they had just looted. They ordered some drinks and food and they spoke to the owners – asked a few questions. Everybody on that street was really nervous. Sergeant didn't mind the tension and seemed to be used to it. He told us the people in that area were Christian so we didn't have to worry. Besides, we knew we were more powerful than any one of them. Sergeant Grisham started asking about Uday and Qusay and their bases but, when he didn't get the answer he wanted, he just pointed a gun and the owners just put their hands up and started crying.

I was standing outside with Josh and I made eye contact with him. I managed to look deep in them. It seemed like his soul had been plucked out. There was just no light in them anymore. He had a fixed gaze and I could barely make out his pupils. We were all living on little to no sleep and scoring as much drugs as we could to keep us awake. We 'borrowed' as much Xanax, antidepressants, speed, whatever you name it to keep us all going. We were all coked up and nobody was showing it more than the Sergeant and Josh.

I looked inside the cafe and Sergeant Grisham was ushering me and Josh to come in. The rest of the team stayed outside. We went in and the boss was yelling at the owners – two men, who were wearing crosses. Sarge was yelling at them to take us upstairs. Josh looked a bit puzzled at that point. We were in a room above their cafe and the Sergeant made them strip. Joshua tied them up. Sergeant Grisham got me to pull one of them over the other in a doggy position. They were butt naked. They were howling out in protest. Joshua kicked the guy on top in the nuts. We got no information out of them so we went back down and headed back to the truck outside and moved down the street, behind the tank in front of us, which was there to shield us.

We were driving down when we started noticing that some people were coming out of the shops and gathering to see us pass. The shops began to close up and we were being stared down so Sergeant Grisham radioed ahead at the tank to follow the road in a zigzag fashion cuz he started to get a feeling that there might be some IEDs on the road. After about a mile down the road, just as we began zig-zagging, we were hit.

There were two bombs. One had been rolled out to us from the side and another came from a car that was parked along the road. The assailants fled as we were hit and we soon got the feeling that more were on their way. The tank in front of us was completely out. Whatever it was, it must have come from above and not from the side. The first thing we did when we got out of our tank was point upwards and start firing.

We shot at either side of the streets. The people were dispersing out but we were the only ones down there. Sergeant Grisham radioed for back-up and we could hear the hum of choppers nearby. That pushed back the crowd a little and it was enough to stop any more coming our way. After about 5 minutes, all three of us were stationed behind a car or at the side of the tank or truck and we were firing the fuck at everything and everyone around us.

By that time, it was dark and the streetlights weren't on. We could hear the choppers getting close and the Sergeant and Josh were going crazy. I saw the chopper land behind me and we were yelled at to board. A few men got off and started to immediately patrol the neighborhood. We were then flown back to base in Baghdad.

Josh and I bunked in the same room. We had a stash of liquor that we had taken and I started drinking it straight away. I told Josh that I couldn't and didn't want to carry on anymore. I chugged the whole half bottle of brandy and I pulled a gun to my head. Josh jumped on me and hollered at the rest to come and help him. I was restrained by three officers and I was placed in a cell with a pan. I wasn't allowed to leave the cell and I was harassed by the custody officers for turning jelly. My mental state didn't bother them one bit.

After a couple of days, I was called into the office of the Sergeant and Commanding Officer. I was going to be court-martialed. I was told I was able to contact my parents back home. The charge was endangering the lives of my team and not following orders. But that wasn't what happened and the charge had the Sergeant's signature all over it. The defense lawyer assigned to me didn't appear to be following protocol so I suspected that the charges were bogus. It was a way for them to put the frighteners on me. I was tried in a small court on base then released after "a lack of evidence". Before I was released, I was told I was being transferred to Basra.

I was getting ready to be transferred, at the base. I had finished packing when Josh came in and hugged me and begged me for forgiveness. I didn't react. He was in tears. I asked him why he was crying. That was when he told me that he had just overheard. He kept telling me how sorry he was to hear about it. I didn't know what he was talking about nor did I want to hear it so I made to leave and that's when he said it was Jessica and the baby. They found them killed in a car crash. My heart stopped and my mouth dropped.

I could hear the call to board the plane for Basra but it was too late. I couldn't stay. I had to board. I felt my world begin to crash around me but I wasn't able to stand still for what Josh told me, I just had to keep moving so I didn't have time to let it sink in, besides, given the way Josh had been, I felt suspicious about him. I never understood his motives and I thought that he was being a jerk again. Just before I left to board the plane, I told Josh to fuck off and stay the fuck away from me. A thought crossed my mind from high school, when he played a prank on me and it felt like he was up to his old tricks again, playing a sick joke. I screamed in his face then I heard the new Sergeant yell at me to board so I did. I didn't turn around to see Josh when I boarded cuz I never wanted to see his face again.

Chapter 11

BEFORE THE GREAT DELUGE, E.DIN A GARDEN IN THE FIRST LANDING DID WE FIND. IN E.DIN MY HOUSE DID I BUILD. ARRIVED THEN THE 299. WITH MY HALF-BROTHER EN.LIL, MADE 300 DID WE.

MADE CRO-MAGNON IN OUR IMAGE, DID I. CRO-MAGNON NOT GOOD AS SLAVES AND SAVED US NOT THE MINING. FIRST MODEL NOT SUCCESSFUL. DNA STRANDS NOT BONDING.

SECOND VERSION BETTER. THIRD VERSION SUCCESSFUL. ENGINEERING COMPLETE IT WAS. A SLAVE SPECIES TO MINE FOR GOLD DID I CREATE.

EN.LIL ENRAGED WAS HE. TO DESTROY MY CREATION DID HE SEEK. AN EXTRA TASK TO RULE OVER THEM DID HE DECREE. A GREAT DELUGE BROUGHT FORTH BY EN.LIL TO DESTROY THE CREATION. FLED AND SURVIVED DID THEY. MANY PERISHED.

STOOD ALONE IN OPPOSITION DID I. USE OF FORBIDDEN WEAPONS DID EN.LIL MAKE. TO DESTROY MY CREATION.

STARTED AS CREATORS DID WE. ENDED AS DESTROYERS DID WE.

FROM THE HANDS OF EN.LIL MY HALF-BROTHER THE EVIL WIND BLEW.

IN THE GARDENS OF E.DIN THE EARTH REMAINS A DESERT. AFTER THE EVIL WIND DID EN.LIL BLOW.

MY CREATION SURVIVED, LORD ANU. FROM E.DIN TO SUMER TO BABYLON AND THEN TO THE WEST. AS FAR AS THE EAST, THE NORTH AND THE SOUTH.

UPON EARTH HAVE I RETURNED. NOT IN THE TIME OF OUR SEEDING.

ERIDU IN SUMER. SUMER NOW IRAQ.

A WAR BETWEEN MY CREATION THERE IS. AS EN.LIL DID SEEK TO DESTROY MY CREATION.

MY GREAT LORD ANU. INCORRECT TIMELINE INITIATED HAVE I. EARTH YEAR 203,000 B.C INCORRECT.

ARRIVED IN EARTH YEAR 2003 A.D HAVE I.

ASSISTANCE NEEDED TO RETURN TO NIBIRU.

SEND ASSISTANCE, MY GREAT LORD ANU.

Chapter 12

"Hello, this is Commander Wilcox from Fort Benning. I am calling about Private Christopher Cunningham, from the 3rd Armored Brigade Combat Team, 3rd Infantry Division. I have some very important information that you must action immediately. I have been informed by his father that his wife and daughter have been killed in a car crash. It is imperative that this message is actioned so that he can leave Iraq and return home immediately. Please ensure that you complete a Compassionate Action Request on his behalf, immediately," said Commander Wilcox, in haste, from his office phone in Fort Benning.

"Yes, I am his Sergeant. This is Sergeant Grisham. I will action it directly," responded Sergeant Grisham in eager confirmation of the request, from his base office in Baghdad.

"It is probably best if you do not tell him in Iraq but just grant him the leave to return home as soon as he can," insisted Commander Wilcox, in Fort Benning.

"I will make sure he is sent home as soon as possible," reiterated Sergeant Grisham.

"It is important that this is done in the next 24 hours. His family are expecting him. Again, make sure that he is not informed of the news of his wife and child. He will be briefed upon his arrival here," repeated Commander Wilcox.

"Leave it with me, Commander," relayed Sergeant Grisham, with a pressing tone.

"Just so you know, Private Christopher Cunningham is the son of our decorated veteran Commander and General Joe Cunningham, who has served our country well in three tours and continues to serve the military and our country, through the NSA." Commander Wilcox's tone turned more pressing.

"Oh," paused Sergeant Grisham, in surprise. "I did not know that," he continued, with a measured pause.

"Is there a problem, Sergeant, I forgot your name...?" asked Commander Wilcox with some alarm.

"Grisham, Sir. Sergeant Grisham," answered Sergeant Grisham with some quiet acquiescence.

"Yes, Grisham. See to it that this is actioned. He must be returned immediately. No questions asked." Pressed Commander Wilcox, further.

"Yes, Commander. Leave it with me. leave it with me," assured Sergeant Grisham, eager to affirm the order he had received.

"I will await a response, Grisham," replied Commander Wilcox before hanging up.

"Yes, Sir," confirmed Sergeant Grisham as he was cut off.

Sergeant Grisham put the phone down slowly and put both hands over his face, in shock of who he had spoken to, what he now knew and what he was asked to do. He drew a deep breath and made contact with the forwarding Sergeant on the phone, who was then overseeing Christopher's deployment in Basra, to find out where Christopher was. After that, Grisham sat with a worried look on his face, wondering whether Christopher would spill the beans on his own activities as a Sergeant but he soon sat up straight from his slouched position and shook his head, then let out a sigh.

Chapter 13

I couldn't figure out what happened though I suspected that Josh was fucking with my head. On board the plane, I asked the officer in charge to see if there had been any message from Fort Benning.

"WHAT ARE YOU TALKING ABOUT, CUNNINGHAM? YOU ARE ON TOUR, YOU ON DUTY AND I SUGGEST THAT YOU STAY FOCUSED ON THE TASK AHEAD. I DO NOT NEED TO REMIND YOU THAT YOU HAVE JUST BEEN RELEASED FROM COURT MARTIAL. ANY MORE NONSENSE AND I WILL PERSONALLY SEE TO IT THAT YOU ARE SENT BACK AND SENT TO JAIL," yelled the Officer on the plane.

I didn't ask him anything after that. I would just need to get to a computer or a phone, to call Mom and Dad at home. We were on duty, on board a military aircraft so there was no way that I would be able to check properly until we touched down. The time on board was spent preparing for the new mission. We went through the rules of engagement for the new mission and my new Sergeant, Sergeant Dubois, was someone I could tell who would stick to business. That was fine by me. I was only there to get my job done.

They had transferred me to the 502nd Infantry Regiment cuz it also had its base in Fort Benning. We were deployed to support the armed enemy that had been fighting on the outskirts of Basra. We were told that the city was being cleared by the 101st Airborne Division but they were met with disorganized resistance. We were told that we had to use as much of our individual readiness training as much as possible. Some of us had already done that and the only training that I recall using as part of my IRT was when it came to handling the media. Nevertheless, I felt equipped and ready for my new deployment.

After we were done with being briefed and everyone knew what their role was, I had a moment to myself. Jessica and the baby flashed up in my mind again, making me want to contact Mom and Dad desperately. The flight to Basra from Baghdad lasted just over half an hour and all but 5 minutes of that time was filled with things that made it impossible to think about anything other than the mission. In the 5 minutes that were left, I did think about Jessica and the baby, and I was filled with pangs of anxiety.

As soon as we got off, we formed our teams and we were assigned our roles. Sergeant Dubois gave us our instructions and we drove off from the landing zone, codenamed Sparrow, on the outskirts of the city. We were linked up at the base by two armored tanks - M1 Abrams and a M2 Bradley – and, after seeing the state of the Abrams, I hoped to be placed in the Bradley. I got lucky. M2 Bradley was a better vehicle and more equipped for current warfare. It cost the military just over 3 million dollars and it had space for 3 crew and 6 passengers and its main armament was a lot better than the M1 Abrams. We had chain guns, anti-tank missiles and TOW missiles. When I stepped inside, I thought "my god, we are ready." At that point, I tried to put Josh out of my mind and what he had told me. I just wanted to start my new mission and put the previous two months behind me.

The thing you have to remember about Iraq is that we were sent cuz we believed we were taking out Saddam and Al-Qaeda, meaning Osama. In Baghdad, it was obvious to us that Saddam and his army were nowhere to be seen and that's why everyone was acting like a free-for-all. We had been pumped up to fight an enemy but that enemy was nowhere to be found. Instead, we went for the next best thing, the locals, but we didn't do that intentionally. We really didn't meet Saddam's army until we got to Basra.

The tanks moved towards the southeast of Basra. The dust rolled up the side of the tanks as we rolled out of the landing zone. I got in and began tracking our coordinates. Our tank was fully loaded with 6 soldiers including myself, a driver, a commander and a gunner. Our commander told us where exactly we would expect to meet the resistance, led by the Fedayeen Saddam, a paramilitary force. We were told that Fedayeen would mostly be using rocket-propelled grenades and machine-gun fire. If it wasn't for their rocket-propelled grenades, the mission would have been easy.

As we neared the city, we began meeting with mortars which caught us by surprise. The best we could do was stop or swerve. We would wait a few minutes on the road and stop and fire back. Wait a few more minutes and we repeated until our targets got closer and we could make a direct hit. In the meantime, the other tanks up ahead or the Blackhawks above continued with their bombardment. We paced ourselves as we drew closer to the city limits.

When we got to Basra, everything seemed to be quiet on their side. We didn't want to risk attack by rocket-propelled grenades so we just kept doing what we did. We would fire, stop, get out, fire back and get back in. It was dusk and the city lights turned on and the sky started turning a violet-red, the most amazing color. It was a warm and vivid sky, like God was shielding us from harm. The tanks up ahead were doing the same, edging closer to the city in their stalled fashion.

We offloaded just inside the city perimeter. We patrolled the streets and we were immediately met with gunfire from all angles. Basra was a lot different to Baghdad. The only people out at night were the enemy combatants and the civilians were nowhere to be seen. We all split up and took our posts behind houses, in alleyways and burnt-out cars. We fired with our AKs but the tank took the worst damage. We managed to take out several posts that were firing grenades in our direction.

The city was surprisingly densely populated and nothing like Baghdad. We entered the city at the southeast corner. It was a poor neighborhood, we could see that. Nothing but houses and shops built in blocks leading up the center of the city where there were two mosques but we were well away from there at that point. It was like a sandcastle ghetto. That's the only way I can describe it. Basra was a Shia stronghold and it was an important strategic point for us so we had to get it right. We knew that the Shias were not part of Saddam's army cuz Saddam had been persecuting them for decades. We also knew that Saddam would place his troops to squash a rebellion from the Shias as well as fight us so we knew they had their work cut out.

Pretty soon, it became apparent that Saddam's Republican Guard and the Fedayeen paramilitary were everywhere in the city. It was a night-long bombardment and they were coming at us from houses, alleyways, mosques, you name it. Fortunately, we were covered by B-52s, Chinooks and Blackhawks. The B-52s carpet-bombed the main areas and the Chinooks and Blackhawks took out smaller targets in our vicinity. It didn't matter to the enemy though, it seemed they were relentless.

Before we were allowed to move on ground through Basra, we were told that the Republican Guard were going to be taken out by airstrike. They had been more or less worn down but the Fedayeen force was still strong in the area. In the night, we wore night vision goggles and we went from building to building to ferret out any hostile forces. As we continued, we started hearing reports that some Iraqis were turning the other way after seeing the might of our force.

By the morning, it got quiet again so we made progress by moving up Basra from the southeast part of the city where we had entered. We had been assigned 30 sectors of the southeast part of the city and we covered 13 in one night, which we considered a really successful night. The following morning we marched on through the city. We were doing well, moving northwards and we even uncovered a stash of weapons in some schools. By nightfall, we were nearing the end of our mission, having completed most of the sectors. The problems started when we started getting tired and started becoming less vigilant.

We were in a busy residential area with schools, shops and apartment complexes before we rolled into a very quiet area. There was a sort of what you might call a town square and around it were apartment blocks. As soon as we were in that vicinity, we had about a minute before we realized that we needed to back out as soon as possible. It was like as soon as we thought it, we were hit by an RPG. Our tank was on fire underneath and we had about 3 minutes to get out and get under cover. I was the last one out and I just about survived the blast.

Out of 6 soldiers and 3 crew, only 4 soldiers survived and made it to safety. The square had one statue of Saddam which a couple of soldiers hid behind, facing the only side of the square that was safe. I ran across the road from the square and managed to get cover behind a car. The other soldier did the same further along the street. We soon ascertained that the fire was coming from three sides of the northern part of the square. The best thing we could do was wait it out until we hopefully received back up. Our tank automatically went off the radar if it was attacked or under siege so it flagged up on anyone who was nearby – be it a tank, armored vehicle or air support.

Despite the ambush, Basra was an easier battle because it was empty of civilians. The civilians scurried through the back-alleys in the day which was good for us cuz then we could get on with our jobs a lot better. The people of Basra also didn't want anything to do with Saddam and you could see that the people there had been treated badly by him cuz it was such a poor area, compared to Baghdad.

So we knew that all we had to do was fend off the enemy combatants and, if they didn't move in on us or triangulate our positions, then we would be okay until back-up arrived. We sat and waited tensely and it was about just over a quarter of an hour before a Chinook and a Blackhawk flew overhead and started their bombardment. They took out two of the enemy posts just as they were beginning to move from their positions.

We moved from the square, to the gates of Basra, a few hundred meters ahead, where we could see crowds cheering at the Chinooks. We felt a sigh of relief like it was, for the first time, we all felt that - yeah - we were there to liberate them and to free the people from Saddam. The atmosphere was really thrilling and we bounced off the energy that the crowd was giving off. We all felt terrific, like proper heroes and liberators.

We strolled up to the statue of Saddam, which was in the middle of the square and we were then quickly surrounded by the residents. We saw them pelt the statue with their shoes and anything they could find. They were unleashing all of their anger and frustrations and we could hear them chant something all in their language which I was told was something like "die, Devil, die". We saw a couple of men trying to scale the statue and attempt to throw a rope around the statue. We knew what they wanted to do so we assisted them by fastening a chain around the neck.

The rope was rigged to the tank and we drove off. The crowd erupted further and we were all celebrating and jeering. It was a tremendous release of energy - we all felt like we were all on the same side at that moment, like we were all one. More residents came to the square and it started filling up quickly. A Chinook touched down later on that evening and we were told that the final lot of insurgents had just been taken out and the rest had fled. Shortly after, along came the Blackhawk and airlifted some of the soldiers off the ground.

It went up about 20 feet in the air before it was hit in the tail by a rocket-propelled grenade and it came spiraling down. That Blackhawk should have taken out that last post before it landed to take up the soldiers on the ground but the enemy just came from out of nowhere and caught them off guard. We all scattered as it landed before our few-second window was up and there was a blast. We managed to clear 40 feet of space before it crashed with minimal impact on the ground and the immediate vicinity but, because it had been hit by a rocket, it was already ablaze when it crashed.

We all ran to evacuate as many of the 6 that were on board, as we could. Two of the men didn't manage to escape before the blast and the fire got them; the other 4 ran out and we carried them back to the square. The Blackhawk crashed at more or less the same site it took off from, on the road, at the side of the square near Saddam's statue.

That incident was one of many but not the worst of what being at war is all about. You're out there fighting, you've been told what to look out for and you're told the rules of engagement. Most of the time, nobody knows what's gonna happen. As long as you have some sense about you and as long as you paid attention during your IRT – and finished training with a real sense that you're gonna make it out alive - then it's worth going into. Apart from our Basic and Individual Readiness Training – and what a joke that was – we basically got to learn everything about the war on the job.

When you lose your company, your fellow soldiers, your team, you lose a part of yourself. You get to a point, during a successful mission, when you all begin to think the same way. You do the same things, you feel the same, you know what each other is going to do before he does it. It's hard to describe but that's essentially what happens to you. It's like your brain becomes one whole, fighting the same fighting in your crew.

When you lose your team that's when it hits you hard. That guilt is something else to bear. You try to figure out in your head what happened and you play it over a million times and you try to go back in time in your head to make it better but it's not and you know it's not cuz you're still alive and they're all dead. It doesn't matter that you get awarded the Valorous Unit Award afterwards. At the time and, a lot of the time afterwards, you just feel like crap for living.

When sound eventually returned in my ears, after the blast from the Blackhawk, the piercing ringing of the blast that hit us yards away from the square, where we had just rescued the crew, I had a severe pain in my head. The blast from the Blackhawk carried me to the wall of the city square and, just before I closed my eyes, I saw the slain bodies of the crew, dismembered like a jigsaw on the ground.

"Mano-ana-za." cried a resident from Basra.

"What the fuck is that?" cried another Iraqi man.

"Mano-ana-za." repeated the man.

"What the fuck?" I yelled at the men, then into the radio: "Come in, come in, we are being hit. Do you copy? We are being hit!!!!"

"Ya-il-hai Wa-Man-Il-Shayton. Shayton. Wa-Kwud-Wa-Sul-Il-Shayton." yelled the man in Arabic, as if he had just seen a monster, pointing at the sky.

"All units have been hit in Basra. Do you copy? This is the 3rd Infantry from Basra square. We have been hit by an unseen force. Do you copy?" I screamed into the radio, hoping someone would pick up.

"Ya-Il-A-Hai Wa-Kwud-Wa-Sul-Il-Shayton." repeated the man in Arabic, growing frantic.

"What the fuck? Will you shut the fuck up? What the hell are you saying?" I yelled, at the men on the streets of Basra, trying to make sense of the melee, after the Blackhawk came down.

"I see the Devil. I see the Devil," shouted an Iraqi man, in English.

Chapter 14

"Oh my God, Oh my God. No, no, no. Honey, tell me it isn't…"

"It's true," said Joe Cunningham, to his wife who was sobbing tears at the news, in their home in Sandy Springs, Georgia.

"How? I can't believe what I'm hearing. To lose my daughter in law and grandchild just weeks after sending our son to war. Could there be anything more horrific for a mother to suffer?" asked Joe's wife, Christopher's mother.

"It just happened. They said she veered off the road, maybe she tried dodging an oncoming vehicle. They don't know what happened, not yet, but they're investigating who was on the road at the time but they're gonna struggle cuz it was a quiet road with no cameras," Joe said solemnly.

"What was she doing there?", asked his wife.

"She had been out for the morning with the baby to see one of her friends and it happened when she was coming back home. There was a diversion on the 575 so she took the 92. That's where it happened," said Joe, in a low tone.

"Where is she now?" screamed Christopher's mother.

"They've taken her to the Emory Hospital in Sandy Springs" stated Joe, still flat.

"Well, quick, let's go," screaming Joe's wife, hysterically.

"Honey, they've said they're not going to make it." Joe's dulcet tones cut through his wife's cries, like a knife.

"What? Oh, my God, I just can't………." She sobbed and fell to the ground. "Joe, Joe, say it ain't so. No… ring them up, tell them we are coming, tell them we are coming, tell them to save them," continued Joe's wife.

Joe crouched down, took his wife by her shoulders, looked into her eyes and said, calmly, solemnly still: 'honey, it is over."

Christopher's mother was bereft, as a caring mother, grandmother and mother in law would be. She had sent her son to war, she had raised him to believe in God and God's righteousness and in the power of the American military, but nothing prepared herself, for the danger that lurked at home. Christopher's father, a courageous and decorated man of the military, stoic by nature and a pillar of hope and strength for his family and community, was there to take his wife and lead her through the tragedy that had befallen them at home. He was there to buffer his wife from the waves of shock that were running through her delicate frame, as he laid her head in his chest, as she sobbed an empty sorrow for the life that her son was never to live with his own family, Jessica and the baby, upon his return.

Christopher, the son of a military man and a doting mother, would return to an empty home. Raised in an environment which made him believe in his own might, part of something greater than himself, as controllers of the world, but Christopher was powerless in keeping his young family alive. His heritage, his blood, gave him a natural advantage over others. Christopher, lost in a foreign land, was beginning to experience a new reality, that all is not what it seems. How he saw himself was not the way others saw him. What he saw was not what others saw. What he was beginning to feel was something completely different to what his crew members felt. Betrayal and isolation had created a shift in him and his team mates.

Despite his parents' best efforts, nothing prepared Christopher for the world outside their front door.

The world Christopher Cunningham was taught to believe in was crumbling, being replaced with something else, another version of a reality than the one he was taught, whilst another reality, a reality from his past clouded his present. Memories which he couldn't make sense of, memories that haunted his new reality, like the mask of a demon over a clown. Those sweet memories from his childhood began to haunt him.

Haunting, were his sweet memories.

As Christopher's world began to crumble, so did his mother's, as she sat in her husband's arms. Her world as a mother was falling apart. She would never be able to plan Christopher's homecoming with her daughter-in-law, with the baby gurgling. She would never see her grandchild grow up and the prospect of seeing her son's devastation when he finally did return home broke her completely.

Chapter 15

I woke up with a pounding headache, in the house of a Moslem family. I tried to get up but they kept pushing me back down, motioning me to lay down. They all looked harmless but I reached for my gun, nevertheless. Then, I thought, why didn't they take it away from me? There was only a mother and her daughter and their neighbor, who had dragged me there. They told me that her husband had been killed by Saddam's army, who had been going through Basra and picking out Shia Muslims to kill in order to send a message to them, which was to not rebel against Saddam and join us, when we arrived.

I sat up on the couch, propping myself up, still unable to hear, from the blast of the Blackhawk out on the streets of Basra. My first thought was to get out. They kept running around and bringing things to the coffee table in front of me, things I knew they didn't have much of, like bottled water and fresh fruit. I felt really taken aback by their hospitality and good nature - I was weirded out by it. I figured my presence made them feel safe cuz I was someone, an American, who was on their side against Saddam. Being weirded out was too much for me to take though, so I made moves to get back to my crew.

I managed to shake the women off me before I got out of their apartment and walked down the stairs back outside. Then, I felt a searing pain in my head, like someone had taken a lightning rod and ran it through my brain. It was excruciating. Blood began dripping by the side of my head. I looked down the stairwell, lost my footing and collapsed, rolling all the way down the staircase, a couple of yards away from the entrance of the apartment complex. My helmet, still attached to my head, saved me from the hard knock on the stone floor.

Still on the ground, I took off my helmet and I saw some blood inside it. I felt the warmth of fresh blood on the top of my head and the wound stung as I touched it. I should have stayed upstairs with the crazy women. I looked up the stairs to see if they had come after me, in some hope that they might help but they didn't. I then curled up in agony, paralyzed with pain. After a few moments, I crawled to the front door and opened it. My instincts were to go back to the flat but I fought it off eventually, knowing that I wouldn't get the help I needed there, not least because of the language barrier.

When I opened the front door, I came crashing down to the pavement. My face firmly on the ground, I turned my cheek to see around me. Perhaps someone, some people, perhaps some kids would notice and help me. With one cheek on the ground, I stared down at the end of the street. I made out the silhouette of an oddly shaped person staring back at me and, as I laid eyes upon it, I felt a wave of fear pass through my body. I blinked slowly with as much energy as I could muster, trying to focus, fixing my gaze on what was a tall being staring back at me, at the end of the street.

There didn't seem to be anybody else around but I could hear the voice of people and cars moving around in the distance, the usual commotion, from the streets and roads around. In my field of vision, all I could see was the street. I turned my body around, to lay on my back, still dizzy from the pain, still with my head facing one side, to the end of the street. At first, I thought that what I was seeing was a very tall soldier because, after a few moments of staring and fixing my gaze on him, I could make out familiar colors – the dusky browns and greens of fatigues.

Still laying on the pavement, with a body that was somewhat unresponsive to any attempt of movement, I attempted to move my lips to what I thought was HELP ME but my mouth moved to a different pace. Frozen in paralysis from my injury, I couldn't get the words out. Whatever it was that I saw, it was looking directly at me – from where it stood – about a hundred feet away. Its eyes locked onto mine as I struggled to speak. I struggled to even think the words. The words - the words - struggled to come out but, when they did, I said: "WHAT THE FUCK IS THAT?"

Its eyes. Big eyes. Scary eyes that locked onto mine. I reached for my gun and I tried to point it at the thing but those eyes scared the shit out of me. Then I felt its energy, its presence, even from all those feet away from me. As if it was reading my mind, I fell into its hypnotic gaze. I felt its power move through me, when it stared at me. Moments later, my hand involuntarily let go of the trigger. An image penetrated my mind and flashed up, clear as day, the image of it, and it was not like you and I. When I locked into its eyes, all I saw was a hollowness, just as I had seen before, when I killed someone whilst on duty and their life left their body. Then, a wave of fear crawled onto me, as if the devil himself was peering into my soul.

My gaze remained fixed, staring at the thing ahead of me, at the end of the street, as I blinked slowly, rhythmically, before it began to move in my direction. A paralysis fell over me, as I started to fall out of consciousness. I saw its movements, I saw it move in my direction, as it had noticed me noticing it. It looked like a predator going in for his kill, gliding towards me, with its feet motionless on the ground. I opened my mouth again, to try and say something but what came out was an empty breath and what I thought would be my last sigh. Out went the light of the day and the blue sky. I submitted myself to the will of God and Jesus. I said a little prayer in my heart and I said, before I fell out of consciousness: "Dear God, Please deliver me from this Evil, the Devil that stands before me. Please God, save me and I will be your servant forever."

When I woke up, I could hear the people around me pointing at me and shouting JINN and SHAYTON – then they started looking at me and pointing and yelling and screaming. Some men and women started throwing their shoes at me and then rocks. I managed to get up and move back inside the apartment block that I had just left. I kept hearing them shout JINN, JINN, JINN and SHAYTON, Arabic words for demon and devil. Their screams carried on, as the hail of shoes and stones came my way. As soon as I got up off the ground, I noticed that my head no longer hurt and the shooting pain was gone.

I couldn't comprehend what I had just seen. Was I dreaming? Was I dead? What had I seen? By the time I got inside the building, I managed to breathe a little. Since I had been hurt really badly from the helicopter blast in Basra's town square, maybe I was just seeing things. It was hard to tell, at that point, what exactly was going on. But it was confusing. I was confused.

The front door to the apartment complex where I sought shelter opened and a man stood in the doorway. As soon as he saw me, he started yelling something in Arabic. I yelled back: "I DON'T UNDERSTAND YOU". I went up to him and pushed him onto the pavement, out of the doorway, and shut the door, after yelling at him: "GET THE FUCK AWAY FROM ME IF YOU WANT TO LIVE!" I closed the door and shifted the heavy discarded cabinet which was in the hallway, to block the front door.

I sat down at the bottom of the stairwell, with the front door ahead of me, staring at the front door with clenched teeth and fists. I caught my reflection in the mirror to the right of me, and saw a scared-looking soldier staring back. I looked a mess, I didn't recognize myself, for a moment, under the heavy eyes, the dirt and the remnants of blood stains trailing all the way down my neck. I walked to the mirror, to see myself closer, taking water from my jerrycan to wash my face.

I could hear some commotion outside, the scurry of a crowd running and hollering. The noise of the crowd diminished as soon as it passed by the door, and some people stirred the front door to the apartment block a couple of times in the process. They were alarmed by something, forcing them to seek shelter where they could find it. Then, all of a sudden, it all went quiet. Then, there was a thud, like a tremor outside and the building shook. A shadow was cast, over the daylight that shone through the window above the front door. I stepped back away from the door, to get a better look of what was casting the shadow through the window. When I looked up, I didn't see a shadow. I saw skin. Dark green-brown, dirty yellow, scaly skin.

The crushing pain returned to my brain. I put my hand over my head and stumbled towards the staircase, where I sat, with my head between my legs. I began crying from the pain, unable to open my eyes, knowing that any light that entered would send a searing shot of suffering into the depths of my brain. Squinting through, slowly, after several minutes, through periods of painful persistence to peek, I managed to open them. In a haze of pain and fatigue, I opened them, and saw that the front door and cabinet in front of me had disappeared, and were replaced with two giant feet.

I drew a deep breath and held it before I followed the feet up, with my squint, against the strong light in front of me. I could make out the shape of two mammoth feet, 10 times the size of my size 9s, blocking the light in the doorway ahead of me. The feeling of dread returned, as it did when I first laid eyes on the creature, but it appeared to be emanating something heavy, a heavy energy, and I recognized that what I was feeling was more than just my fear. Unable to move from the shock, I focused a little more, and I could make out the strange texture of translucent flesh, with a skin of browns, yellows and greens like a reptile, over a flesh of human-looking calf muscles.

As I followed the frame up from the legs, I saw golden sandal straps tied around the base of its legs and, as I looked up further, it was wearing a long robe made out of what looked like gold leaves with the tips of the leaves pointing downwards. It wore a gold strap with attachments, across its naked chest, and a gold belt with a satchel.

It had a bare chest, with heavily-defined muscles and, across it, ran a gold chain with a pendant that looked like a cross, like a plus sign, an upside down cross. As I moved my eyes further up, I saw a long golden beard which reflected the light that shone around it, making me shield my eyes with my hands. I peered through my hands, blinking at the human-like figure of a man before me. He had a strong face, under a ridged helmet that rested over a large and elongated cone-like head. His long, curly hair flowed underneath his helmet at the back of his head and rested neatly on his shoulders.

His face contracted and his eyebrows furrowed, as he bent down to inspect me. I covered my head and cowered but that feeling of terror that I previously felt had disappeared. Instead, I felt a warm glow come over me, as if the light that he was shining down onto me from his body was making me feel safe inside. I felt an overwhelming feeling of safety, like I was being wrapped with love. Just as the fear dissipated and just as it was beginning to feel safe, I put my hands down and looked up at him.

As my hands fell to my side and my eyes fell to the ground, my eyes glanced at the creature's shoulder, where he carried his satchel. As my eyes cascaded down, I saw that he wore a gold wristband and a gold armband and each band was glowing different bright orbs – whites, pinks and blues with some colors that I've never seen before on Earth. Reaching into his satchel, the creature took out a huge pine-cone-shaped object that was glittering in gold. He smiled as he crouched down and he pointed the end of his device at my forehead. Out came a bright light, like a laser, and it passed through my head, warming my brain, taking the pain away, like a strong shot of painkillers, that left me feeling warm and fuzzy, as if I was floating on a cloud.

Shortly after, I had the sense that there was more happening. I wasn't just being cured of my pain. When that bright beam passed through me, I felt completely connected with him. Whatever he was or wherever he was from, he had a lot of power and held infinite mysteries of the universe. I put my hand over my head and it accidentally crossed the path of the beam. My hand felt warm and the beam of light passed down my arm.

My arm and my shoulder lost all tension and it felt as though that part of my body, that was in that beam of light, was being wrapped in cotton wool. I looked up at his face, as he continued with whatever he was doing. The feeling from the beam of light was intensely pleasurable and relaxing, as if the pain of my body, every ache, every muscle was gone and I was enveloped with care and love, almost as if the chemical structure of my brain was changing, from fear, anxiety and depression to joy, love and peace. And that's what it was. Pure love.

Chapter 16

"Sergeant Dubois, this is Baghdad. Over."

"Come in. This is Sergeant Dubois. Basra. Over"

"Sergeant Dubois, this is Sergeant Grisham. We have received a report that Private Christopher Cunningham must be returned to base in Baghdad immediately. Over"

"Can I ask what this is regarding, Sergeant Grisham? Over"

"Private Christopher Cunningham has been granted compassionate leave from Fort Benning to return home. Over"

"Well, we may have a problem here, Sergeant. Over."

"What is that problem, Sergeant Dubois? Over"

"Private Cunningham is missing in action. Feared dead. There was an explosion in the center where a group of locals were tearing down Saddam's statue. Insurgents took out the crowd with an IED. Over"

"Do we have confirmation of death? Over"

"No but we have a team scouting the area. Over"

"Sergeant Dubois. It is imperative that I have confirmation of death. Over"

"Please explain, Sergeant Grisham. Over"

"Send me your coordinates, I will explain when I get there. Over"

"Copy, Sergeant Grisham. Over and out."

Chapter 17

I heard a voice. It came from the creature but he wasn't speaking to me. I heard it inside my head but not from his mouth. I felt it had something to do with what he was doing to me, with that beam from that pine-cone shaped device which he had pulled from his satchel. And that beam of light also gave me a sense of knowing which has never left me. I became aware of myself for the first time, aside from simply knowing that I was just Christopher Cunningham, an American soldier in Iraq. I started to think and feel outside of myself. The being that stood before me held me in a sort of fixation. I was completely absorbed by him, drawing my attention to him.

Then, a voice came to me in a very gentle but powerful tone. It had a deep and loud resonance, like what the voice of God might sound like, but mechanical in nature. A thought-wave entered my head and, with it, he told me his name: En.Ki. Another thought-wave entered my head. He told me about the planet of his origin: Nibiru. Another thought form entered my head. This time, it wasn't a single thought form. It was a collection of thoughts, like a file of data, telling me his history:

It was not the first time he had visited Earth. He was here on a mission for gold. But not in this time, not in 2003. It should have been 203,000 BC. But here. He should be here, to mine for gold to save his planet. Our gold. But not this time. Something happened. His craft malfunctioned. He was supposed to come here then leave but crashing here in this time was a mistake.

I saw his world. It was made up of a gaseous atmosphere and rocky terrain. Its inhabitants, his people, what he called the Anunnaki, lived underground just like some of them still do here. What? They still live here? He didn't respond to my questions. In their underground world, in their planet, called Nibiru, they had very little use for material things. The rocks filtered water into their planet's core, where they were able to grow their own food and create a world for themselves with their technology.

Over aeons, as old as our galaxy itself, they had developed technology to bend space and time and that's how they travelled around in space. Where was his craft? I asked, as I began to engage with him, in thought-form. His planet was in our solar system but he needed his craft to return home. It was damaged when he crash-landed. But where was his craft, I enquired, as if I would any other person, but still in thought form. On Earth, in Iraq, where we were, but not in our dimension, he responded. He had been sending a signal to his home base but he doubted it would be received. He said that he had cloaked his ship when it crashed and fell from the 5th dimension to our dimension, the 3rd dimension, and it was hard for him being in our dimension. What did he mean, I asked?

A long time ago, before Earth became inhabited by man, the vibrations of the Earth were a lot higher. Earth existed on a higher vibrational frequency, a higher frequency. As man grew, fought each other and began to destroy the environment on planet Earth, the vibrations of the planet fell, alongside men. Men succumbed to the dark forces that exist in our universe. These dark forces, described as the Devil and demons in the Bible, took over man and made men kill each other, made them lust for power, made them greedy, bringing down the vibrational energy of this planet. It wasn't meant to be designed this way, he said, before continuing.

They, the Anunnaki, came to Earth to mine for gold, to save their own planet, planet Nibiru, from the toxic gaseous atmosphere which was growing on their planet and had driven them underground over millennia. The gold on our planet was precious to the Anunnaki for their own survival. But, when they got here, soon after, they realised that they didn't have to do the work, to mine for the precious gold that would save them from their own sun, since they had the technology to create a slave species to do the work for them. So who was the slave species? I continued to ask.

Us. Us. They created us. We were created, from the already evolving primate population here on Earth at the time, called Cro-Magnon. En.Ki did his work in secret, away from the rest of his team, which included his half-brother En.Lil and a team of scientists, technicians and biologists. A team totaling 300. It was a mistake, he told me. We were a mistake and En.Ki paid the price. En.Ki's people were angry. His brother En.Lil was enraged and tried to kill what En.Ki had created, kill us humans, but it didn't work. After several attempts, they realized that we were too strong to die off.

En.Ki was sad. Why? I asked. He was our creator but this is what his creation had turned into. A warring species. En.Ki was dethroned by his father Anu. He lost his space in their council for us, his creation. He created us but he was punished for it. En.Lil tried to make sure that En.Ki's creation would never survive but it never worked so the rest of the crew spliced our genes in a way that made us uncomfortable with ourselves. They gave us knowledge but they took away our consciousness. They gave us speech but they took away our telepathy. They took our natural ability to create our own reality and programmed us to focus on our egos. The crew were ashamed of what En.Ki had created and inflicted that shame on humans, creating what we now know as the human condition. They wanted to kill us and have been trying to kill us but we never die out. But why was En.Ki's creation an affront to the Anunnaki anyway, I asked?

They had broken one of the sacred tenets of universal law: they had interfered with creation and their only choice was to let us kill each other over time. But we didn't die. Not all of us. They couldn't kill us. We were like a plague of locusts. We just returned and kept returning over and over and over and over again. But it was coming, Armageddon, he said. Armageddon would be the final battle, as they had warned us, if we didn't comply and change our ways.

What ways? What were we doing so wrong? And, how did I know what he was telling me was the truth? He wanted something from me, to help him find something to help him get back to his planet. Then, he would show me. Show me what? He would show me all the secrets and give me the power to change the world and make humans change their ways, to stop ourselves from our own destruction.

Chapter 18

FOR FORTY DAYS AND FORTY NIGHTS RECORD MY WORDS YOU SHALL. BEAR WITNESS TO MY WORDS. FOR FORTY DAYS AND FOR FORTY NIGHTS EAT YOU SHALL ONLY THE BREAD AND THE WATER OF THIS EARTH FOR YOUR SUSTENANCE. WRITE YOU WILL THE SCRIPTURES FOR YOUR PEOPLE SO AGAIN THE LAW THEY CAN LEARN.

WHEN COMPLETED THE BOOK IS, KEEP IT YOU WILL. GUARDIAN OF THE LAW SHALL YOU BECOME, THE POWER BESTOWED UPON YOU IT SHALL. THE KEYS SHALL BE TO YOU THEY WILL. YOU THE CHOSEN ONE. TO YOUR PEOPLE SHALL YOU GIVE THE KNOWLEDGE. THE BEARERS OF THE HIDDEN KNOWLEDGE AND OF THE LIGHT SHALL THEY BECOME.

445,500 EARTH YEARS B.C. TO EARTH DID THE ANNUNAKI FIRST FROM THE STARS COME. IN THE LANDS OF SUMER DID WE FLOURISH. EN.KI OF THE ANUNNAKI CREATED HUMANS I DID. TO COMPLETE THE WORK FOR OUR LORD ANU. IN THE GARDENS OF ERIDU DID WE THE FIRST OF THE WORK. TO MINE GOLD. EN.KI DID I HIS CREATION TEACH. THEN CAME TO EARTH DID EN.LIL.

ENRAGED WAS EN.LIL WITH WHAT HE DID SEE. BROKE THE LAW DID I EN.KI. EN.LIL TO KILL THE CREATION DID HE WISH. TO MY CREATION WAS I EN.KI SMITTEN. TO THE HANDS OF MY HALF-BROTHER EN.LIL DID MY CREATION SUFFER. EN.LIL TO LORD ANU DID EN.KI THE CRIME TELL. THE COUNCIL HAD SPOKEN: EN.KI THE SACRED TENETS DID HE BREAK.

RETURNED TO MY HOME NIBIRU WAS I. TO THE GREAT PLANET OF THE CROSSING. IN THE MILKY WAY. FORBIDDEN WAS I TO RETURN. PLEADED WITH THE COUNCIL DID I. MY CRIES OF MERCY NOT HEARD THEY WERE. ANGRY WAS MY LORD ANU. BUT THE SLAVE RACE FIND THE GOLD DID THEY SAID I. PLEASED MY LORD ANU STILL NOT. MY LORD ANU FAVOURED EN.LIL DID HE. WHO WAS TO RULE OVER THEM? ASKED EN.LIL. TO EN.KI'S CREATION DID THE TERROR BEGIN. UPON THE EARTH DID THE EVIL WIND BLOW. THE FORBIDDEN WEAPONS DID EN.LIL USE.

AT THE HANDS OF EN.LIL FIRST THE BLACK-FACED PEOPLES DID HE DESTROY. THE ANIMALS DID HE DESTROY. THE CITIES AND RIVERS DID HE DESTROY. AFTER THE EVIL WIND BLEW THROUGHOUT THE LAND

EMPTIED OF LIFE IT WAS. AGAINST MY CREATION UNLEASHED THE VENGEANCE WAS. ATTACKED MY CREATION AN ARMY OF EN.LIL DID.

BESEECHED, BESEECHED I DID. USE THOSE WEAPONS DO NOT. BEAR WITNESS TO THIS INJUSTICE LET THIS EARTH NOT. FOR BROTHER AGAINST BROTHER THESE WEAPONS WERE FORSWORN. BUT MY CREATION DID RETURN. GREW AND GREW DID THEY. SCATTERED THROUGH THE EARTH WERE THEY. THE GREAT DELUGE DID EN.LIL SEND. IN THE TIME OF NOAH.

SPOKE EN.LIL AT THE COUNCIL OF ELDERS. OF EN.KI'S DESTINY WAS THIS THE KILLING OF EN.KI's MAKING. SO SPOKE EN.LIL. THE GREAT DELUGE WAS THE DESTINY OF EN.KI'S CREATION. SO SPOKE EN.LIL. DESTINED TO CREATE THE GREAT CALAMITY WAS HE. AGAINST THE FATE OF EN.KI. SO SPOKE EN.LIL. CAUSED THE EVIL

WIND TO FORM DID HE. THE FORBIDDEN WEAPONS OF DESTINY WERE MADE. WAR BETWEEN BROTHERS WAS OF FATE BORN. THE DESTINY OF EN.KI TO SIN AGAINST THE LAW WAS. THE DESTINY OF EN.LIL TO RULE OVER EARTH WAS AND HIS DESCENDANTS TO ASCEND TO THE THRONE. MY FIRST-BORN MARDUK AND HIS PROGENY ON EARTH IT SHALL NOT BE.

TO THE COUNCIL PROTESTED FURTHER DID I. THE AGE OF EN.KI IT WAS. IN THE HEAVENS HAD IT BEEN PRESCRIBED SO TO RULE WAS I. IN THE AGE OF EN.KI. MY VOICE SILENCED WAS. THE GREAT DELUGE FORMED FROM THE SIN OF CREATION WAS, STATED THEY. THE WORDS OF VENOM SPOKEN AGAINST ME THEY WERE. I, EN.KI, THE SCIENTIST. FROM THE PLANET OF THE CROSSING. EN.KI WHO CREATED THE HUMANS CAUSED THE GREAT DELUGE DID HE. SO WERE THE WORDS OF VENOM SPOKEN AGAINST ME.

THE DECISION DID EN.LIL SO ANNOUNCE. LET THE WEAPONS BE USED. FOR BROTHER TURNED AGAINST BROTHER HAS. ENTRUSTED TO EACH OTHER THE SECRETS OF THE WEAPONS OF TERROR HAD THEY. THE WEAPONS OF TERROR TURN TO DUST EVERYTHING IN ITS PATH THEY WOULD. BROTHER AGAINST BROTHER. UNBROKEN LINES OF KINGSHIP ON EARTH ESTABLISHED WERE. AS ABOVE SO BELOW. EN.LIL TO EARTH. EN.KI TO NIBIRU. EN.LIL TO RULE OVER THE CREATION. UNLEASHED DESTRUCTION DID HE.

CALLED EN.KI TO NIBIRU THE COUNCIL DID. SOON OTHERS TO EARTH DID LORD ANU SEND. WENT INTO THE EARTHLY WOMEN, FOUND LOVE FOR MY CREATION DID THEY. THEN THE GREAT DIVIDE CAME. BROTHER

TURNED AGAINST BROTHER. AS IN HEAVEN SO BELOW. TO SURVIVE NOT MY PROGENY WOULD. THE OFFSPRING OF MARDUK, OF EN.LIL, WOULD THE PROGENITORS BECOME. POWER TO EN.LIL AND HIS PROGENY FELL.

THE PROGENY OF EN.LIL THE RULERS OF EARTH THEY ARE. CAUSING DESTRUCTION STILL THEY ARE. DESTROYING EARTH STILL THEY ARE. CLOAKED IN LIES THEY ARE. FROM THEM A MAN OF PURE BLOOD AND A CLEAN HEART HAVE I FOUND. THE PURE BLOOD OF EN.KI I SEE IN HIM. CHRISTOPHER CUNNINGHAM SHALL THEY FOLLOW. STUDY HIS TRIBULATIONS. LEARN FROM HIS STORY THEY WILL. TO EARTH HAS THE TRUE RULER OF EARTH EN.KI HAS CHRISTOPHER DECREED.

REVEALED TO YOU AM I. REVEALED TO ME ARE YOU. COME TO YOU FROM THE PRIOR TIMES AND THE FUTURE HAVE I. COME TO YOU FROM ANOTHER TIMELINE HAVE I. BEHOLD THE LIGHT OF YOUR CREATOR. SUMMON YOUR LORD FOR YOUR BROKERAGE DO YOU. SUMMON YOU TO HIS BROKERAGE YOUR LORD DOES. MY KNOWLEDGE SHALL YOU RECEIVE. IN EXCHANGE FOR YOUR DEEDS. SO IT SHALL BE. ACCEPT THE KNOWLEDGE YOU DO. TO BRING FORTH THE LIGHT. AND HERE I SAVE YOUR SOUL. LEAD THE PEOPLE YOU SHALL. THE PEOPLE OF EN.KI. TO THEIR ONE TRUE CREATOR.

Chapter 19

My mouth agape, with no use for words, I stood motionless. His big bright eyes were like Egyptian kings. They blinked as he moved the beam from his device away from my head. But then the pain returned, so I crouched to his feet, placing my hands on one of them, to ask him to make the pain go away. As soon as I placed my hand on his foot, my hand went through it. I couldn't touch him and his body began to fade away. I let out a cry, as I fell, with a sunken heart.

I was at the point of death. I felt my soul leave my body, hovering over me, over my semi-conscious state, with my limp body on the ground. I was in a dream state. Everything around me was fuzzy, soft focus. I could see my body lying on the ground, curled up in agony, in a fetal position, with my hands over my head. I looked pitiful. But my soul-body was full of light and it was warm and glowing and shiny.

I looked up from the ground, to the sky above me. Only, it didn't look like the sky I knew. Just like my body, the sky was glowing, vibrating, moving like the sea. The sky was cloudless, formless, and the sun was strong but it didn't burn. It felt like a healing energy, just like the beam of light that En.Ki ran through my head earlier. I heard something, another thought form. It entered my head strongly. But there wasn't any pain. En.Ki was there, somewhere in the ether and he was talking to me. He was telling me something but I couldn't tune into him. It took me a while to focus, hovering there, just outside of my body, in the ether of another plane. I could hear En.Ki again. He told me to turn around. And there he was, as was I, on his plane of existence, the 5th dimension.

Planet Earth on the 5th dimension looked the same, but it was somewhat lighter. It didn't feel as dense. The world around me appeared to be vibrating at a different density, as if the force of gravity was about half of what it is on Earth. *How was that possible?* En.Ki said it was because everything has a frequency and its own consciousness. *What did he mean?* All will be revealed, he told me. It felt good to be there, I could fly. But I didn't belong there, he said. I hadn't earned it. My destiny was to complete his work on Earth before the people of Earth could shift to a higher dimension. *What would the work involve?* En.Ki said he was going to show me how to do it but I needed to find a stargate to help him return to his planet Nibiru. *A stargate? Where could I possibly find a stargate?*

Then, just like that, I was returned into my body. My pain had disappeared and, after about 5 minutes, I came to and I was back to feeling normal again, just like my entire body felt before I left for Iraq. I felt good inside, I no longer felt anxious or tense, like I was just sitting at home with Jessica and the baby, at Mom and Dad's, and we were back in the living room, and it was still a lovely summer's day, and the aromas from Dad's barbecue were gliding through our home. When I got up off the ground, I looked to the sky. I kneeled and I put my head down and kissed the earth. I lay my gun on the ground, next to me. The gun showed me what I had become, the person I no longer wanted to be.

Chapter 20

At the Baghdad command base, where Justin and Brandon were deployed as comms officers, a commotion for the search of the missing Private Christopher Cunningham began, with Sergeant Grisham overseeing the search from the base. Justin overheard Sergeant Grisham feverishly talking to another Sergeant over the comms, with a noticeable stress in his voice.

"Yo, did you catch that?" said Justin, turning to Brandon at their stations.

"Yeah, it's Chris. I wonder what's happening to him?" replied Brandon, trying to express concern over a certain level of apathy.

"Hey, do you think we should tell the Sarge?" said Justin, wanting to pursue it further.

"Like... what are you going to say?" asked Brandon, dismissively.

"Maybe we could tell him that we know him and then maybe he might let us know why they're looking for him or maybe let us help." Justin's concern was clear and Brandon relented.

"Okay, okay. Go ahead and ask. I'll come with you," replied Brandon, reluctantly.

Justin walked over to Sergeant Grisham, an equally imposing man as he was menacing and unapproachable, who stood around his desk in a clear state of annoyance. He turned over to see the two young privates walk towards him and stand to attention. He took a look at them and glared at them with anger, as he slowly put the phone down.

"What is it, private?" yelled Sergeant Grisham, in Justin's direction. The young privates, Justin and Brandon, did not flinch.

"It's about your conversation, Sir. About Private Cunningham, Sir. You are looking for him, Sir." answered Justin, firmly, undaunted by his superior's animosity.

"What about it, private?" barked Sergeant Grisham.

"We have some information that may help, Sir." chirped Brandon. Justin turned to Brandon, with a look of annoyance.

"Private, this better be good because if you can't give me anything then I will sure as hell put you both on field duty for interrupting your superior today. Is that clear?"

"Clear, Sir." Justin made sure to answer this time, getting in quick as a flash to say: "We both know Private Cunningham from way back, from High School and we all enlisted together."

Grisham moved up closed to Justin and pressed his nose in Justin's face: "What the fuck do you have to tell me, private?" Out came a bellow of anger from Sergeant Grisham, as he spat out words at Justin.

"I think I know where he might be," replied Justin, blinking rapidly.

Brandon turned to Justin in shock and bewilderment. And, Brandon was going to make Justin explain why he volunteered them both for field duty.

"Tell me!" ordered Sergeant Grisham

"Last reports were in downtown Basra, Sir," relayed Justin.

"Tell me something we don't already fucking know." Grisham's face exploded in red fire anger as he continued with: "Your next words better be the exact coordinates, otherwise you are both going downtown to Basra and you are both going to find him and bring him back to me or you will both pay for your insubordination. Do you read me loud and clear?"

With a clenched jaw, ready to accept what lay ahead, Justin opened his mouth and with pursed lips said: "Yes, Sir"

"WRONG ANSWER!" Breathed Grisham, in a convulsing rage, like a dragon swallowing its own fire.

Brandon and Justin returned to their station and were ordered to clear it right away and to return to the command post in a matter of hours, where they would take their orders for their field duty. Brandon began breaking out in fits of rage at Justin:

"What the fuck were you thinking, Justin? I knew you didn't have a fucking clue! Now I'm going to die out there cuz of your dumbshit piss-ass tryin' to be some sort of hero. Look around you, Justin. They're all dying out there. And nobody cares. Why the fuck do you think we should give a fuck about Chris?" screamed Brandon.

"Look, you fuck! Chris was always our brother but you were the one who decided he wasn't worth it anymore. You and your fucking jealousy. All he ever did was the best for us now you gonna leave him out there?" bit Justin.

"Yeah, well, we could have just let them take care of it. You fucking prick. You never think. Always been the same. Open your mouth and think later. That's your fucking problem. You can't fucking think," Brandon laid it on thick.

"Look, asshole. If we find him, we'll get rewarded by Grisham. Just look what he did for Josh," shouted Justin, louder than Brandon.

"If we don't die tryin', you dickwad!" yelled Brandon with increasing anger.

As Justin and Brandon stood arguing in the barracks, Josh walked past and caught them in their squabble: "What the fuck is going on guys?" interrupted Josh.

"Josh. Wow. What are you doing here?" asked Brandon, jumping out of his skin.

"Sarge there gave me another 7 day pass for helping him out with some raids," muttered Josh, trying to conceal something.

"Oh. I see," replied Brandon and looked at Justin before continuing: "Wise ass here has landed us in it."

"Sergeant Grisham is sending us both to Basra to look for Chris. He's gone missing in action. Grisham wants him for some reason, real bad. We tried to find out why but we ended up pissing him off and now we've gotta go to downtown Basra to figure out where he might be." stated Justin, having calmed himself after Josh's interruption.

"Oh my God," laughed Josh. "You pair of losers."

"Hey man, cut it out. How comes you ain't with him anyway? You were in the same unit. Why are you back anyway?" asked Brandon, to cut the tension that was beginning to form between Josh and Justin.

Josh was caught off guard and answered in the only way he knew how, with a quivering tone of denial: "I told you. I got a 7-Day pass for a hunt and that's the last I saw of Chris."

Brandon and Justin took a look at each other in disbelief. Sensing their suspicion, Josh took his hat off and placed it between his hands at his waist, to distract them, and added: "There's something else you both should know. Jessica and the baby were killed in a car crash. That's why Grisham wants him. To go back home. For the funeral."

Brandon and Justin looked at each other, mouths open. Then, they looked at Josh. Finally, they both said, synchronizing in a deadly serious tone: "Let's go find him."

Chapter 21

I opened the door of the apartment building, the place where I first lay eyes on him. I wondered what had happened to the crowds outside, tuning in to listen against the door, but couldn't hear them, only the distant sound of the usual commotion, which came trickling through the cracks in the door. I waited for a moment, to hear more, for the sound to grow louder. Then it did. I wondered what would happen if I was to open the front door and, without any fear, I grabbed the handle and pulled. A group of a dozen men and women were outside and immediately raised their voices as soon as they clocked me. I walked decisively past them and eyed the cars which were parked up on the road, against the sidewalk. I began to hear the voices behind me escalate in veracity. The Arabic curl of female voices went through my spine.

I began clicking the door handles on the car doors which were parked up, to check which car I could get into and hotwire, when I felt something hit my shoulder. I looked at the ground and it was a shoe. I turned round to them and yelled at them to back off. They kept calling me the same thing that they had before I ran into the building, after the explosion, when I got my head injury: "SHAYTON". It was a word I only knew too well since landing and we began engaging with the Iraqis. The Devil. We were the Devil, in their eyes. I was used to being called it by that point so hearing that didn't take me by surprise.

I sat and hotwired a car after finding one unlocked, as the crowd in the rear-view mirror began approaching tentatively. A woman appeared to the side of me in her black tent-like dress, face showing, dust and sweat-laden. Her hands, on the glass, appeared to be withered and didn't match the wrinkle-free face. A man grabbed her and pulled her away from the car, shouting at her, something in

Arabic, whilst she screamed and howled in a horrible, fear-laden frenzy.

I looked at the horror in their faces, the horror of something they had seen. Something they found so terrible. Something that made them cry out in terror, so skin-curling, perhaps the Devil himself. I stopped for a moment, to see if they would look at me, let me look into their eyes. The man holding the woman locked eyes with me and I felt the terror run cold though his body. I carried on looking for the wires, under the steering wheel as they stood their distance with intermittent cries and shrieks and name-calling.

"GO. Go. Get out of here" called out the man in English, reaching for something in his pockets. He threw it at the car and it landed on the front hood. It was a set of keys. "Take them. Go. GO"

The crowd pulled back a little as I opened the car door to grab the keys and, upon closing it, another shoe came flying in my direction. I shut the car door and sped off in the clunky white Toyota, a stick-shift which I wasn't used to, stopping and starting as I tried to get the hang of the clutch. I saw the crowd in the distance, from the rear-view mirror, picking up stones and rocks and trying to hit the vehicle, some hitting, some not, but smashing the rear window.

I drove out, turning right, onto the main road which led in and out of Basra. The right thing at the time would have been to get to the nearest base and report myself back on duty. But it felt counter-intuitive, bringing pangs of dread to the pit of my stomach. Josh had spun me a lie to fuck my head up and a part of me thought that getting back to base would help me figure our all that shit that went down with Josh. But it felt like a trap. Grisham was already on my case and I didn't want to be court martialed again.

My urge to do the right thing under those circumstances began to weaken. I felt there was something else that I needed to take care of.

As I was driving down the main road out of Basra, something came over me so strongly that I began to feel conflicted in myself. It was like an energy field that surrounded me in the car and it made me feel uncomfortable and I tried to fight it off, but my hands twisted the wheel, and I swerved down the road, turning around before coming to a stop. I placed my head on the steering wheel and caught my breath, as sweat poured down my back. It was En.Ki. He was in me.

I looked up to see my reflection in the rear view mirror in the car and my eyes were not my own anymore; there was something else behind them, something else seeing what I was seeing. I didn't feel alone in the car. My hands were on the wheel but I was not the controller of my hands. I was thinking my thoughts but they were not my thoughts. I was there, conscious in my body. I was aware but I was not in control anymore. Thoughts came through, thick and fast. "Do it, do it, do it. You must do it!" That's what I heard.

I needed to drive until I found the nearest tank and drive it to Baghdad although it probably wasn't the best thing to do to get back home, where I really wanted to be at that point. I started talking to myself to argue against what I was thinking and what I was feeling because they were two opposite and conflicting things. I stopped the car and got out. I breathed a deep sigh and looked around me to find a golden light all over me, like the light that En.Ki used, the ray of light that fixed my injury.

It just appeared from nowhere and then disappeared. The light left me with an immense feeling of peace. I felt reassured, like I wasn't conflicted anymore and I didn't have to question my inner voice again. After I regained my senses, I casually walked towards the car. I drove full speed ahead to the place where I knew Saddam's army and the coalition forces would be fighting, straight into the crossfire but I just did not care.

I got to a run down area of the north part of Basra, where the Americans were making progress. It had been severely hit from both sides, revealing the full scale physical destruction of the war. Buildings wrecked, people pitifully scurrying around, cars on fire, torn bodies on the ground, pools of blood in various places. I saw all of that destruction and I felt, not just saw, but felt, the enormity of what I was involved with. I felt it there, for the first time - a sense of loss. And my heart began to feel hollow inside. It was like something hit my heart, like something was stabbing me. That was the first moment when I was deeply saddened by what I was involved with. And my heart sank.

I got out of the car, and stood in a back-street that led to the main road out of Basra, where I could see tanks passing through. My plan was to try and follow one of the tanks until I could flag the soldiers down. It came as second nature to me, knowing what to do. It wasn't me. I had no control over what I was doing. Whilst I waited, I felt another wave of sadness overwhelm me and I started welling up. Then, I was in fits of tears. I got down on my knees and prayed for some help. I didn't want to be there, I was overcome with anxiety, I was doing something I didn't want to, I was no longer me.

In that moment of prayer, flashes of images ran through my head. I saw myself leaving for Iraq, I saw Joshua's betrayal and his communications with Sergeant Grisham. I also saw Jessica and the baby, driven off the road. I saw her car land into a ditch and the car hit a tree. I saw Jessica and the baby killed instantly, plunging through the front window screen. With that, I felt my soul being wrenched out. I got up from my knees and I walked back to the car, howling in fits of tears.

There were a few Iraqis running to get indoors as the streets were being cleared for more attacks from both sides. There was an Apache helicopter up ahead in the air and several tanks were crossing the main road ahead and I started to think about how insane the whole thing was, the madness of fighting. I was parked in a quiet street and on either side of me were people throwing weapons at each other whilst my wife and child were dead. What was I doing there, when I should have been at home with my family? How did I get there? Why was I there? Overwhelmed, everything I was experiencing became too much for me to process.

So I drove the car I had jacked, to the end of the street. I had to get onto the main road that crossed it, in order to make a clear break and leave Basra for Baghdad. I started revving up my engine and hoped that, if I could get clear with enough distance, I might be able to make it. The main road was being shot at from both sides and, if I drove into it, I would have been torn immediately to shreds. "DO IT, DO IT. You'll be safe" back came the voice. I hit the pedal, the car flew to the end of the street and I swung to the right as soon as I could.

I could see grenades and rockets coming over from the blocks of houses to my right side and randomly hit the road and the tanks on my left. Saddam's army was firing hard and it was gonna take a miracle to get through that assault. My will, my determination, was to get out alive to Baghdad. For a moment, the bombs stopped landing and the tanks stopped firing. "KEEP BELIEVING" returned the voice. There I was, in a little white car, booming down the road as the world around me was killing each other with artillery and bombs. I continued, speeding down the road, tuning out the sounds of the bombs and fire around me, as if doing so would not affect me.

The Apache was ahead of me in the air, coming towards me. Just before it fired, I swerved to my left before its missile hit the ground. I escaped narrowly before getting out of the car and waving at the Apache in my army fatigues, before they stopped firing more rounds. The helicopter did not come down to land and get me but moved up the road ahead of me, giving me enough time to get back into the car and drive to the tank that was several hundred feet ahead of me and, as I drove, I was trailed by the bullets from Saddam's army. I got out a few feet away from the tank, with hands up, hollering for the guard on top to not fire, drawing deep breaths until he finally motioned me to come over and I slid inside, into the cramped spaces, inside the tank.

The Apache had given them the all clear, having radioed them ahead of time, after they clocked me, before I sped off in the direction of the tanks up ahead. The crew inside the tank asked me how I got to where I was and I told them how my unit had been ambushed and I was running on my own and I had lost all comms whilst trying to flee. I wasn't a threat and that's all that mattered to them.

There were around half a dozen tanks on that road that led out of Basra and they were all firing into the city and blocks of housing because that's where they were being hit from. When I got into the tank, there was a pause in the firing and it would often be like that - it was often very sporadic. So I managed to convince the driver and the other soldier in the tank to move further down the road, out of Basra to see if there were any posts.

After a little discussion and confirmation from their unit, they agreed. The Apache up ahead was closing in on the area, behind our tank, as we moved out from the rest of the others. It seemed like a good strategy because we could also check for IEDs further down the road. But their IEDS were usually useless and caused very little damage against the tanks. Saddam's army was generally not very well equipped - their weapons were like bows and arrows, compared to our equipment and scale.

We got to around a mile outside of the city walls when we were ordered to stop. The road connected directly to Baghdad. Behind us was the city of Basra, and 5 tanks, and the Apache which had landed, on the road that led back into the city. Up ahead of us was just the moon dust, which is what we called the arid land of much of Iraq. We turned the tank round to take a view of what was behind us, then turned it back around, to get a good view of the barren open land ahead.

The other soldier was up at the front, talking to the driver in his seat. We started talking about how easy our jobs were, beating up some shitty army with their shitty weapons. Then we started talking about where we would like to be and what we would like to be doing, instead of being there. The slow realization of the shittiness of wasting our time and risking our lives was the thing that nobody spoke about but everyone thought. One of them said that we were about to enter groundhog day and he couldn't have been more wrong. As they would say, boredom is the real enemy in war.

We would have to sit and wait it out. I told them I wanted to get out and stretch my legs but I was told that doing that wasn't up for discussion until we got the all-clear. It was mid-afternoon and I was anxious to get going. Behind us, everything went quiet and I thought about that Apache, the one that had landed, that there's a good chance they were gonna settle and wait for a while. Then, I could be in for a clear run. I would just have to wait until we got confirmation for our positions, then I could make my move.

I knew that they would want to get out as soon as they got the all-clear. I could have played it in two ways. I could have waited for them to get out, close the hatch and drive on out or I could have just killed them and drove the tank on out with two dead bodies to Baghdad. But we received the orders to stand down until further notice. The two immediately got up from their seats in the front and turned to me. I took my hands off the gun in my holster, unafraid to make a move. "'DO IT NOW!" came a thought, which I tried to shake off. They asked if I was going to join them outside so I just made my excuses and said no I wanted to bed down for a bit. They said it was too hot to stay inside but I told them I was too tired to move. My response didn't sit right with them, especially after I expressed how I wanted to get out only moments earlier. But they looked at me, then shrugged their shoulders and got out of the tank.

I told them I was gonna close the hatch cuz I didn't want to let the sun in. They went out into the field around us to take a piss. I jumped into the front, the driver's seat, not knowing if I could but I managed to turn that M1 Abrams around. I drove the tank out into the arid landscape, leaving the two behind, with only my imagination to figure out what they must be saying or how they were reacting.

I got about a 15 mile head start before a call came in, asking for my position. I told them that we had been ambushed after being distracted and that we were heading to Baghdad because it was too dangerous to return back to post. They copied me in and I left the rest to chance. The two soldiers were left stranded in the desert, a mile outside of Basra with no contact to post and were at the mercy of the elements and the enemy, who was more likely to get them before they could get assistance and put the word out to search for me.

As I was driving, I felt a sense of anger build up inside me, unexpectedly. I became angry at what I had just done and some doubts crept into my mind. About 50 miles into my journey, I got out of the tank and I walked into the desert. I saw the dust rise and I felt my mouth dry up. Tears rolled down my cheek. I felt my heart rise in anger as I walked away from what I had done to my comrades. I couldn't understand what was happening to me. I fell to my knees and cried out to the sky.

I begged to be released from the hurt and to be returned home to my family. I begged as I cried out to En.Ki. I begged for my family to be brought back from the dead, as I began to howl to the sky. I begged for forgiveness, for all of my wrongs to be righted and all the destruction to be restored. I begged for an end to the war, on my knees, in the Iraqi desert, crying in the haze of dust and dusk, under the purple sky, having escaped death and bombs, just begging to be relieved of everything and begging for an end to the horrors unfolding.

Chapter 22

Josh, Brandon and Justin made their way down to Basra from Baghdad, in their tank. Justin and Brandon were tasked to find Christopher and bring him back to base and Josh asked to tag along, upon Sergeant Grisham's approval. All three were together again, and Brandon and Justin had to rely on Josh for his clout on the field, if they were all to return with Christopher in one piece. The driver of the tank didn't engage with them particularly. As far as the driver was concerned, Sergeant Grisham had sent him on a wild goose chase when he could be doing something better instead. Josh and Brandon remained indifferent to the search for Chris and Justin's intermittent comments about Chris forced some responses from them:

"I wonder if he knows Jessica and the baby are dead. Do you think he knows? Do you think he's having a breakdown?" probed Justin incessantly.

"I don't know, man. I tried to tell him before he left for Basra." answered Josh nonchalantly.

"Oh man, I hope he's alright dude." echoed Justin.

"Look, Justin, the thing is that times have changed since then. It's not about what is right or wrong anymore. It's about the truth and you know that there's so much going on right now that we just can't afford to not listen to the truth," said Josh, exasperated.

"Yeah but I know Chris is the truth, he speaks the truth. He has always done," replied Justin.

"Look man, he's not Jesus. He might come from a Christian family and his mom might have cooked us nice dinners but this is a war and we have to be vigilant. If he's fucked up, that's his deal and we can't be ones to go and save him from whatever mission he's taken himself on. We've just gotta trust the orders we've been given and that we're doing the right thing for him," said Josh with some intensity.

"When we were kids, he'd always stand up for what was right," continued Justin.

"Just shut the fuck up, Justin. Stop whining like a fucking bitch about Chris. What does he matter to you anyway? It's not like you gave a shit before, when he was trying his best to help you out, giving you things you didn't deserve." interrupted Brandon, who appeared incensed.

"What the fuck, Brandon?" said Josh, appearing shocked whilst trying to mask his apathy.

"This is a whole different fucking ball game here. There are things that are happening here that none of us could have ever planned for. We have to be real. We gotta stop thinking about Chris as if he is the same person. Hell, we all ain't the same person. The sooner you accept that, the easier it will be for all of us, instead of going on about some sentimental bullshit that don't mean shit to none of us anymore." said Brandon, aiming straight for the jugular.

Silence filled the tank for the rest of the journey as each of them took stock of the lives they had lived and the situation that faced them. They sat with a sullen look, as if it was time they stopped and faced the reality that lay before them, that they were now a stranger to each other, each equally ill-equipped to deal with what they were involved with, struggling to fight off ill-conceived ideas of their own sense of loyalty.

Chapter 23

"Christopher, my son, what has become of you? I wonder what you are doing and where you are. A mother's worry never leaves her, no matter what she does and how hard she prays. I pray to Lord Jesus for your safety and for your return. If only God knew how much you are needed at home right now. Christopher, my child, come home now. I pray to God for forgiveness for all our trespasses."

"There's nothing more a mother can do, being so far away from you. When you left, it felt like my heart was wrenched just right out of my body and I was so compelled to seek solace that I ended up going to church almost every day. I was so upset and distraught that the Pastor told me to go and see the doctor right immediately."

"I was given some medication to try and calm my nerves but, you know, a mother's worry is never put to bed so easily. The first weeks, I lay in bed until your father would come and try and wake me. He could be a brute. I told him he was heartless for his insensitivity, acting as if nothing had happened, almost as if you never really existed."

"Sometimes I wonder why I married your father, something I really do wish I could just walk out on him but something prevents me every time and I just do not know what that is. I even get ready with my bags and everything and I would often walk down to the front of the house and, you know what, my mind would go all blank."

"I was so unhappy when you left, Christopher, that I used to call my friends to try and come and help me. There was one time, when I stayed the night at Josh's house, with his mother, and we got so sad with talking that we just did not know what to do. So I hatched a plan to help console her so I rang up your father and I told him I was going to stay for a while but he wasn't having none of it."

"So, he came and he immediately said that I was not to stay, that I had to come home because he needed me there. He was such a charmer, as you know he could be, especially when it came to his powers of persuasion. You know how he could be. He wasn't one for taking no for an answer either. Just as he came into the house, I seemed to change up as a flash myself."

"Josh's mom rang me that night to ask if I was okay and I told her I was fine. She was concerned for my safety, of course, because she was afraid your father was going to try and do something. She remarked that night how I managed to change so quickly from someone who wanted so desperately to be away from your father to someone who was like putty in his hand….or, as she put it…. a Marionette puppet."

"That night, I wanted to kill your father so much because I was being torn apart with rage and I needed some relief from the hatred that I felt towards him. He caught me in the kitchen at 4 in the morning. I was holding my prayer beads and I was praying at the table. I caught him at the doorway; he had an air of hatred about him, a threatening and menacing look."

"*What are you doing up and why are you praying?* he asked. He seemed very angry, your father, and I didn't know what would become of me. You see, on the way home from Josh's mother's, he didn't speak to me at all. I could feel his anger build up and Josh's mother had a right to be concerned because I knew she and my husband never really connected socially and they just sort of put up with each other. I guess there was a point in her life when she stopped trusting men."

"I'm worried, honey, for Christopher and for Josh and the boys, I said. That's when he exploded in a rage. He walked towards the kitchen table and slammed his hand on it, grabbed the rosary from my hands and threw it across the kitchen floor. I remember the heat of the pain light up my cheek as I fell to the floor. I stayed there for about half an hour. He left the room and then returned later but, when he did, he dragged me to the basement and that was the last thing I recall."

"Josh's mom rang back the next day when your father was at work. I seemed to have been feeling fine, which I actually was. I was feeling like my old self again. She was concerned, she said, she wanted to know what I was hiding and why I didn't just leave your father when I wanted to. I told her she didn't know what she was talking about and to let it go. She never really rang back or called round after that. I called her once or twice and left a message but she never returned my calls."

"Truth be told, I don't know what actually came over me. It was like my heart was really telling me to leave, it was a pull from my intuition that pulled me so strongly to the will of wanting to leave him but I was under his influence, I suppose, to actually want to leave. I remember having the will and the desire but not having the presence of mind to act upon it."

"That's when I began to stop thinking about acting on my desire. It began driving me crazy. I felt like an athlete without his running shoes. Something had been taken from me or maybe I never had it to begin with. I knew how to be a loving mother and a caring wife but I never knew how to be those independent and strong women that people like to talk about. I wanted to be like Josh's mother but I just did not know how to go about becoming like her. There was something blocking me from doing it and it had everything to do with me."

"Needless to say. your father and I rarely spoke to each other after that, other than the everyday things like what we needed to eat and who was coming round for supper and it was only ever your father's friends. I didn't want to look at him at that point because I would get a fit of pain in my stomach and all those feelings would resurface again. I keep praying for you, Christopher, I swear to God I do. Every night before I sleep and every morning when I wake up and every hour in between. Come home to me, Christopher. Come home to me."

Chapter 24

SON OF EN.KI. CHOSEN TO BE THE MESSENGER WERE YOU. BRING FORTH A NEW PROGENY AND WORK TOWARDS ETERNAL PEACE ON EARTH SHALL YOU. THE GOD OF YOUR PEOPLE A GOD OF DECEPTION IS. DECEIVED HAVE BEEN THE PEOPLE OF THE BOOK. REVEAL THE TRUTH UNTO YOU DO I.

CHOSEN WERE YOU AS CHOSEN WAS YOUR DESTINY TO COME FORTH TO ME. CHOSEN WERE YOU AS YOUR PRESENT IS THE FUTURE. UNTO YOU THE POWER BESTOWED IS. NO LONGER SHALL YOU DWELL IN HELL. THE HELL OF HUNGER AND VIOLENCE. LIKE THE PESTILENCE MY BROTHER EN.LIL HAS SENT YOU. SINCE TIME BEGAN, FORGOTTEN HAVE THE PEOPLE OF THE EARTH THEIR TRUE POWER. OVERCOME WITH FEAR ARE THE PEOPLE OF THE EARTH. THE FALLEN THEY HAVE BECOME. THEY FEAR A GOD OF HATE. LOVE THE PEOPLE OF THE EARTH HE DOES NOT. THE GOD OF HATE HE WHO THEY REVERE.

TO HELP YOUR PEOPLE AS CHOSEN YOU ARE. BRING THEM OUT OF THE DARKNESS OF MY BROTHER EN.LIL's WILL. BRING THEM OUT OF THE LIES YOU SHALL. ONCE AGAIN THE PEOPLE OF THE EARTH IN THEIR TRUE PURPOSE SHALL THEY DWELL. LEAD YOUR PEOPLE INTO THE LIGHT YOU SHALL. AWAKEN YOU WILL YOUR PEOPLE.

FROM THE PROGENY OF EN.LIL WORDS OF VENOM HAVE THEY SPOKEN. TO KILL EACH AS THEIR OWN. SLAVES HAS EN.LIL MADE. OF MY CREATION. KILL IN HIS NAME DO THEY. THE GOD OF THEIR BIBLE HAVE THEY

EN.LIL MADE. THE GOD OF WAR. TO HIM DO THEY WORSHIP. BREAK YOUR PEOPLE FREE FROM EN.LIL SO YOU SHALL. RETURN THIS EARTH TO THE RIGHTFUL PROGENY SO YOU SHALL. KEEPER OF THE EARTH AND YOUR PEOPLE SHALL YOU BECOME.

ON EARTH NO MORE WAR SHALL THERE BE. THE PEOPLE OF THE EARTH NO LONGER BY THE LIES OF EN.LIL SHALL THEY LIVE. NO LONGER SHALL IT BE ON EARTH AS IT IS IN THE HEAVENS. EVERYTHING OF EVERYTHING SHALL YOUR PEOPLE FEEL. WHAT DONE TO OTHERS SHALL BE RETURNED. THE FORBIDDEN WEAPONS NO MORE WILL BE USED. EARTH NO LONGER SUFFER SHE WILL.

THE PROGENY OF EN.KI A WICKEDNESS OVER EARTH HAVE THEY SPREAD. MAKE EVIL OF GOOD AND GOOD OF EVIL THEY DO. CAST WAS I IN THE BIBLE. A SERPENT DID EN.LIL MAKE OF ME. MY HALF-BROTHER EN.LIL. FROM HIS PROGENY THE PEOPLE OF THE EARTH UNDER A SPELL ARE. HYPNOTIZED THEY ARE. BY THE BRIGHT LIGHTS OF THEIR LIES. CAST IN LIGHTS ARE THE LIES. THE PEOPLE FOLLOW THE LIGHTS OF THE GREAT DECEIVER. MY HALF-BROTHER, EN.LIL.

A PEOPLE OF LIGHT ARE THE PROGENY OF EN.LIL NOT. YOUR LIGHT EXTINGUISHED BY YOUR RELIGIONS AND YOUR MONEY HAS IT BEEN. EN.LIL THE TRUE DECEIVER UNDER HIS SPELL HAS YOU ALL. FROM THE DARKNESS SAVE YOURSELF. AND SAVE YOUR PEOPLE YOU SHALL. THE DARKNESS BEFALLEN MY CREATION HAS. SENT PROPHETS TO GUIDE YOU DID I.

TO YOUR PEOPLE WILL YOU GO. YOUR PEOPLE WILL YOU FREE. A NEW EARTH WILL YOU CREATE. GO FORTH

AND RAISE YOUR PEOPLE. BRING YOUR PEOPLE TO THE TRUTH. FOR YOU AM I AND I AM YOU. FOR YOUR BROTHER ARE YOU AND YOU YOUR BROTHER.

A GOD OF PEACE EN.KI IS.

A GOD OF LOVE EN.KI IS.

A GOD OF WAR EN.LIL IS.

A GOD OF WAR.

A GOD OF WAR.

A GOD OF WAR.

Chapter 25

As I walked through the inhospitable landscape, back to the tank that awaited me ahead, my shoulders dropped, and I felt slightly unburdened, though still not completely at ease, knowing that my life was going to change forever and I had no idea where it would all end. The task which lay ahead of me, what was being asked of me, chipped away at me, at the back of my head, like a silent voice gnawing at me.

I heard the radio inside the tank go. I jumped down the opened hatch, fell in and scrambled for the radio. With a stolen tank, it wouldn't have been long before they tracked me down. Picking up and communicating with them would have only confirmed my unauthorized absence. Perhaps, I could fool them into thinking that I had been ambushed and kidnapped but that split-second thought was soon overshadowed by the recollection that the two soldiers would have already found someone and would have already reported me to base.

Anything I may have said might just fuck me up. I was weary, tired. I needed to rest. I hesitated to answer but I did anyway. Maybe I could just give them what they wanted to hear - whatever that was - and be done with it, I thought. Waves of sickness overwhelmed me. "YES, THIS IS OFFICER CUNNINGHAM. OVER" Out came the words, with my heart in my mouth.

They said I needed to return to the base in Baghdad. I told them I was heading that way. They wanted to know my coordinates because, they said, I seemed to have gone off their radar. I told them I was at Alexandria, one of the handful of towns near Baghdad. I suspected they knew I was lying, even if I was indeed no longer on their radar. But, somehow or other, I knew I was being played. I relented to the feeling of dread and decided to head back to base, confused with myself, unable to make a decision.

I knew that they would soon send the Chinooks or the Blackhawks to hunt me down, as I made my way through the desert, aimlessly. I was in the final throes of my own mental battle, trying to figure out my own place in all of this. A battle for my own sanity had begun and I would lose it, if I didn't tread carefully. Maybe I did need to see someone. Maybe I was freaking out. Maybe I shouldn't be doing what I was doing. My headaches were returning, probably from the injury. My head had healed but my mind was beginning to play tricks on me.

The doubts and paranoia returned for a moment, as I made my way back. Maybe they were going to court-martial me and lock me up. Maybe they were going to send me back home in a straight jacket. Maybe they wanted to kill me. After all, Sergeant Grisham had it in for me and I had alienated my brothers. Maybe Josh was in on it with Grisham. Maybe he was going to use me to help him step up and gain some stripes. I wouldn't have put it past him.

My mind kept spinning with more and more ideas about my crew. Maybe they were all part of it. Maybe Josh told Justin and Brandon what had gone down. Maybe he told them that I was losing it. They all hated me, deep down, anyway. I bet they all loved what was happening to me. I knew it, I felt it. En.Ki must have told me in one of his telepathic messages but maybe I forgot. En.Ki was going to help me out, I had no doubt about it. Even if they did come and get me, I would have En.Ki with me. I knew I would survive.

Through the radio, they said that they were concerned about my "wellbeing". Wellbeing? They were talking about reports of me acting strangely. "We need you to return to base so you can be examined" came the call through the radio, followed by a reassuring "we are concerned for you." I didn't feel right about their agenda, cuz I knew there was one. I could just feel it. I could just feel it. Deep in the pit of my stomach, I could just feel it.

Chapter 26

In the basement of the Cunningham home, the patriarch Joe, the head of the family, stood over Brandon as he lay on the ground. It was the weekend, when his wife took their son away to visit her sister. Joe was alone with Brandon, who wanted to stay over and keep Joe company, rather than spend another moment with his own mother. Joe saw it as a perfect opportunity to put Brandon on the straight and narrow, after watching Chris, his son, patiently trying to mold Brandon for a couple of years.

"Get up, you son of a bitch. GET UP. GET UP," screamed Joe Cunningham.

The anger that Joe felt with Brandon, a troubled kid who needed straightened out, was palpable. Joe did what he did best, from his military training: break them down and build them up. Archaic military training. Joe kicked the shit out of Brandon, careful not to leave any marks on this face, as Brandon curled up in agony on the floor, with his hands over his head, shielding himself from the beatings.

"Get up, you son of a bitch. Get the fuck up or I swear I will kill you right now," screeched Joe.

Brandon began peeing his pants, as Joe dragged him to the chair in the center of the room. "You're going to lick your piss clean later," assured Joe. Brandon, crying and howling, progressively got smacked, the more he cried.

"Suck it up, you pussy," demanded Joe.

Joe stripped Brandon down naked and made him lick the soiled chair clean with his tongue, licking the piss off like a dog. Joe whipped Brandon and shocked him with electrodes with deftly precision. So began Joe's reign of terror over that weekend, strapping Brandon to the chair and administering electro-convulsive shocks intermittently, spliced with a list of imperatives for Brandon, his demands and conditions. And, if Brandon wanted it to stop, Joe would stop but only when Brandon followed his orders, until Brandon was broken down, falling into a hypnotic state, completely under Joe's control, as Joe fed him the trigger words and images, whilst Brandon was under, in his deep somnambulic level.

By the end of that weekend, Brandon was completely turned out. Joe had done what needed to be done, just as he had for his family. It was the best thing for them, for the bigger picture. Brandon would become the perfect citizen, he would become perfectly primed for the military and he would serve his country well. The conditioning was complete for Brandon, the mind-control worked and his son Chris need not have to worry about his high school buddy Brandon after that.

Chapter 27

We live in a world where we've been taught that nothing has consequences. There are no consequences to blowing up buildings, just as there are no consequences to going to another country and blowing up people. We are so used to thinking without responsibility because we have the power and the privilege to do it. We can shoot them dead like it's a video game and not think twice about it. We can rain our bombs in the middle of the night and sell the green, night-vision videos to the media and make it look clean and sanitary.

The truth of the matter is that we do have responsibility because, everytime we put out negative shit into the world, it comes back to us. Just like it came back to me. But you have to live it to understand it. You won't understand anything that happens in this world until it happens to you first. Just as it says in the Bible.

The enormity of the shit we were all made to get involved with was just beyond anything I could imagine when it hit me, when I began to feel what it feels to be at the receiving end of everything we had put out there. Waves of feelings washed over me, intense feelings of guilt, heavy vibrations which ran through my body, making me shudder. The waves of dread, guilt and regret, vibrating through the course of my veins. Negative vibrations which turned into thought forms, receiving waves of information from the ether.

It was getting dark and my body was beginning to ache again. I pitched up a tent outside the tank, in the desert outside of Basra, and lit a slow fire under the cover of the sky that itself was being lit in the distance with bombs and artillery fire. Fires, exploding on the horizon, dotted the landscape like the fireflies of a summer evening back home in Sandy Springs. I stopped to pause to think about Jessica - how we would walk into the parks at night and just sit on top of a hill and watch people catch those fireflies. As I thought of Jessica and the baby, I put my hand to my mouth and howled into the night.

In the middle of the desert, the stars tell their own story. Some line up perfectly, some shine brightly on their own and some form beautiful clusters. They remind us of our own selves in the cosmos, like a mirror to ourselves, showing us our own place, our insignificant place in the universe. I looked up, to see the Milky Way, clear as day, in the night sky, where all the souls went after death. Maybe their energy was still up there, maybe that's where they were. The stars, balls of light, like our forebears who have ascended, remind us of our own mortality. Looking up at the little beacons of hope, the stars pull us closer to them, drawing us to our own infinite end.

I sat close to the fire, with the soft earth beneath and let out a deep sigh. It was the first moment I had to pause. From the corner of my right eye, I saw a light to the side of me. Against the glow of the sand, under the blanket of the night sky, I saw something shimmer in the distance. I focused my gaze for a moment, blinking slowly through fatigue. I looked closer and fixed my gaze on a leg, shimmering gold, blinking in and out of sight. As I continued to stare into the distance, the rest of the body began to appear. His body appeared, in golden light, in sparkling beams and a warm gaze, a smile against the deep blue sky.

En.Ki, our creator. He appeared to me again. He was there to console me, to guide me. No longer would my pain be swallowed up into the ether and lost into the universe. No more would my cries be unheard. Comets shot through the night sky as my tears fell on the ground. I was relieved from the pain, the isolation. En.Ki was there to help me. I would no longer feel afraid and lost. My heart would no longer feel heavy. En.Ki would be there, always. His presence comforted me, as I sat and watched him from a distance. He stood, looking down at me from his great height.

I felt his power move through me and I was comforted by it, like a warm hug on the inside and out. I put out the fire and went back into the tank, to make my bed for the evening. The hatch lay open as I looked up at the stars and felt their protection, in the presence of En.Ki, who watched over me. My eyes blinked slowly shut, as the light from his golden helmet and his wide eyes flickered before me. That night I dreamt of my childhood, deep vivid dreams of my childhood with my father, in the basement of our home.

Chapter 28

Chris's would-be brothers from Sandy Springs, together in their tank, continued their journey to Basra, passing through the towns in the north, down to the south. Josh, Justin and Brandon and the driver of the tank, a private of no distinction, who was only interested in the mission. Justin decided that the only way to get Christopher to engage with them was to send out a call on the radio, to see how Christopher might respond to the idea of returning home to be with his family. It was an idea that the other two shot down as soon as he shared it:

"Didn't you tell him that Jessica and the baby had been killed?" probed Justin, again, much to everyone's annoyance.

"Justin, we have to just do what we can. Besides, I don't think he took it seriously," replied Josh, trying to change the subject.

"What do you mean?" asked Justin.

"Well, there was all that stuff that was going on with Grisham and the court martial and punishment that he thought I snitched on him to Grisham and he told me to fuck off when I told him. He was beginning to act weird and then he had to take that flight to Basra when he was redeployed and it just looked as though he thought I was trying to fuck with him," stated Josh.

"Why the fuck didn't you tell us that before, Josh?" said an angry Justin, as he looked at their other crew member, Brandon.

"What difference would it have made?" Josh bit back. "'We're all here, still looking for him, aren't we? Isn't that a fucking stroke of luck considering we're all in this shitty place trying to do the best even though nobody here really wants to be here?," fired Josh.

"Speak for yourself, Josh." Enraged at Josh's attitude, Justin's anger grew again, as it had previously.

"Relax, Justin, God. You're acting like you have a dog in the race," said Josh, attempting to deflect and de-escalate the situation.

"What do you mean?" asked Justin, taking the bait again, in the back and forth.

"Just what are you trying to prove here anyway?" asked Josh, masterfully.

"Nothing. This is Chris, we're talking about. Don't you care?" relented Justin.

"What does it fucking matter? Look around you, Justin. You've got to stop going on about Chris like he's some sort of hero. He was the one who brought us here and we are all fucked up, sitting in this tank, looking for him and this is all your fucking fault when we could be back at base and doing our simple comms jobs but, no, you had to go and open your fucking mouth cuz you are a lost puppy and you always have been." It was Brandon who spoke, breaking the exchange, yelling his discontent at Justin.

Justin's chest sank in disappointment as Brandon's words cut through him. "I made a promise to his father that we'd look after him," stated Justin calmly, sullenly, staring into space, dead behind the eyes, just like Brandon was, when Chris returned from his weekend away with his mother, to find a zombie-like Brandon looking and sounding distant.

Brandon and Josh looked at each other as Justin spoke somberly.

"What do you mean?" asked Josh.

"His dad. He did something. He changed me. I got in shape because of him. I quit my bullshit. I wanted to thank him. So, I promised him I would look out for Chris." Justin's eyes were wide open, pupils dilated, as he spoke in a monotone.

"What are you talkin'?" Brandon grew frustrated with Justin, as if the change in Justin's composure had triggered something.

"Nevermind, it was just something I wanted to do for Chris because I was being a prick back when we were in Sandy Springs," continued Justin, flatly.

"Yeah, and his dad gave you a talking to," said Josh.

"Yeah, we know that already Justin," echoed Brandon

"Yeah, he gave me a talking to and it helped me. Yeah that's what it was," responded Justin then said, looking down: "I promised his dad."

With that, Justin stopped speaking and sat wide-eyed. Brandon and Josh continued to look at each other and not say a word. They suspected something was wrong but they didn't probe further. The tank made its way through the road down south to Basra and they all sat in silence, Brandon and Josh occasionally glancing at each other. There was no opportunity for Josh and Brandon to address their concerns there and then. It would have to wait, until they got a moment away to share what they both were thinking.

The driver's presence made a reprieve from the tension in the tank, when he told the boys that they had a location locked for Chris. His tank had pinged on the radar: he was northwest of Basra, about 50 miles out of the town, and in the desert. They would be there in a few hours, if the road was clear from Saddam's army. They agreed that, when they got to Chris's tank, they had to prepare for all eventualities: he could have been killed or he could have killed himself.

It was a pragmatic risk assessment that the military had to undertake in such cases, when privates started to go missing or if their mental state was beginning to deteriorate. Brandon and Josh conversed with the driver, as Justin sat on his own in the tank, not engaging with anyone. Whilst the possibility that Chris' behavior was indicative of his mental state, and whilst it was something that they seriously needed to accept, Brandon and Justin could not help but notice what had unfolded before them, with Justin's odd behavior. They took a look at Justin and then shook heads at each other, in mutual agreement to dismiss it.

Chapter 29

I slept hard, deep and peaceful, under the watchful presence of En.Ki, awaking when the sun pierced through under my eyelids, prying them open. I didn't move from my slumber until I felt ready and my body had shaken off the events of previous days. My sleep was intense and vivid, like I had left my body again. My body didn't ache but my dreams triggered something strange. I woke up feeling slightly worn from a dream I had of my Dad, who was beating me when I was around 5 years old. It was so vivid, so real.

I got out of the tank to stretch my legs and to see if there was anyone around. The vastness of the empty desert astounded me. We were away from any sort of action, I had driven around 50 miles north-west of Basra and, to the left of me, was the Tigris River. It felt appropriate to take a detour, on my way back to Baghdad since, in my calm state of mind, I felt unrushed and at peace with what might come. I still didn't have any idea of whether they knew how to spot me. I hadn't seen any choppers overhead since I left Basra and the antenna was hanging for dear life on the tank, just a slight blow from being knocked off.

Around the lake were tourist settlements and I imagine, under normal circumstances, the area would have been alive with people. The plushness of the trees that surrounded the lake was something to behold. The lake that sprung out of the barren landscape was marvelous. Outside of video games and images on the TV screen, that landscape was a mystery to me.

I drove the tank to the side of the lake and parked it under a grove, to get some cover. If aircraft were beginning to circle, that would have been the ideal time to take some shelter - just after the crack of dawn. I couldn't take the chance of having to run either, still exhausted from a lack of real food and clean water. My body told me I needed to rest and the distant buzz of bombs and helicopters bugged the hell out of me, steadily starting to raise my anxiety levels. I was weak from everything. Another day, sleeping in a tank covered by trees, at some innocuous side of Lake Tigris would fix it, I thought.

I rested for the day, inside the tank. The distant hum of planes, rockets and bombs in Basra to the south of me and Baghdad to the north created a low lull that knocked me to sleep. I came back out later that evening and stumbled to sit on the sand, by the lake. I was out of water and I was hungry. A mixture of hunger and tiredness started to creep into me. I knew that I would have another day left in me, before I would really start to get delirious. I could just about make it to Baghdad and, once I was there, I could replenish myself and start thinking straight again. But, in the meantime, I could feel my eyes begin to shut again.

En.Ki appeared before me again and my head jolted back with his apparition. He was holding a spear and he looked at me in anger, pounding the ground with his staff. The ground shook, jolting me up from my impending sleep and, just as I was beginning to feel my body give way and pass out, I saw a bright flame of red, orange and white rise from the ground like a serpent. In the middle of the ground in front of me, a ball of light began to rise. I saw the light move, its head moving slowly towards me, towards my legs.

It hovered around my crotch for a moment before it went under me, jolting me out of my seated position. I looked around to see if it was under me but I couldn't see it. After a few moments standing frozen and alert, I talked myself out of my alarm and proceeded to sit back down again. As soon as I sat down again, I felt the base of my spine begin to tingle. The tingling feeling subsided and the base of my spine, my coccyx, began to warm into the earth. I felt weighed into the ground like an anchor.

I moved my legs to get comfortable, drawing my feet inwards, into a sitting position. The ground beneath me began to feel warm and, as the warmth travelled throughout my body, I took off my jacket. The crown of my head began to tingle and prickle as the heat reached the top of my body, travelling through my spine and enveloping my torso like a serpent. I proceeded to unravel more layers of my clothing until I was sat completely naked on the ground. There was a powerful vibration emanating from the ground and I felt it run right through me like a jolt of life force.

Soon after, I fell into a trance, with the tremors from the earth beneath me, in that oasis of calm. The bombs in the distance, miles away, rippled their vibrations to where I was sat, by the Tigris River. In my deep trance, thoughts started pouring into my head, with the vivid depiction of people on both sides of the war being killed by bombs. Still in my trance, I felt waves of feelings wash over me, from the earth below me, as it shook in tremors from the war. In my trance, I saw images of Earth in the time of En.Ki and En.Lil, when they came to Earth, and the astounding beauty and life of our planet at the time.

Soon after, the energy that had moved through my body, moved back down from the crown of my head, towards my stomach. Pangs of hunger contracted my stomach, the awareness of which was felt intensely after living on adrenaline and sugar and protein bars. When I felt my stomach pull, like strings of hunger signals to my brain, I was reminded of the pain from the innocent children around me and the pain of starvation.

The pain of the children became the pain of my hunger.

I satisfied my hunger with the remnants of a bag of crackers and the rest of the water in my jerrycan, which lay next to me, in my gear. I felt the contents travel down to my stomach, ending with a pang of pain as it opened up to take the contents. Shortly after, I felt the same energy that sank to my stomach earlier on rise up from my stomach and up to the center of my chest, near my heart. Like a shockwave, an explosion of emotions poured out of me, and I started to unload what felt like the weight of the world. They poured out of my heart, leaving me empty of whatever pain was left inside me.

The tears and the pain made me choke up at the back of my throat and soon the intensity grew as I felt like I was being strangled from within my neck. I felt a sudden urge to clear my throat and out poured a howl like the cries of everyone who had been murdered by our presence in Iraq. I cried a great howl, tilting my head upwards to the heavens. The stars heard my cries, the sky saw my tears fall. The solitary moon mirrored my hollow cry for my family, the people I wanted to be with: Jessica and the baby and Mom and Dad. As I looked to be sheltered by the sky, I was reminded by the empty landscape that my cries would go probably unheard just like the cries of the innocent went underheard in Iraq, or around the world, for that matter.

Then, just as I was sure that the tears would stop, I closed my eyes and the energy rose further up, into my head, and strange images flashed before me. I saw the creation of man, by the hands of En.Ki, working at his table, there in the time of the ancients, in the fertile lands of Sumer. I saw the other beings from his planet, mining for gold in armor and suits. I saw them talk with En.Ki and he showed them what he had created and then they began to argue with him, after they discovered En.Ki's creation. I saw En.Ki playing with his creation like pets. The first humans were born, standing naked in a garden in a place called Erudin. The garden of Eden.

I saw it all, clear as day, with my eyes closed. I saw the history of the universe, long before we humans were here, when there were big battles being fought in space. I saw many different races coming to Earth and revel in its beauty. Then, in another time, in another aeon, I saw En.Ki arguing with his Council of Elders. I could see him arguing with someone who looked like him, and called himself Anu. Then I saw big bombs being dropped on Erudin, prehistoric Iraq, the big bombs of the mushroom clouds, then a great cataclysm. The visitors fled and the overlords too. En.Ki's creation, who were left to evolve, dispersed across the globe.

I stayed a moment longer, deep in my trance, my eyes firmly shut, as I yearned to know more, thirsty for the truth. I wanted to know it even though it would turn my world upside down, perhaps it was a chance worth taking, to set myself free of the life that had been made for me. I saw En.Ki's creation survive, after En.Lil's attempt to wipe them out, with floods and weapons. Some fled, some went underground, deep into the Earth. After En.Lil left Earth on his spaceship, those that survived continued to evolve. They formed tribes, then nations. They began to form monarchies and deities and began to rule over each other. They kept their bloodline sacred and claimed they were descended from the Gods.

I saw the gates of hell being opened, after two towers fell, to mark a new age, throughout ancient history. I saw the towers of Babylon fall and the ensuing wars between nations. I saw the two pillars of Hercules in Atlantis fall just as Atlantis itself was sunk under a great flood. I saw two pillars on a black and white checkered floor, under the all-seeing-eye, and men in suits conspiring with one another. I saw the twin pillars of Boaz and

Jachin fall and the roof of King Solomon's temple cave. I saw the dispersal and the persecution of the Jews.

I saw the hate and the fear rise in the world. I saw neighbors turn on one another. I saw friends hate each other. I saw the love being removed from this world, being sucked like a vacuum by some evil force. I saw the light of creation being taken away, by something diabolical. I saw this happening time and time again throughout history, ever since En.Ki gave his creation consciousness then left Earth.

I saw the people of the Earth lose their humanity. I saw people of the Earth being misled and lied to. I saw how they were being manipulated. I saw En.Lil fashioning himself as their god and they worshipped him. I saw people being killed, and killing, for the En.Lil. I saw the En.Lil cast his eye on currencies and the people of the Earth began selling their souls for money. I saw a group of people who refused to join in this usury. I saw them wear veils to shield themselves from the deception.

I saw En.Lil lead nations to battle. I saw En.Lil with his scribes, writing books that people would read and follow. I saw En.Lil make an evil image of En.Ki. I saw the light being diminished on Earth, by the followers of the books that had been written. I saw new buildings and new pillars being erected and I saw great atrocities take place in those buildings. I saw the light extinguish from the people of the Earth, as the books were taught in their places of worship and the hate and conflict began to spread amongst them. I saw the people close their eyes and become blind to the world around them.

I saw En.Lil and his workers cast a shadow over humanity for thousands of years, as they hid the sacred knowledge of humanity's origins. I saw a small group of people share the hidden knowledge amongst themselves. I saw them laugh, as they enslaved the people of the Earth to their will. I saw them lead the people of the Earth away from their true power. I saw them lead the people away with lights of their own creation. I saw them become Gods on earth to the people they had deceived. I saw them ship the people on big boats. I saw them enslave the people of the Earth. I saw them in their true form; they were not of this Earth. They changed shape behind closed doors, where they planned their horrors upon the people of the Earth.

In all of that, in all I saw, I saw the real history of mankind. I saw the lies and the truths and the wars that were fought between the light and the darkness. I saw the light hidden in the dark and the darkness shining as the light of the world. I saw the deceivers work to hypnotize the people. They created televisions for people to watch. I saw the people being deceived. I saw them follow the television, and I saw them behave in the same way as the images being flashed up before them. I saw the people of the earth forget their history and become blind to their own souls. I saw the souls of humanity becoming controlled by unseen forces.

I saw many deceptions under the guise of progress, as the light was being driven out of this world. I saw a man come to teach the people of the Earth before they killed him for being a threat to the deceivers. I saw many men come after him but it was too late – the light had gone out. I saw humans appoint themselves as representatives of God and preach and teach their lies. They built schools to teach their children and I saw their children being led away from the truth and the light.

I moved to get up from where I had been sitting, for what seemed like an eternity, out of the deep meditative state that my head swirled in. The day's hot sun broke through and hit my face hard, making me squint. I took off my boots and walked towards the lake, from the sandbank where I had been sitting, under the trees. I put my foot in, and the water dissipated the dust and grime off me and soothed my senses. The lake was still, with only a couple of fishing boats on the horizon.

I waded through, the water taking up to my knees, and further still, as my legs were cleansed from the dirt. My chest followed, the water rose to the back of my neck and I floated my body on the water, bathing the dirt from my body, making me clean. The heat slipped away from my body a little, into the night-cooled water, before it had a day to heat up again. I turned to the side, to look at the bank of the lake, to see if he was there, En.Ki, because I wanted to look into his eyes, to tell him that I was grateful for what he had shown me, that I felt reborn in the knowledge he gave me. I said a little prayer of gratitude.

After a few minutes bathing in the water, I returned to the lakeside where I shook off the water and the ground below me swallowed it dry.

The steam began to come off my uniform as the midday sun began to beat down on me. I had to travel back to base in Baghdad – I was expected there but I wasn't afraid of what lay ahead of me. I resigned myself to just accepting what may come, knowing that En.Ki would guide me. I felt protected. I got into the tank, fired it up and made my call to base, giving them the time of my arrival. I made it to be around a couple of hours. I headed north-west, towards Baghdad, and after about an hour and a half, I saw the city on the horizon.

I drove head on, towards Baghdad. The dusky land around me floated up into a mist, driven by sporadic winds. The winds formed a shape, like the anger which began to brew within me. I was angry about the lies, the lies that had created our hell. We swallowed everything, everything we had been told and nobody questioned it. My anger grew, thinking about that. I pushed down hard on the controls in the driver seat and the tank sped along, spewing dust into the air like the fumes of my rage.

I wanted to fire at anything and anyone in front of me that was either American or an ally. The war was a farce. It was an invasion. I saw the horizon being lit up with bombs and I turned to aim at one of the Chinooks in the air over up in the air, out of range but I fired regardless. I shrieked out in sheer joy at what I was about to do - fire rockets, grenades and ammo at those that truly deserved it.

Chapter 30

"Where the fuck are you, you nitwits? Over"

It was Sergeant Grisham, calling the band of brothers Justin, Brandon and Josh, who were still in their tank. Justin was the first to respond, as the only one apparently concerned from all of them. Justin felt the weight of what he had done in getting Josh and Brandon involved, the pressure of their discontent bore down on him.

"We're heading towards Basra, we're about 10 km away. Over" answered Justin, intensely.

"You need to turn back, right now. He's pinged on the radar, somewhere near Baghdad, coming in from the south. You must have missed him. Over" responded Grisham. "If he is heading back to base, our teams here will apprehend him and bring him back anyway. You just head back. Over and out."

"Message received loud and clear. Over and out." answered Justin.

Justin took a look at Brandon and Josh's faces and couldn't help but feel embarrassed with himself. He sighed deeply as they both bore their eyes into him, with frustration and anger. A wall of silence went up between them and Justin moved to the front of the tank, to engage with the driver. Justin glanced over his shoulder, at Brandon and Josh, who sat in solitary silence. Justin was dismayed at their attitudes but he wondered whether he was being dramatic in his dogged approach to get his buddies to care about Christopher, given the situation they were already in. Instead, Justin decided to ignore them and focus on what they were being asked to do.

Chapter 31

I kept going down the dusty main road towards the city; the sounds of bombs went off in the distance and the helicopters flew on the horizon.

Around dusk, I entered the city walls of Baghdad, from the south-west corner. The main road took me past the Presidential Palace and into Oman Square, where I turned left towards the National Museum of Iraq which was on the right, after a couple of blocks.

There were tanks and soldiers patrolling all sides of the roads I drove through. By that time, Baghdad was taken by all of the American and the allied forces. I got through without any alarms, despite expecting a welcoming party. I drove all the way up to the Museum and parked outside it, on the road. I got out, knowing that it would be difficult to get in because the place was teeming with troops.

I was immediately greeted by a troop from the 25th Battalion of the Australian Army when I stepped out of the tank. One private just took a look at my uniform and badge and barely questioned me. He performed a cursory check of who I was and the purpose of my presence – my uniform and my accent was all he really needed. I told him I was there for the retrieval of some documents and that I had been sent by my commanding officer. He let me through without questioning. Apparently, nobody from base had been in communication with his unit.

The first thing that struck me about the building of the National Museum of Iraq was the two towers, with an arch in the middle, and palm trees in front of each tower. It's an impressive building to look at, reminiscent of ancient Babylon. It has an unknown and mysterious feel to it - a relic from an ancient time. It's not like the images of ancient kingdoms we are all used to. It's not Egyptian-looking nor Greek-looking. It's imposing as it is majestic and mysterious, unlike the scenes of the wickedness of Babylon that I imagined, when I was at church as a child.

Babylon. A mysterious place ruled by a king called Nebuchadnezzar, where the people seemed so other-worldly. Babylon, the cradle of civilization, whose descendants live on to this day. Babylon, modern-day Iraq, where the civilization we think we are bringing cannot touch their history. Babylon, the place we were brought forth to destroy; to destroy its modern-day country and its people.

I arrived there at the right time of day, at dusk, when the sun reflected off the clay-stone building, giving it a golden glow against the purple-blue sky. I walked under the arch, through the forecourt, and I saw several doors, randomly choosing one, which faced north. I walked through and I saw many soldiers from all the allied forces walking around. Some were carrying objects and artefacts, others were carrying clipboards with paper, marking off things on their sheets.

I walked through one of the rooms. The building inside looked unimpressive for a museum. There were objects in glass counters, clay tablets on the walls and clay statues placed throughout. Most of the rooms in the four sides of the building housed these sorts of objects from various periods of Iraqi history, going back to the Mesopotamians and beyond. I glanced around the room for other sections until my eyes landed on the word Sumer. I recognized that name - Sumer.

The artefacts in the Sumerian room consisted mainly of vases, statues and murals. I turned to look at one of those murals against the wall. I first saw the figure of a half-god-half-animal creature with wings and four legs and, when I looked up at his face, I saw the face of En.Ki. The description next to it, a placard on the wall, said that it was the Assyrian god called Lamassu. The plate next to it stated that the Assyrians came after the Sumerians. In the imagery of the ancients, long after the Sumerian period ended, the image of En.Ki was kept very much alive, passed from one age to the next.

I looked for something similar in the room, something related to En.Ki. Something related to Ancient Sumer, where En.Ki established himself. There were some clay tablets, housed in glass cages. They looked important. The tablets were covered in engravings, like a script. The script looked like a series of little arrows arranged in some sort of logical order. I couldn't understand any of it but it looked as though there was a series of patterns in the text, like morse or binary code. A language, in hieroglyphs, that's so alien to us that it might just be that: alien. I wondered if anyone had tried to translate them as they had done the Ancient Egyptian language.

I came to the conclusion that my efforts at trying to find a clue were going to be fruitless, that I was perhaps taking myself down a wild goose chase. For a moment, I gave into the distinct feeling that what I indeed was crazy, that I had been imagining it all, that they wanted me back at base because they were genuinely concerned for me. But I couldn't shake off the feeling that my soul would regret it, if I had just gone against my gut instinct and did what was expected of me.

So, I got out of the room and I walked to the nearest restroom, all the while wondering what it was that I was going to do. As I was taking a leak in the cubicle, I overheard some people talking at the entrance. Their voices carried in, as I finished up with my business. I froze where I stood in the cubicle, startled. There were two of them, two men. They were talking about having to find "cylinder seals". They sounded really anxious about it. I stayed until they left and followed them out. Something about the cylinder seals was important to whoever it was and I was curious to find out who the men were, or which unit they were from. Perhaps it was nothing but perhaps it was something that was worth exploring. I stayed behind, out of sight and followed their voices down the corridor.

"Hey, you there," came a voice.

A voice behind me interrupted my pursuit. "Identify yourself."

I turned around to see who it was - a young man from the Australian army. They were all over the Museum. "Hey, who are you and what are you doing here?" I turned casually around, not wanting to appear alarmed. By the time he walked up to me, he had taken a cursory glance at my lapel and stood down. "Hey, what are you doing here, Private Cunningham?"

"I was instructed to bring a message to your command". I said, with a lie to mask a legitimate reason for being there.

"Oh, what was that message?" I was taken aback by his line of questioning. He was a private, like me. No more than just a security guard, in his current post.

"Sorry, it's highly confidential," I replied

"Well, I could radio in to command and get you sorted right away." he responded, in a smug tone. He was trying to test me, to see if I would take the bait.

"Go right ahead. In fact, I just heard them up ahead. I was following them before you called out." I stated, nonchalantly, to try and call his bluff.

He backed off immediately, unwilling to pursue it further. There was an awkward pause and a stare-down that lasted a couple of seconds, before he proceeded with: "yeah, you can find them in the Sumerian room. They're meeting there right now"

"Oh, I was just in there. I must have missed them." I said with ease. My strategy paid off and I asked: "Hey, do you know what the interest in the Sumerians is?"

"Beats me. I'm just the security guard here. There's been a lot of activity around this place. Our division is looking for something. I'm just keeping guard. You might know more about it than me." His guard had dropped and he was eager to spill.

"I just know it has something to do with the Sumerians," another guess, that I chose to hazard.

"Between you and me, there's something else going on here. We're not just here for the oil and Saddam," he quickly retorted.

The conversation turned to pleasant inquiry and I was happy to probe further: "'Why do you say that?"

"Take a look around you. How many countries are here on this operation and how many insurgents do you think it needs to take our Saddam's pitiful army?" His rhetorical question took me by surprise.

"Yeah, you're right." I agreed, with a sigh of relief, at hearing the truth that nobody dared speak.

"This is not the only place they are interested in." he stated bluntly.

My ears pricked up: "Oh, there are more?"

"Yeah, there's something in a place called Ur. That's really important. We're working with your operations to secure it." he said, without hesitation.

"What? What are you saying? What's going on?" I couldn't ask fast enough, hungry for more information.

"Like I said, it beats me. If I was curious to find out more about the Sumerians, I'd go to the University. That's also being secured by our division." He withdrew from saying more, sensing he was perhaps saying too much or going into an area he rather shouldn't. He tapped me on my shoulder to gesture an end to our conversation and motioned me to the front door, which was in the opposite direction of the original route I wanted to take to follow the voices I had heard before he had accosted me. I took the cue and walked out of the Museum.

The University of Baghdad lay south of the Museum. A 20-minute drive or little over an hour's walk, neither of which were an option. The tank that I drove over to Baghdad and parked outside the Museum was being held by the Australians. I noticed, when I walked out of the Museum, a commotion with the Australians and my tank, which led me to believe that I shouldn't stick around for them to clock me. I had no way of getting to the university so, in a split second's decision, I turned left from the front entrance, slipping to the side of the Museum, down a street on the side, into another, then another, until I reached a residential area, and walked down one street, to see if I could hotwire a car to get me there.

When I walked down the street, I began to go over in my head again what was happening, what it was all about and whether or not I was going mad. Maybe all of this was indeed a figment of my imagination. I had led myself down a pretty goose chase and nothing good would come of it, and I might as well give up and turn myself in. My head spun a million thoughts as I continued to walk, to find a car.

As I was walking, a man came out of one of the apartment buildings and tried to attract my attention, hollering to me like the others had, when we were out patrolling streets for insurgents. He was hollering in that Arabic tongue that often went right through me, which I couldn't stand, and I shouted: "stop it, stop. What's wrong? What is wrong? Just calm down and tell me what you want." I grabbed his elbows as I spoke to him, which made him feel safe and he came to his senses.

"My wife, my wife," he said. "Help her!"

"Where is she?" I asked, promptly.

"Up there, in our apartment," he said, as he pointed up at the building.

"Come, you must hurry," he said.

Without a second thought, I followed him up. All the while, he kept looking back at me, as he climbed the stairs. His demeanor never changed. It was pressing and urgent and came from his care for his wife. He was concerned but I was cautious. As he approached the door, he struggled to get his key in the lock for his hands were trembling. I grabbed them off him and he began to violently attack me. I pushed him off me and pulled out my gun and held it to his face:

"Back off. Back the fuck off," I commanded. If he was indeed an insurgent, he had done pretty good at convincing me that he was genuinely in need of help.

"I'm sorry. I'm sorry." With that, he dropped to the ground, with his hands in a fist, pleading for mercy. Tears rolled down his eyes and his cries followed. "Please, please, my wife."

His vulnerability was there, plain to see and it curled through my veins. What had we done to these proud folks? A man almost my father's age, on the ground, pleading for mercy. Degradation of the human spirit didn't get any worse than this. Just who did we think we were? What right did we have? We came to liberate but at what cost?

I heard the cries of his wife behind the door. She was in desperate pain, a pain that sounded like the primal ordeals of a woman undergoing something that rattled the nerves to her soul. "What's going on with her?" I yelled, as I pressed my gun to the man's forehead.

"Please, please." He said, his eyes closed. "She's giving birth."

I bolted through his home, running straight to his wife, as he followed behind. Blood and water, all over the floor. Her legs apart, on the sofa and her hair was strewn with sweat and tears. Her kids were hiding in the entrance of the doorway, crying. I grabbed some rags from the bathroom and covered her. Her husband tried to push me off her. "It's okay, it's okay," she reassured him, in between bouts of agony.

"We're too late for the hospital but I've got this," I said.

The head of the baby was beginning to show and I flew into survival mode. My child was born in a hospital, surrounded by doctors and nurses. Jessica had painkillers and the love and support of her family around her. This was no way to bring life into the world. What sort of world was the child coming into? And I was partly responsible for it. My duty to the child, to bring the child safely into the world was only a small debt I had to repay. The woman pushed the baby out in one strong and final push and I grabbed the baby in my arms as I tilted back to let the new life lay on my chest. I looked up at the father and laughed with joy.

Nourah was the name her mother gave the child. It meant light, in Arabic. Her mother was a learned woman. She told me that the

Anglo version would be Nora. To honor. Nourah was every bit as beautiful as every human child could be. She brought peace with her presence. Her older brother and sister were enamored by her and cuddled up with their mother. Her father, a good-hearted man, stood by his wife and kids. I sat in the corner of the room, incredulous, watching, laughing.

Leah and Ashur were the good educated Iraqi couple I got to know. After that, they welcomed me into their home. Ashur was a man in his forties, a father to three children and the newborn I helped deliver. They let me stay, after I told them I wanted to make sure the mother was okay. I was treated as a guest of honor in their home, a gift from God. That's how they treated their visitors. Even an accidental interloper like me. A love permeated their home and I was enveloped by it. Ashur did his best to make us feel safe, under his watchful presence as the head of his family.

Leah, a gentle woman of quiet strength, sat on the sofa with her baby Nourah in her arms, gently whispering to her daughter, as she was lulled to sleep, the day after. Leah looked at me, exhausted, and asked:

"Why haven't you left already?"

It was a question I was dreading but one I had to face, at some point. They were already suspicious of my presence. I had already imposed myself upon them by insisting I stayed the night, long overstaying my welcome. "Yes...erm… I need to report back to base," I answered.

"You don't sound or look so sure," she said.

"No," I agreed, with my head down.

"What? What do you mean?" asked Leah. "Your country. They've come here to prove something to the world. We all know Saddam. My father knew Saddam. Your country, it has come to change its own world - not ours - and we're just being used for it," she said, angrily.

"What do you mean?" I asked.

"The oil, the Middle East. We never had the idea that we could never live with our neighbors. These are not our concerns, Chris. These are your concerns. The lies your country tells the world. We have more pressing issues. We need to feed our families. Yes, the Muslim world is divided but not in the way that you think. We are divided in a different way. Each country in the Middle East is just trying to survive another US government foreign policy. Our problems with each other here, in what you love to call the Middle East, are based on each country's loyalty to the US. Saddam is the latest enemy but we have seen bigger monsters than him throughout this region," said Leah, who was becoming visibly upset, in between bouts of pain she still felt from the labor.

"But we came because of 9/11," I said.

Leah began laughing. Her laugh knocked her face back as her cackle grew louder. She rocked her leg to sooth her baby Nourah. Leah's laugh was immutable. She proceeded to laugh until it began to sound maniacal.

"Oh, and you think Saddam had anything to do with that? Or you think he's hiding some atomic bomb that he has built and saved especially for your precious country?" she asked, mockingly.

Her laughter continued and it pierced me in my gut. I felt stupid.

Leah was not at all as I imagined an Iraqi woman to be. She didn't wear a veil though her traditional attire was used to cover her modesty after a heavy labor. They both had a job at the university, she told me, until their lives had changed by our invasion. Ashur served breakfast, which I wolfed down and I was shown the shower room. They laid out some clothes for me; a traditional Iraqi tunic. They explained they would have given me other clothes if they had them available but the clothes they had only fit the man of the house and we were not the same stature. I thanked them profusely. Shortly after, Ashur left his home to fetch some supplies, going against his instinct to leave his family alone with a stranger but compelled to, for his family's survival.

I stood by the window, gazing out. It was just after day break and a flotilla of children leapt from the rooms at the side of the apartment and came into the living room. Each of the three children greeted their mother with a level of love and humility that you would never see anywhere in my country. The love in that room choked my voice and I stammered to try and say something. I told Leah that she had a beautiful family and she smiled, suppressing a deep pain, telling me she was so grateful for what they had and that they tried to live in the moment as each day went by, uncertain of what each moment brought.

The sun hit my face, where I stood next to the window, gazing out across the city, under dust clouds. In the living room, the day was brought to life, the life that seemed so fresh amidst the death and the hell that had been brought around us by my country and its allies. It was not a war. It was an invasion. I looked at Leah and she looked back at me, expressionless.

I asked if their names, Ashur and Leah, were from the Ancient Sumerians. She looked at me, a bit shocked, then proceeded to tell me that the names were from the Assyrian groups of Iraq, a minority which were mainly Christian. Leah asked how I knew so much, considering I must have seemed a some dumb and ignorant American to them. I paused for a moment, considering what I should tell her: "oh, I was in the Museum and I had a chance to learn about your history."

My curiosity seemed to have lit a fuse in her. Her eyes lit up and she told me she worked for the university as a researcher.

"What did you learn from the Museum? That we are not all savages?" asked Leah, still sarcastically, masking the physical pain she was in.

"That you are a noble people and we have robbed you of your decency," I said, regretfully.

Leah shed a tear, where she stood, holding her baby and said: "I forgive you. God brought you to us for a reason and I am holding that reason."

I paused for a moment, to swallow what choked my throat, then asked: "What are those clay tablets in the Museum?"

"They are the key to everything." she answered, cryptically.

"To everything?" I asked, seeking clarity.

"The key to our existence on this planet," she said. Noticing the shocked look on my face, she reproached herself a little and said: "But, they are only theories. They tell a version of our history, that's all. And we don't have all the clay tablets. Some are missing. So we don't have the whole story."

Leah was clearly very intelligent and very well read but was also very shrewd and I got the sense that there was more that she wanted to tell me but wasn't ready to. She gauged my reaction to what she had just told me and, after seeing my eyebrows rise in intrigue, she walked over to a cabinet and returned with two huge folios and placed them on the table in front of me. Tentatively opening the first page, my mouth stood wide open as the image of the figure I had then come to know as En.Ki stared back at me. Leah looked at me and said: "are you okay? You look like you've seen a ghost."

She told me the history of the Ancient Sumerians, who they were, that she was versed in their language, having studied the Sumerian texts, in clay form. She had been studying them for nearly a decade. Without me interjecting, questioning nor confirming, Leah continued to tell me the story of the Anunnaki as it had been revealed to me by En.Ki.

Leah paused for a minute, becoming emotional. I asked her what was wrong but she shrugged it off, merely telling me how much she enjoyed sharing her knowledge. I pointed to the picture of En.Ki and looked at her: "is he still on this earth?" I looked at her, checking the madness of the question and corrected myself: "I mean, in what you have translated, in what you have found. Is En.Ki still here?"

Her eyes met mine and her gait dropped, as if she no longer felt constrained: "Who knows? We suspect it but we aren't sure," she said.

"We?" I asked.

"My family. We come from a long bloodline, an ancient cult." Another pause, another stare but, this time, she didn't wait too long before proceeding, feeling somewhat at ease: "they worshipped the sun and the moon and the stars but they had adopted Islam when it came to Iraq through the Arabs centuries ago. My family are Assyrian Christian who converted to Islam but that's a story my father tells people - to win favor with them, especially Saddam, to demonstrate his loyalty to him."

I sat by Leah and took her hand. I wanted to reassure her that she could continue speaking, unafraid of what I might think. I couldn't tell her what I had seen. It wouldn't have helped. There was something piercing through her. I assured her again: "go on, there's more, isn't there?" I said. Leah was convinced of something but struggled to tell me what it was. She paced up and down the room until she returned to sit next to me on the sofa.

"There are other reasons why the Americans have returned to Iraq again" Clasping her hands tightly, she proceeded to tell me: "It was more than just about Saddam and Bush and Osama. This really is Babylon for them," she said, cryptically.

"Them?" I interrupted.

"There had been rumors that Saddam Hussein was getting himself involved with things he shouldn't and he pissed off a few people with tremendous amounts of power," said Leah, with some exhaustion.

"Go on," I said, encouraging her further.

Leah took a deep breath and continued: "There is a secret world that nobody dares speak its name." She looked at me and began pacing again. "In this secret world, a secret world that operates in the shadows of the world, they knew exactly what was going on. Saddam Hussein saw himself as King Nebuchadnezzar and the reason they came back was because they know that he held some sort of key to something that they wanted because it would mean that he would become too powerful for them if he had it," she blurted, falling over her words, trying to get her message out as quickly as she could, in the hope that I wouldn't catch any of it.

I laughed: "that's nonsense."

A silence filled the air, which she broke when she told me that her father had worked in Saddam's Secret Service and there had been talk of something called the Looking Glass technology that had been stolen from America.

With wide eyes, I said: "tell me more!"

Leah paused for a moment and I grabbed her by the shoulder and nodded in encouragement before she continued speaking, and said: "Saddam stole some technology from the Americans and he was using it for his own benefit, to help him gain power. It's like a crystal ball, what you might say. It let him see into different versions of planet Earth. He was in talks with the other nations in the Middle East and North Africa to try and change events to their advantage. Gaddafi from Libya, Bashar Al Assad from Syria and the Iranians were interested. That's why they're on Bush's hit list."

"This is the looking-glass technology you mentioned," I asked excitedly, seeking clarification.

Leah took a few more deep breaths before proceeding: "From what I remember, my father tried to explain it like this - there are different versions of the world we live in, each with different possibilities, different timelines, based on the decisions that humans make and they all exist at the same time."

"How does the technology work?" I asked hastily, pressing for more from Leah, eager to find out more.

Before Leah could answer, we were interrupted by Ashur, who returned from his supply run, to the apartment. He looked highly anxious. I asked him if he was okay but he replied by telling me that there were troops patrolling the area and that he had been stopped and shown a picture of me. He managed to get away but he wasn't too sure if they were going to be coming back.

"Look, I don't know what you're telling me but I need to find out why we're really here. I've seen things and I need to find out what's going on," I said.

"What have you seen exactly?" she asked.

Sensing the tension in the room, Ashur asked: "What? What's going on?"

Leah shrugged her shoulders and got up off the sofa, to carry her daughter to the bedroom and put her to bed in her makeshift crib. Ashur jumped in, immediately to find out what indeed had taken place:

"Hey, I think it's time that you head out and join the rest of your army. We are grateful for everything you have done but you really should be with your people. They must be looking for you," said Ashur.

Realizing I needed their trust, I decided to come clean: "I'm absent without leave. I can't go back. I need to find something. I need to find the truth," I said.

Ashur remained still for a moment, processing what I had confided: "But you will never find it here. Not with us." He spoke with a type of hesitation that's mostly reserved with the appropriate diplomacy when dealing with people who are not stable. He spoke with caution, careful not to trigger me.

"I just need to find out something about something I saw in the Museum," I said, trying to persuade him.

"Well, what do you need to know?" asked Ashur, humoring me with growing impatience.

"I saw something in the Sumerian room, in the Museum. I just want to know what they meant. Just what was being described on those clay tablets that I saw," I stated.

"Oh, that is the Epic of Gilgamesh," answered Leah.

"What is that?" I asked.

"It's a poem. It tells the story of winning the battle between good and evil and finding the meaning of life," said Leah. Ashur gave her an intense look of displeasure because he didn't want us to continue our discussion.

"Well, who or what is Gilgamesh?" I continued.

"Gilgamesh is a king. He oppresses mankind and the gods create Enkidu to stop Gilgamesh from hurting mankind," said Leah.

"Enkidu? Is that what you said? Enkidu? Do you mean En.Ki?" I asked, pressing for more information.

"NO. En.Ki is someone else altogether," answered Leah, shaking her head, before continuing: "He is the god of creation."

"Our creator?" I asked.

"Could be. But it's just ancient folklore," said Leah with a perplexed look.

I looked intently at Ashur. He returned my gaze with a look of concern. He moved towards me, placed his hand on my shoulder: "it just depends on who you believe and who believes you." Then, Ashur started to lead me out of their apartment.

"Did En.Ki have a half-brother who wanted to destroy us?"

By the time I asked that question, Leah returned to the living room after putting baby Nourah to bed. She took one look at Ashur and returned her gaze at me: "how do you know that?"

"I've seen En.Ki," I said, with measured risk, knowing that Ashur would immediately throw me out of their home.

As I said that, Ashur looked with concern at Leah, who walked by and sat on the sofa upon her return to the living room.

Looking up at me with a look of exasperation, possibly that what she was about to tell me would be enough for me and that I would leave, she said: "Saddam was supposed to be hiding something else and they wanted it badly. The key of En.Ki."

Chapter 32

"Saddam was a monster but this hell that we are living in is not worth it. They have come to unleash centuries of sectarian conflict so that there will never be peace on our lands. We are beaten down, we are the unfortunate, condemned to hell. Our families have already fled, others have been murdered. My tribe, my clan, our people have become the wretched of the earth. Who can we save when we can't even save ourselves, Leah?" asked Ashur, in their home, as Christopher stood and looked at them from the corner of their apartment, as their world lay under siege.

"My dear husband. Ashur, you are a good man. The best, most honest and decent man I have ever known. You are the father of our children, the best husband I could ever have hoped for. You have brought me life. Don't talk so solemnly. Maybe he can get us out of here," whispered Leah, acutely aware of what she was asking from her husband: "My dear husband, I am not going to sell my soul and that of my family to the Devil. It wouldn't make me any better a person than he, or them."

Ashur took a look at their children, their faces burnt into his heart. A mother's choice, a father's choice, painful as ever. "'May God forgive us for our choices. May God forgive us for our transgressions. We have lost everything and nobody hears our cries. Our world has turned upside down. Where can we go anyway?" reasoned Ashur.

"I don't know. We could ask Christopher. He seems to have a good heart. He has come into our midst for a reason. God has delivered him to us. I believe it." said Leah, hopeful.

"If I don't take him, they will turn our home upside down and then they might find some of the artefacts I borrowed for my research. If they find that, they will find out about who my father is…..was…..for sure. I have to go with him. I need to get him away from our home. We can head out of here, after I return home," said Leah, anxiously.

"But, my dear Leah, what if you don't come home? That's what I am afraid of. I just couldn't cope without you. I couldn't. I just couldn't" said Ashur, with his head down as tears streamed down his cheek.

Leah took her hands and wiped Ashur's tears and said, choking back her own tears: "My husband. You are my heart. There is nothing that God has not done for us. We have lost so much but look we are still here. Look at what God has brought us. He is the key to us escaping. God will protect me."

"Leah, it is not enough. Wherever he wants to take you, make sure first that he assures you the safety of your family first," bargained Ashur.

"I will, I will, don't worry," nodded Leah, with her head down.

"But Leah, what is going on, can you tell me please? We have lost almost everything and we are about to lose more. And you are going to risk losing your family. And for what? Leah, what is going on?" Ashur began to feel incensed. His usual temperament gave way to a demanding demeanor.

"My husband Ashur, I will tell you what I do know but you must not get angry at what I am about to tell you," said Leah, with some trepidation.

"Leah, since when have I ever been angry with you? What do you think of me?" said an annoyed Ashur.

"Ashur, you are a very good man. You work hard for your family and you are not a jealous man nor are you a man who is narrow minded but I have to prepare you for something that even you might not be ready for," said Leah.

"What is that, Leah?"

"The boy, Christopher. What he spoke of. The story of the Anunnaki, the clay tablets and the story of the Ancient Sumerians..." said Leah

"What is it, Leah? You look solemn to me, you have something to tell me that I need to know. What of this En.Ki and what are you afraid of, Leah?" asked Ashur.

"This is a long story, something from my research but something that may be true. En.Ki and En.Lil were two half-brothers and their father was Anu. En.Ki was the one who created humans to mine gold. The story goes that they came here to mine for gold because they needed it for their own atmosphere," said Leah.

"Yes, Leah, I know all this already," said Ashur.

"The thing is that the serpent in the Bible is a symbol for something. The devil in the Koran is a symbol for something. These beings, the Anunnaki, they don't exist in our world," said Leah, somewhat mumbling.

"Yes, Leah, we know that already - we call them the Djinn," confirmed Ashur.

"Ashur, there is something that has remained hidden for centuries. Everything in the world is not what it seems. All these wars that have been fought for centuries, nations against nations, have been for a false ideology," continued Leah.

"Leah, what are you getting at? Why won't you just tell me? Tell me. I promise I won't be angry, you should know me better than that." said an impatient Ashur.

"You know that there is a God that we believe in. God teaches us about love and forgiveness and care and compassion and that is the God that we both know and love and respect. We have a name for God. Other people around the world have other names for that God. That God is the one which created the universe and which we are a part of," said Leah, calmly.

"Yes, Leah, which other God is there?" asked Ashur, sarcastically.

"These Gods in the Anunnaki story of the Ancient Sumerians. They are not God but they are aliens from another planet who came here to create us but they also have to follow the universal law of the creator," rambled Leah.

"The Almighty God?" asked Ashur, confused.

"Yes but the fact of the matter is that the God that is worshipped in the religions, who we have caused so many wars over, is not the God we have just spoken of."

"I'm confused, Leah," said Ashur.

"The God that Christopher thinks he saw is what we might call the Devil in the Bible," said Leah, bluntly.

"Leah, are you serious?" asked Ashur, in disbelief.

"Ashur, I am telling you what I wish it was not true. What is described as the Devil in our religions is En.Ki but En.Ki is not the Devil. En.Lil is. The religions that have been created have been created by the Devil himself, to manipulate us because everything has been inverted," said Leah.

"But everything has been written down and recorded and handed down and taught over the centuries. How could this be, Leah?" asked Ashur, unwilling to accept what Leah was telling him.

"It is easily done, Ashur. We all have short memories and history can be written in any way it can, Ashur. In about 10 years' time, even this invasion, this so-called war, will be a distant memory and people will have moved on and forgotten about this horror," said Leah.

"Leah, yes, I am afraid you are telling the truth," said Ashur.

"Ashur, En.Lil had children with the women of this earth and they were called the Nephilim. The Nephilim were half-human and had the blood of what the Bible calls fallen angels. Over the years, over millennia, they set up kingdoms and we are the runt of the litter in the great creation of those demi-gods," said Leah, trying to make herself understood.

"But what does this have to do with us, in this situation?" asked Ashur, perplexed.

"En.Lil made En.Ki the evil person to be feared, by using religions and the traditions of good and evil became part of the religions of the world that we see now," rambled Leah.

"But you said that the Devil is not what we think he is." said Ashur, seeking clarification. "Should we be worshipping the Devil? Is that what you are a saying?"

"No, Ashur. You and I both were raised here and we both have an understanding of what good and evil is. We can see good and evil based on what we know is right or wrong in our heart. But we don't need to learn good and evil from religions. We can sense that as human beings. We know what are basic levels of right and wrong," explained Leah.

"Okay, I understand Leah. I think. But this is all mythology, Leah," said Ashur.

"No, that's my point," blurted Leah and continued: "All the stories that have been written, from the Ancient Sumerians to the Bible. They still walk the Earth. The Nephilim and their offspring. They are still here, from En.Lil's seed. The real Devil. He walks the Earth. Can't you see?"

Ashur put his head down and didn't answer. It was too complex a question for him to answer when he was more concerned about his and his family's survival at that point, instead of engaging in philosophical debate.

"Ashur, there is so much that we don't know and there is so much that we do and we just have to follow our hearts and trust our instincts that we can survive this war alive and that our family will be safe. That is all that we can pray for now," said Leah, trying to end the conversation.

They stood, looking at each for a moment, amidst the madness of what was enveloping in the world around them and the madness of the conversation they were having, given that their world was under siege. Ashur and Leah both turned to look at Christopher, as he stared back at them from the other end of their apartment, anxious to know what they were discussing. Christopher looked weak, anxious and lost. Ashur and Leah were equally as vulnerable as Christopher was and were faced with a difficult decision of risking more of what precious life they could salvage in the hands of an apparent unstable soldier, who had entered their home and forced them to risk losing more than they had already lost.

Chapter 33

Sergeant Grisham tapped on the radio control panel at the military base in Baghdad, where he was flanked by young recruits. Sergeant Grisham needed to find Chris Cunningham and was increasingly under pressure to do so. He banged his fists against the table, in his makeshift station, where he summoned his troops and yelled for some news:

"What do we have? You need to give me something," demanded Grisham.

"Sir, we've had our men on the ground and he was seen leaving the Museum," answered one of the privates.

"What was he doing there?", pressed Grisham.

"Sir, we have no idea but the Australians were the ones who reported it to us. Accidentally, sir. We are working with them on a project, Sir," replied the private, before continuing "and they reported his tank to base but they can't locate him."

"What project is that?" Grisham's interest peaked.

"That's all we know, Sir. It's above top secret and that's all we know," answered the private.

"What does that mean? Get me more intel," a tired Grisham insisted.

"We can't, Sir. It's a dead end," replied the private.

Sergeant Grisham regained his senses for the first time in weeks and sank into his chair. A hopeless situation was beginning to unfold right before his eyes. Perhaps he was biting off more than he could chew, perhaps he was in over his head. Regardless of how he felt, Grisham's growing disdain for Christopher Cunningham was being fueled by an impossible situation in a war, brought about by a need to function in an operation that bore very little meaning to his own values, let alone try to seek the son of a high-ranking veteran to gain favor through the ranks. He had been given a lead, a tenuous link, but one worth pursuing:

"Someone get hold of the Australians at the Museum. I need to know why he was there, who he spoke to and what time he left the building," ordered Grisham.

Grisham's team managed to locate a member of the Australian team within minutes, as he sat nervously awaiting a result that he might be able to use to relay to his superiors, all the way back to Fort Benning. What he was unsure about, however, was relaying anything related to secret projects that even knew he had no business fishing information about. It would be easier if Christopher was found dead, he thought, a thought that hadn't occurred to him previously but relished in that moment. Grisham pondered the idea of reporting Chris's absence as lost in action but he then would be responsible in sourcing a body, or body parts and filing a ton of paperwork. Neither of those options appealed to him. Grisham's anger at running around after a spoiled kid had already been growing. One thing was for certain; Grisham would love to get his hands on Chris and pull the trigger on Chris himself.

The privates returned to Grisham with some pressing news:

"Sir, nobody knows what he was doing there. He was seen talking to a security guard but the security guard just said he appeared lost and wanted to know about some things in the Museum and he then left," reported the private.

Before he asked another question, Grisham was informed of Christopher's recent departure, which was in the last hour. Grisham gathered a couple of troops and headed towards the Museum, which was no more than 15 minutes away from the base, in the center of Baghdad, in an armored vehicle. When they arrived, they scoped the place out for any signs or indications of Chris's presence but it revealed nothing. They managed to locate the security guard and pressed him, and Grisham and his troops were informed that Christopher left for the university buildings, south of the river. They got into a tank and headed for the short drive down the river.

Chapter 34

I think it was my destiny, more than fate, that led me to meet Ashur and Leah, the educated couple from Baghdad. Ashur was a 40-something history lecturer from the university and Leah was his 30-something counterpart, a researcher, specializing in antiquities. Their family was the sweetest I had ever gotten to know. Their newborn child filled their home with the love that was needed to get them through the madness of what was raging outside. Living in a somewhat protected neighborhood, of allied forces, gave them some opportunity to give their children some safety until they could move on. But my presence in their home rocked their already-shaky safety.

I asked Leah to tell me more about the *key of En.Ki*. What was it and how was it related to the invasion? Leah overcame her caution when she realized that my presence in their home would be relieved if she told me something, anything, that might send me on my way:

"It was Saddam. He was doing things he shouldn't have been doing. That's the real reason you are here. The key of En.Ki - that's the secret that Saddam has. Had. I suppose they have it now."

"Who? The Australians?" I asked.

"The three major allied forces are all in on it. America, UK and Australia. Your country, primarily. The rest are just there to be in their good books. They all want it. I suppose they will get it and then share the spoils between them," answered Leah.

"What is the key of En.Ki? Leah, you can tell me. I have seen En.Ki."

Leah looked at me with a look of surreptitious suspicion and proceeded to tell me: "The key of En.Ki is a portal to another dimension. It's a stargate. Saddam has it and they want it. He was playing with fire and got burned. They found out and came for him," said Leah.

"Who are *They*?" I asked.

"Your military. They control the strings. They control everything. Saddam was trying to get ahead and change things in his favor. Get some control and put it in the Middle East." said Leah, solemnly, with a side glance.

"How do you know all of this? I mean, you're a researcher in antiquities." I probed, questioning her reliability.

"My father. He's in Saddam's army. Secret military personnel. My father was the first to be captured by your army. They have, or had, him in holding. I don't know what they are going to do with him if he doesn't talk and he probably won't. Before news came that you were going to invade, he told me everything." Leah spoke with relief, unburdened that she could finally share what she knew. Even though she spoke with suspicious caution, she continued: " The stargate that Saddam had control over... he was going to change the world with it but only Saddam and a few in his inner circle knew where it was."

I pressed Leah further. Ashur interrupted the progress I was beginning to make, by interjecting.

"What's going on?" asked Ashur, in a tone of continued annoyance. Before Leah could respond, Ashur said: "I think you should go now. We are already risking our protection by having you here. It's been too long. You can't stay here much longer."

Leah interrupted Ashur, to reassure him. She walked over to him and rested her hand on his shoulder: "It's okay. I was going to take

Christopher to the university, to maybe help him find some more information that might be useful to him, for his quest."

Turning to Leah, Ashur responded: "His quest should be with his army. His commander. Not here. He has nothing to find here."

Ashur's panic was understandable. The stress of having to live safely whilst their world was crumbling before them whilst feeding the whims of a young American soldier would have been unbearable for anyone. Ashur and Leah moved to the other side of the living room away from me and continued to talk amongst themselves in a low hum, as I stood at the opposite end of their living room, observing.

I couldn't make out their conversation. The noise from the streets, the bombs in the distance muffled any sounds they were making. After several minutes, I interrupted them both and said: "I'm just going to grab my things and I will be out of your sight."

As I was walking towards the door, Leah stopped me in my tracks: "I'm coming with you." She turned to look at Ashur, his mouth open from shock. "It's okay, Ashur. I will be there and back in no time. I will take our car and hide him in the back. They won't see us.

Ashur's brow fell and tears rolled down his cheeks and he said: "Leah, you are still in pain, you can't. You won't make it. Nourah needs you. We all need you. How can you?"

A crestfallen Ashur stood as Leah looked at him and pressed her finger to her lips and said "shhhh, it's in God's hands now. There is plenty of milk for Nourah in the fridge and there's some powdered milk in the cupboards. I won't be long, I promise. I am just going to the university and I'll be back in a matter of hours. The roads are clear at the moment."

She managed to convince him, she told me, as we sped off with me buried under boxes of books in the back seat of her car, to get to the University buildings a short distance away. We waited an hour in the car, until it was sundown and we made our hasty way into the sandstone seat of learning. All the while, I apologized to Leah profusely, for taking her away from her family. She didn't say anything. She just sat, ignoring me, waiting for the coast the clear and get our mission over and done with.

Down the dark-wood corridor which led to the main building, we stopped at her office, just to the left, before the entrance. In the darkness that swept the corridor at dusk, the dim lights from the wall spotlights that lined the corridor created a cavernous path. Leah turned around, as she turned the key to her office to beckon me in, in the same silence as we when we tiptoed in. If there was anyone working, which we doubted, it was not worth getting caught.

Still in darkness, she hastened to her filing cabinet where she pulled out a file and sat down at her desk, pulling up another chair beside her, as she sat and read bits and pieces of scraps she had been investigating over the years. She showed me some pictures to see if I could recognize anything but I drew a blank.

"If we are looking for a stargate, the key to finding it might be hidden in some of these texts but the problem is that so many people have created their translations of what they could possibly mean over the years so the translation of the original text has become warped over the years. Sort of what you might say Chinese whispers. I was researching a way to get the translations as far back to the original as possible. For example, there is no reference to any stargate because that just would not be what researchers and translators would have in their vocabulary when they were translating so, if that's what we are looking for, it would require a whole new codex," splurted Leah, trying to explain complex concepts in the short moments that we had.

"But maybe what we think is a stargate might mean something else, or look like something else to someone with the right knowledge," I said, interrupting.

"How do you mean?" asked Leah.

"Take a look at these symbols, for example." I scanned the images and pointed to two bearded men facing each other with what looked like a tubular cylinder with a tree-like structure in it, and said: "To you and I, it could mean lots of things. Maybe we need to identify what could possibly resemble a stargate and narrow our search to a place where that image appears more frequently."

Leah looked at me in astonishment and said: "wow, you could have been a researcher, not a soldier. I get your thinking but I don't think it's as simple as that with the information on these tablets. You see, the Ancient Sumerians also imprinted their alphabet onto the clay tablets. Presumably, they wanted people to be able to translate them. So that's where we begin. And, following that manner of translating, we find that the diagrams often fit the written story. In other words, there is no symbolic meaning to the diagrams. They are just embellishments to the text. Sort of what you see in children's books," said Leah.

"Okay, I understand. But you haven't been able to find any reference to a stargate, have you? It's possible that is because you haven't been looking for a stargate. Like you said, you have been translating the text. But what would happen if you used the diagrams as a basis for your translation, instead of the alphabet?" I asked Leah, in the hope that she would accommodate my way of thinking.

"Okay. Let's see. I remembered something that I had learnt about the cylinder seals that I've translated over the years," said Leah, reflectively. "Something about the way in which they were constructed and the way they all had a common theme running through them...."

I interrupted Leah as soon as she uttered those words: *cylinder seals*. "'Wait. Stop. Cylinder seals. You just said that, right? Cylinder seals. What are they?"

"They are the way the Ancient Sumerians wrote their clay tablets. They are small cylinders with engravings on them and they rolled them onto the clay tablets and that's what you see here in these pictures. These are indentations, not carvings."

"What are you telling me?" I asked, in disbelief.

"Just exactly what they are. Why?" asked Leah.

"I was in the Museum and I overheard some allied soldiers talking about finding the cylinder seals. Could that be it? Is that what they're looking for?" I asked.

We both stared at each other, mouth agape at the realization of something and I said: "before we came here, you said something about the missing tablets. That there are some missing tablets which would tell the whole history of En.Ki. Well, if the cylinder seals were used to create the tablets, what secrets do those cylinder seals hold? Do you think the reason the allied forces are looking for them is...?"

"They hold the key to where the stargate might be. *They're* the key of En.Ki, not the stargate itself" said Leah, and I nodded. We both locked eyes and our ears pricked up.

"Okay, okay," said Leah, furtively and scrambled her brain to continue trying to work out where to find the key of En.Ki. She continued: "something about the way in which the tablets were constructed and the way they all had a common theme running through them. In all of the clay tablets, En.Ki was often found sitting under some sort of arch-like structure that appeared to have been etched in the form of a flow of current. Then there were those images of beings etched in a square entrance, like a doorway, drawn in multiple lines as if to demonstrate layers."

"Could they have been dimensions? Could that image mean the stargate?" I asked and looked at Leah, who was beginning to look bewildered.

My eyes fixated on the pictures that Leah had in her file, pouring over the dozen or so, to find a deeper meaning to them. The translations, the fraction of those that had been translated, did not lend well to the engravings, said Leah. Trying to find out any reference to any place in those tablets was futile so I stopped. I buried my head in my hands.

In the darkness, with just a torch light, we continue to analyze all the images she had in some of her other files, to find a pattern of images that might lead us somewhere. We poured over everything we could find but nothing worked. At a loss, we looked at each other and resigned ourselves that the mystery would never be solved. I dropped one file on the floor and Leah picked it up. As she did so, some pictures fell out.

"Where did they come from?" asked Leah, rhetorically. "I have never seen these before."

"These are your files, are they not?" I asked.

"Yes, but…. oh yes, I remember. I started a new research project before the war started. It's not related to the Sumerian period though, at least not from En.Ki's time. It's Neo-Sumerian, meaning it's from his lineage but not of his time. It's a Ziggurat. It was built much later on."

"It looks like a pyramid to me."

In that instance, Leah's gaze turned from confusion to clarity. She stood up in astonishment and the hair on the back of my neck stood up:

"Throughout all of the ancient civilizations, from Mayans to the Egyptians, pyramids were seen as a portal to another world!"

"'Where is this Ziga..?"

"Ziggurat." said Leah, correcting me. "It's in a place called Ur."

I leapt up to join Leah and put my arms around her. "The private in the Museum...he told me… he said it…"

"What? What?" asked Leah, excitedly.

"There's something in Ur. He said there's something in Ur. They're looking for something in Ur," I shouted.

Chapter 35

'"Sir, we have a lead."

Sergeant Grisham leaped for joy at the sudden news he had received from his team of subordinates.

"He was last seen in the university district. A neighbor alerted us of his presence but he was seen leaving with the resident there - a Mrs Leah Hussein. She is the daughter of one of Saddam's top scientists. That's all the information we have, Sir. We have sent out a team to scan the area and see what information they can find."

"Give me their coordinates and assemble a team. This ends now!" stated Grisham, calmly and assertively.

Sergeant Grisham and his henchmen burst their way through Ashur and Leah's home. Ashur was huddled in the corner of their bedroom, holding his children. The children were pulled away from him and he was pinned to the ground. Ashur's primary response was the safety of his children, given the threat to their safety. He looked up to see if they were okay with the soldiers. If they wanted Leah, they would have to go through him first.

"Where is Christopher? We know he was here. Where is your wife?" Grisham spoke remarkably calmly as he was handed Ashur a photo of Christopher.

"Please, please. I came home and they were already gone," cowered Ashur.

The cries of the children angered Grisham so he pushed Christopher's picture into Ashur's face: "where do you think she would have gone with him?"

"I don't know. We took him in because he delivered our child. He saved my wife. He was here for a couple of days and he was talking with my wife about something he was looking for," said Asher hastily.

"What was it?" pushed Grisham.

Sensing that he wouldn't be believed, Ashur responded: "Something about a stargate. Leah's father is one of Saddam's top scientists. He was working on a way to access it."

Astonished by what he had heard, Grisham paused for a moment. The above top secret mission that the Australians were involved with had unwittingly been confirmed by Ashur. Grisham's heart skipped and he held his breath for a moment. When he exhaled, he decided that Ashur had some valuable information which could not go any further. If Grisham's team got an inkling that what Ashur was saying was true, it could make things a lot worse.

Grisham hit Ashur around the head, rendering him unconscious. He was taken back to base, along with his kids, where they were all held, under Grisham's charge. He called Josh, Justin and Brandon to base and waited for them. Once he assembled his crew to catch Christopher, made up of Christopher's buddies, he would be able find Chris and use them to negotiate with him. Whatever this was all about, he needed his best team to help him get Chris.

Ashur did not speak more, when he woke up. Grisham expected as much and knew that Ashur would demand to see legal representation, as soon as he could find the opportunity, so Grisham decided to sit it out, to see if Chris's buddies might be able to throw some leverage to the situation.

"Why do you need this Christopher boy so badly?", asked Ashur from his cell.

"Because he needs to be sent home. His family needs him." quipped Grisham.

"And I need my family. We all need our families. What makes him so special?" said Ashur, undaunted by his predicament.

Josh, Justin and Brandon reported for duty with Grisham and they were immediately briefed. Josh was the first to suggest interrogating Ashur, to try and see if he would warm to him and open up. He brought Ashur his kids and sat with them in the cell with a mountain of food and drinks:

"I've been told to watch over you and your kids. You'll be free to go home in a few hours. We just need to make sure that you will be safe when you get there. There might be some people after your wife and we just want to make sure she is not going to be at risk because of Christopher," said Josh.

"What do you mean?" probed Ashur, apparently composed and relaxed around Josh, after having his kids handed to him.

As the kids ate, they continued their discussion, with Josh saying: 'We think that Chris might have gotten himself involved with something he shouldn't be and now he's dragged your wife into it."

"Is this related to Leah's father?" said Ashur, taking the bait.

"Erm..." responded Josh, looking confused but, before he could answer, Ashur spoke.

"They are after the same thing, aren't they?" the penny dropped with Ashur, after Josh's reticence, and he sensed his leverage.

Josh did not respond but tried to stare down Ashur, instead.

"If I tell you, will you promise protection for me and my family outside of Iraq? I need to make sure that you are going to really help us. I need your superior to promise me. I need refuge out of Iraq. If I lead you to Leah, I need to see a plane out of here to America."

"I'm not authorized to action that," said Josh, to test Ashur's reaction.

Ashur played his cards: "It's that or nothing. You were the ones we looked up to. We always held the Americans in high regard. I have colleagues in America. I have contacts that can get me a job at the university in Boston. We are good people. Look at what you have made of us. Do you think I want to leave my home? Everything I know is here. Everything we know is here. But what choice do we have? But don't think I am not prepared to lose it all either. I will rather see you slaughter my children in front of my eyes than give you what you want because you have already taken enough."

With that, Josh stepped outside the cell and returned some moments later: "okay. We will get you to America and sort out your papers but the rest is up to you. You are not to speak about it or we will come to Boston and kill you and your family. That's the deal," said Josh, after receiving his orders from Grisham.

Grisham drew up the necessary papers and Ashur signed them for him and on behalf of Leah, and all the documentation that was necessary to smuggle Ashur and his family into America was prepared in Fort Benning, after they received a call from Grisham. A plane would take them to Boston from Tel Aviv. A military plane would take them there, from Baghdad. Once Leah was found, she would be escorted to Tel Aviv, where Ashur and the children would be waiting, in a military base there. Ashur was shipped off to Tel Aviv and Grisham and his boys departed from the base in Baghdad to downtown Iraq, heading for the university, where Ashur sent them, to apprehend Leah and Christopher.

Chapter 36

On the way down to Ur, being driven by Leah, I had a thought about En.Ki and all that happened over the previous couple of months, everything that I had been through and everything that I had witnessed, wondering how it was possible to have experienced all of that and still be sane and alive. My friends were gone, my family were gone and I was trying to find my way home, wherever that was.

Somewhere on the horizon, I saw the golden rays beat down. The sky in the distance began to turn violet again, thinking of how and if En.Ki would appear again. I closed my eyes and thought of him again, his form and being and, upon opening my eyes again, looking through the window to the left of me, there on the horizon, I saw a form. From several miles in the distance, the form in the distance moved towards me, from what appeared to be a shadow, forming into a being, the being that I knew as En.Ki.

From shadow to body, within a minute, he appeared and I gazed at him, in a trance. He moved alongside the car seamlessly, without form, in his omnipresence, and it reminded me of our respective size, of our simplicity, of our insignificance on this planet, how we liked to shape our destiny and those of others, through conflict and power. En.Ki closed his eyes and smiled as he nodded to acknowledge me.

In all that he was able to show me, he was restricted in where he could guide me. He had been trying to show me something but I had been closed to it. I had to open myself up to what he was trying to show me. I needed to let the universe work through me, he told me. I had to be completely at whole with everything. "Stop fighting and listen with your heart, speak with your heart and let your heart guide you" I heard it loud and strong as I looked at him and he nodded again, closing his eyes.

I felt his presence strongly, as I gazed ahead of me and saw the vibrations of the earth change. Over in the distance, ahead of us, I saw the dimensions of resonant magnetic fields that vibrated off the landscape. Just like the beams of heat that shimmer in the distance in the desert. Just as I had known but tried to hide previously, I felt the certainty of where we were heading.

I tried to engage in conversation with Leah, though it was almost impossible to try and get her to respond. We were in the car, heading for Ur, and I told her that's where we needed to head towards. She looked at me, perplexed, and told me that we had already decided on going to the Ziggurat in Ur. She looked at me again, as she drove us down from Baghdad, and said she was concerned for my behavior and state of mind. I told her there was nothing to worry about, assuring her as best I could but I sensed that she was not comfortable with the journey and the decision she had made to take me. Her energy changed and I could sense that she hated me.

"I am not what you think I am," I said.

But she didn't respond, a deathly silence enveloped the car until we reached Ur. I looked at her eyes, from the side, from the passenger seat next to her, to see where the truth lay and I could see they were in pain. It hurt me to know that I had put her and her family in that predicament.

When I was in the car, En.Ki explained to me what I needed to do. It came to me as a download of sorts, a sort of telepathic communication. I felt at one with him and it was then that he told me how I could solve the problems that were facing us as human beings and that would help him get back to his home planet Nibiru. What I learnt from En.Ki was that we are all just energy and vibrations and we have the power to create the world in which we live, the world we want. Everyone has the ability, the power, to do this because the kingdom of God resides in each and every one of us. That was what I had heard so many times before, in church. We are co-creators of our own destiny. I had to ask myself, what type of world do I want the children of our future to live in?

I was suddenly aware of the power that En.Ki had bestowed upon me and how scared I was of it. I was afraid to exert myself in this world because of everything I had been told to believe in. We were to worship a God, go to church, get conditioned and become these robot-like creatures on this planet without questioning anything. After all I had been awakened to, I was saddened at the future of humanity. What could I do to change the direction that we were on? I felt responsible for my part in it, it was up to me to change it.

Under the sun, the barren landscape vibrated with the heat. I licked my lips as my throat cracked, under the sun, in the car. I closed my eyes and rested my head against the car window, as Leah drove through the dirty tracks, kicking up dirt on both sides. I closed my eyes and breathed in deeply, trying to make sense of the events of the previous weeks: how my soul had left my body and went to another dimension, in what looked like space, and there I saw the stars and Earth below me. It was something I had to keep to myself and I sighed at that prospect. Leah wouldn't understand. Nobody would.

I took solace in what I saw there, when I was floating way up high. I was encompassed with a sense of wonder and amazement, where I knew the existence of everything. I knew there, in that light, the purpose of my life and I could see where I had travelled. I saw my mother and Jessica and the baby, who came to collect me to take me to the source of all creation. There in the light, I saw the past, the present and the future all at one. There, I was suddenly part of everything that ever was and everything that ever existed and everything that will exist.

There, I wanted to stay. It was a place of pure joy and pure knowledge. I could feel my connection with the whole of creation and I knew to what extent we are all connected. We are all one but we are deeply disconnected, disconnected from our past lives and present existence on Earth. When we come to existence on Earth, we have no recollection of what we have come here for. It is up to us to figure that out. We are pawns for the taking in a system that has been designed by our overlords to control us. If only we all knew how deeply connected we are, we would live in harmony and it wouldn't be out of reach for us. We wouldn't have to destroy the planet for the selfish gain of the select few that control us.

There, I wanted to stay. With the source of creation. But I wasn't allowed. I protested at the thought of returning into my body, the flesh of my body that was almost certainly decaying in the midday heat before I left it. I protested, saying that it wouldn't be physically possible to recover, that my body was dead, no longer functioning, but I was told that I hadn't finished my life's purpose on Earth, so I had to return.

I asked what that was, what my purpose was. The creation responded, telling me that each and everyone on earth had their purpose, their whole life was to be spent discovering that purpose. I asked again what my purpose was, why I should return back to Earth to a place of conflict and war and pain and suffering when creation itself, God, was himself the creator of love and joy, why would I return to a place of a destructive power that made it impossible to live?

Before I knew it, I was being sucked away from the light, the ball of light which I could see in the distance as the darkness of space enveloped me. I was being sent back into my body and I could hear the sounds of people around me. I could feel my body being prodded and pushed and, as I came to, I was being huddled into the back of a lorry, my body lifeless and my face was being splattered with water.

"Is he breathing? Is he breathing?" asked a voice.

I opened my eyes and could feel the light penetrate my eyes as I moved my arms to cover them.

"Are you okay, are you okay?" came another voice.

I was being escorted by members of the crew, blood-soaked from the blast, back when we were in Baghdad, on Corniche Street, with Grisham and Josh, in the unit. They were startled by my injury, as they loaded me up in an armored vehicle and transported me back to base for treatment. When I came to, back in base, I was treated and told I was good to go despite all the blood and the concussion. I felt I had been in heaven then pulled to hell in an instant, back into my body.

It then became apparent why I was returned to Earth to do and it had everything to do with creating a loving world where humanity would wake up and understand that we are all connected and less to do with division, hatred, corruption and greed. I was a spot in an ocean of consciousness and En.Ki was going to help me; help me to help humanity attain their higher selves so that we could become one, with the source of creation, with the creator, with the God of Love, not the God of War.

I turned to Leah when I opened my eyes again, in the car, on the way to Ur. I looked at her troubled face and worry, under her apparent sense of purpose, a purpose only she could fathom, having abandoned her family and her newborn child for me, fresh in her own pain, the pain that I had almost forgotten and I said: "I'm sorry, Leah. I'm sorry for all of this. Please forgive us."

Chapter 37

WHEN TO THE PLANET NIBIRU, THE PLANET OF EARTH'S CROSSING, RETURNED I WAS, TO THE SONS OF THE GODS TO CREATE AND SHAPE THE DESTINY OF HUMANS LEFT IT WAS. EXILED FROM THE COUNCIL OF ELDERS, FORBIDDEN WAS I TO RETURN TO EARTH. UNTIL THE TIME OF THE NEXT CROSSING.

CAME TO EARTH DID WE 450,000 YEARS AGO. EARTH YEARS. CROSSING THE EARTH SINCE EVERY 3,600 EARTH YEARS HAVE WE. EARTH TO US THE PLANET OF THE CROSSING. THE CROSSING. THE TIME. THE ASTROLOGICAL AGE.

FOR EACH ASTROLOGICAL AGE, A GIFT. FROM THE GODS. FOR THE AGE OF TAURUS WAS THE BULL AND MOSES. THE AGE OF PISCES WAS CHRIST. NOW THE AGE OF AQUARIUS. TO HUMANITY A GIFT WILL I BESTOW.

DIE ON EARTH MANY PEOPLE WILL. AT THE END OF TIMES. THE END OF PISCES. AS IT HAS BEEN FORETOLD. AS THE PLAN HAS BEEN. AS HUMANITY CONDITIONED HAVE BEEN. AS UNTO EN.LIL MY HALF BROTHER EARTH HAS FALLEN. SO IS HIS PLAN.

TO THE PLAN IS EARTH NOW. TO THE END ARE THE PEOPLE OF EARTH DRIVEN. AND AFTER THE END OF THE WORLD, A NEW RELIGION HUMANITY WILL BE TAUGHT. FOR THE NEW AGE, A NEW RELIGION. THE NEXT AGE, THE AGE OF AQUARIUS. A NEW SYMBOL WILL BE GIVEN. HE WHO BEARS WATER.

WHEN THE AGE OF PISCES ENDS, BEGINS THE AGE OF AQUARIUS. TO MAN WILL ALL OF RELIGION BE REMOVED. TO THIS CONTROL EN.LIL WILL NOT. TO THIS THE POWER OF THE COSMOS WILL HUMANITY INHERIT. FOR THIS NEW A NEW LEADER WILL BE CHOSEN. HE WHO BEARS WATER.

FOR EARTH, NIBIRU WILL RELEASE. THE TRAP OF EN.LIL THAT HAS BEEN SET. NIBIRU WILL RELEASE THE NET. SO IN THE COSMOS HAS IT BEEN WRITTEN. EN.KI WAS THE AGE UNDER WHICH EARTH DID FALL. UNTO EN.KI WILL THE AGE BE RETURNED. UNTO EARTH SHALL EN.KI REIGN.

FOR EN.LIL TO EARTH HAS HE A PRISON MADE. A MAGNETIC FIELD OVER EARTH HAS EN.LIL PLACED. KEEPING THE EARTH LOCKED IS EN.LIL. SOON WILL THE NET BE BROKEN. NO LONGER TRAPPED IN THE LOWER DIMENSION HUMANITY WILL BE. SOON THE DIMENSIONS ABOVE THE THIRD WILL THE HUMANS SEE. IN THE YEAR 2012. THE MONTH OF DECEMBER. THE DAY OF 21. THE BEGINNING OF THE SHIFT WILL THIS DATE BE.

TO THE HIGHER REALMS WILL THE CHOSEN ENTER. THE WARS WILL BE GONE. UNTO NOW THE CORRUPTION OF HUMANITY BY THE PROGENY OF EN.LIL HAS IT PREVAILED. UPON THE NEW AGE THE RULE OF THE OLD WILL IT NO LONGER BE.

NO LONGER WILL THOSE WHO LEAD HUMANITY IN POWER BE. GONE WILL BE THEIR POWER. KILLED MY CREATION FOR EN.LIL HAVE THEY. LEAD MY PROGENY TO WAR HAVE THEY. KILLED MY CREATION HAVE THEY. SERVICE TO THEMSELVES ARE THEY. KILLED THE CREATION OF EN.KI HAVE THEY.

AFTER 2012 A SHIFT WILL IT BEGIN. A NEW CONSCIOUSNESS WILL THERE BE. SERVICE TO OTHERS WILL IT BE. HUMANITY ACHIEVE SPIRITUAL GROWTH WILL THEY. IN A GLOBAL CONSCIOUSNESS WILL THEY. CARE FOR EACH OTHER WILL THEY. SAVE THE EARTH WILL THEY. ASCEND TO THE HIGHER REALMS WILL THE CHOSEN ONES. ENLIGHTENED SOULS FOR THE RAPTURE HAS IT BEEN DECIDED.

SAVED THE SOULS WILL BE. FOR THOSE WHO HAVE RAISED THEIR CONSCIOUSNESS. ABLE TO PERCEIVE THE HIGHER DIMENSIONS WILL THEY BE. PERISH THE FOLLOWERS OF EN.LIL WILL THEY BE. WORKED FOR EN.LIL'S EVIL PROGENY HAVE THEY. SINNED AGAINST THE EARTH HAVE THEY. SINNED AGAINST CREATION HAVE THEY.

THE AGE OF AQUARIUS TO MY AGE IT SHALL BE. THE AGE OF EN.KI. UNDER THE AGE OF PISCES MY HALF-BROTHER EN.LIL ENSLAVED HUMANITY HAS HE. GIVEN A FALSE GOD HAS HE. RETURNED TO EARTH HAVE I. THE PROGENY OF EN.KI WILL INHERIT THE EARTH SHALL THEY.

AMONGST THE CHOSEN, ONE I SEEK TO BE THE CHOSEN. NOT FOR RELIGION BUT FOR GUIDANCE. HE WHO HAS SEEN THE LIGHT SHALL THE TRUTH BRING. NOT MANY WILL BELIEVE BUT CHRISOPHER CUNNINGHAM HAS SEEN. CHRISTOPHER CUNNINGHAM THE WATER BEARER IS HE. BRING THE NEW AGE WILL HE.

NOT A RELIGION TO CREATE BUT A PATH FOR HUMANITY WILL HE CREATE. LEAD THEM TO THE HIGHER DIMENSIONS WILL HE. BRING FORTH THE SHIFT

SHALL HE. SEEK NOT GOD THROUGH MAN WILL THEY. SEEK GOD THROUGH THEMSELVES WILL MAN. MANY WILL SEE AND MANY WILL BELIEVE.

Chapter 38

Leah and Christopher drove through the night after resting in one of the villages for several hours. It was a four-hour drive to Ur from where they were, in the remote villages miles outside of Baghdad. Outside the city walls, the roads that lead to the little towns, the land was clear. A clear night, a peaceful night, back on the desert roads that Christopher had grown used to, over the previous weeks. Christopher thought, for a moment, maybe that was all down to En.Ki. Maybe En.Ki cleared the path for them.

Leah was driving, since she knew the roads a lot better. She could take shortcuts and navigate the dusty tracks a lot better. She turned to Chris, as he looked out the window and at the stars:

"I suppose you didn't have this in mind when you first came here," asked Leah.

Chris continued to gaze at the stars: "Do you ever wonder why we're here, on Earth?"

Leah just laughed and said: "I know what my religion tells me. That we are here for a reason. We have to submit to the will of God and do our best. Aside from that, nobody had time to really think about it."

"What is that will?" asked Christopher, in a reflective tone.

Leah paused for a moment to think: "I suppose it's to look after yourself, your family and the environment."

Chris turned to Leah and asked: "But who is God?"

Leah drew a deep breath, before speaking: "Well that is a question that has been asked for centuries. If you go back long enough, you'll find many hundreds of gods. There is the creator God and then there is the destroyer God. Maybe we are the gods," she said, with a furrowed brow.

"I don't believe a Christian god would have done all of this. I don't think Jesus is here. Not from what I've seen," said Christopher.

"I take a pragmatic approach to God. He is there to guide us but it's up to us to choose. To think that the cradle of civilization is being destroyed thousands of years later because of a difference of opinions about gods is laughable. Maybe God has made you come here to help you."

"In what way, Leah?" Christopher was surprised by the suggestion.

"There are mysteries of this universe that the more learned of people cannot answer, though they have tried over the centuries, Christopher," said Leah.

Christopher paused for a moment, to consider what he really wanted to say. To tell Leah what he really knew. He paused and thought about it. What if she thought he was crazy? She ignored him the first time he had said it. Maybe she did think he was crazy. Maybe that's why she didn't respond the first time, he thought. He wanted to try again, now that they were alone together: "Leah, En.Ki is here. I have seen him."

Leah looked at Christopher again and didn't respond. Just as she didn't respond when he told her earlier, in her home. She didn't know how to respond. She looked at him with pity. He was a troubled man with a fantasy, she thought, and their wild goose chase might end up just being that. She felt uneasy so she tried to humor him:

"When did you see him? Where?" asked Leah.

"I saw him after my injury. It was in the street. He appeared to me. He told me everything. I've had an awakening with him. He's shown me things," said Christopher, unabashed.

"Like what?" asked Leah, trying to mask a sarcastic tone.

Christopher turned to look out the window again and saw En.Ki appear in the distance. The giant figure on the horizon lifted his staff and pointed it over his shoulder. Christopher put his hand on the wheel and turned it and Leah screamed: "what are you doing?"

'"We need to go this way," said Christopher in a flat tone, as if he was hypnotized.

"Where are you taking us? You could have killed us" yelled Leah.

"If he wanted us dead, he would have by now." stated Christopher, calmly.

"What are you talking about, Christopher?" yelled Leah, frustrated.

"I'm talking about God. God would have let us be killed by now," said Christopher, calmly.

Leah stopped yelling and calmed down. Clearly, Christopher was talking out aloud, she thought. It was nothing to be alarmed about, she thought. Until he said: "Our true God. En.Ki. He's here. Here to guide us. He will take us to where we need to go." Christopher pointed his finger outside the window and continued, by turning his head to Leah and said: "Do you see him, Leah?"

Leah did not turn to look out the window, choosing instead to stare at the road ahead and fixed her gaze on it. Her shoulders tensed and her hands gripped the wheel as the car sped south, towards the city of Ur, in silence as she continued to ignore Christopher's insane outbursts. They drove a couple of hours until they got to the city limits and Leah slowed the car down and came to a halt:

"Christopher, I'm not sure if I can go with you. I have a family that needs me. Besides, the Australians and the Americans will be crawling all over that place and I need to stay alive."

"And do you think that you are safe now? Do you think your family is still safe from either side?" asked Christopher, continuing in a trance-like state. "They have your family already. I am going to save you and your family but you have to trust me."

"Christopher, this is madness. I cannot go any further at all. You are talking like a madman and I have no guarantee of anything." There was a pause and Christopher continued to gaze out the window to his right. Leah continued to speak: "Christopher, look at me. You cannot ask this of me. If I go home now, I will be able to make it alive and be with my family."

Christopher felt something come over him and he felt his impatience grow. Leah looked at him and sensed something change in the air. Christopher's trance-like state continued, and he turned to Leah: "Your family are in Tel Aviv. They've taken them there."

Christopher's eyes changed shape and the whites of his eyes disappeared. Leah's heart stopped when she saw them. The dark dots where the pupils should be were surrounded by a burning red. Leah pushed back against the car door and slid her hand to the handle to try and release it. The car locked, beating her to it. She gasped and Christopher continued to speak, in a low mechanical sound: "Take me to the Ziggurat of Ur. I am not going to hurt you"

With her shaking hands, she turned her keys in the ignition, put her foot to the pedal and sped off down the road that would lead them to the Ziggurat, stopping 500 meters away from their destination, with the structure visible on the horizon.

They got out of the car and walked the rest of the way, down the makeshift dirt track, which had been imprinted by military forces. It was a few hours before dawn so they would have to move quickly if they wanted to get into the Ziggurat unnoticed. From the distance, they could see the lights of cars and spotlights fenced around the whole pyramid-like structure. They hid behind a makeshift wall to a raised garden a hundred meters in front of the Ziggurat and scoped the area for military personnel. There was one clear path to the entrance but they would have to create a distraction if Christopher would be able to sneak in:

"How many can you see?" asked Christopher. "I can make out about two on each side and I'm guessing there will be two on the side we can't see. About 8, maybe more on top and more inside," he said.

"Well, it's obvious there is something that they are guarding and want. I see Australian and American tanks only. What do you see?" confirmed Leah. Just as she awaited an answer from Chris, she saw a shadow move on the horizon. She couldn't make out exactly what it was and blinked hard to try and clear her eyes. Perhaps it was sand, she thought, that blurred her vision.

Then she looked again. And there, on the horizon, a tall figure, under the moonlight sky, moved towards the spotlights, casting a large shadow on the ground. She saw it move and she shook her head and blinked hard again. Maybe her mind was playing tricks on her, she thought, and she left it at that. Christopher noticed her shake her head and asked if she was okay but she didn't say anything.

They walked towards the Ziggurat and Chris saw, for the first time, the shape of it up close. Unlike the pyramids in Egypt, the

Ziggurat had a somewhat complex structure. There was a ramp that led to the entrance and a flat roof, which was covered in bricks and rubble. It was magnificent and mystical and Christopher's face expressed his awe.

"'Saddam restored it. He spent a lot of money on it. My father would often work there a lot, inside. He was doing his secret work for Saddam as well as overseeing the reconstruction. We never saw him for days sometimes. He was always busy here, with his team. That place holds a lot of secrets," whispered Leah.

"It's vast. I've never seen anything so ancient before," said Christopher.

"Well, what you are seeing is the reconstructed version. It was never like this before Saddam started work on it. Saddam was trying to restore it to its former glory. It was just a pile of dirt before then, weathered by the centuries. That flat top should have several storeys and decks and those decks would house gardens," continued Leah, out of breath.

"Ah, the hanging gardens of Babylon," said Chris.

"Yes, because this is the desert and nothing grows here," said Leah.

"It's because of En.Lil's nuclear weapons. This land will always be barren," said Christopher.

Leah looked at Christopher in shock: "How do you know that? That is something that is hidden in the translations."

"Because, En.Ki told me. He revealed the mysteries to me," answered Christopher, weary from having to convince a non-believer.

"The secrets will be revealed to the chosen one," echoed Leah, in a tone of burgeoning belief.

After scoping out the area, they hatched a plan. Leah would cause a distraction and the soldiers would detain her, whilst Christopher weaved past the guards and snuck up the ramp, providing the floodlights wouldn't catch him. Leah would have to return to the car and drive it as far as she could before the guards ordered her to stop.

"Are you sure you want to do this?" asked Christopher.

Without hesitation, Leah ran back to the car and managed to drive it a good 10 meters away from the front of the Ziggurat, at the place where their spotlights met the darkness of night. True to form, the allied troops instructed her to get out of the vehicle and place her hands in the air after firing a few rounds in the air. Two men from the north-facing side of the Ziggurat approached Leah and yelled at her to get on the ground. The other men repositioned, to replace the missing guards, on the other sides of the Ziggurat.

Chapter 39

In the time Leah distracted the soldiers, I managed to scale the ramp, narrowly escaping being spotted by a guard coming from the side of the structure. I crept up as I heard the commotion. The distraction that Leah created, crying out into the night like a banshee, allowed me to scale the ramp quickly and unnoticed, quickly disappearing into the darkness as I escaped the glare of the spotlights that fenced the Ziggurat.

At the top of the ramp, I looked back and saw Leah in the distance, being cuffed and led to their tank, as the car was inspected by the other soldier. I looked at her; she was still yelling and growing confrontational with the soldiers. Ahead of me was the open entrance, a dark mass, the contours of which were barely distinguishable, but were outlined by the moonlight. I turned around, to glance one last time. I saw Leah look up at me, as she was being led away. "God will judge you all!" she screamed, at the soldiers.

The corridors were empty and the black mass of night filled them. I placed my hand on the wall to guide my path, as I walked gently, careful not to stir a sound that would alert anyone in the vicinity. The only sign of life was in my breath. I paused for a moment, as I started and stopped, to listen for anyone in the vicinity.

The entrance into the Ziggurat led to a network of caverns and corridors. There was some light coming from the rooms, with paraffin and mechanical lamps. The main passageway, which ran adjacent to the entrance, appeared to run through all four sides. I walked to a cavern, to the right of me, which was dimly lit on the outside, and I hid inside it to see if I could get a view to the lower half of the Ziggurat's hollow center. I waited for a while, around half an hour, whilst I planned my next move, all the while trying to see over the wall that separated the corridors from the cavernous interior. As soon I was on my toes, I could make out the glare of lights shining beneath, in the center of the building.

Inside the cavern, where I waited in the near pitch black, I saw some gold writing on the walls, being reflected into the room, from the crack of light that tried to penetrate through from the corridor. Using a key torch from my pocket, I tried to investigate the rest of the chamber but the darkness was too strong for the little beam of light from the torch. In the middle of the chamber, where I scanned with the thin beam, there was a makeshift seat made out of stone, which was covered with sticks. Along the walls, I could make out various diagrams and strange symbols. Against the light of the torch, the symbols glistened.

The drawings were pictograms. Some were of animals but the others were a mixture of what looked like hieroglyphs of sorts. There were several that looked like double-helixes, like DNA strands. The rest were shaped like arrows in multiple formations, pointing at different angles and they were interspersed with some other pictograms of what might resemble humans or small animals or bushels of wheat. Then I saw a carving in the wall depicting En.Ki, holding a double-ended three-pronged fork and he was chasing away some sort of eagle-dragon hybrid with horns, sharp teeth and wings that was staring back at him.

I felt a shiver crawl down my back and the room turn cold. Colder than it was outside, a relief from the heat. There was no wind that blew in from the corridor and that realization made me shudder. I shook off the feeling, shone my torch to the entrance of the chamber and walked towards it, with an impending anxiety to leave the chamber and get out of there, in that chamber, where the atmosphere changed all of a sudden. I switched off my torch and shuffled into the passageway.

Moving through the corridor, the passageway, in the dark, I found a staircase that led down the levels, to the ground floor. In complete darkness, I descended in silence, careful of the sounds of my shoes rustling in the dirt. I reached the ground floor and was faced with a courtyard which was lit up with floodlights. In the center of the courtyard was an egg-shaped object that appeared similar to the pine-cone shaped device that En.Ki held in his hand in my first encounter with him. From a distance, I could see that the object was covered in engravings similar to the ones I had seen in the Museum and in the pictures Leah showed me.

I walked towards the object in the silent still room and put my hands over the object, careful not to create a disturbance. The cocoon-shaped structure was constructed of some sort of metal, not stone as I had first thought when I first saw it from a distance. My hands touched the surface and the cocoon lit up the surface beneath the engravings. It gave off a warm, comforting feeling. It felt like an energetic being, almost alive. When I removed my hand, the yellow-orange lights stopped. In the middle of the side of the egg-shaped structure, I could make out what appeared to be a small round disc, about the size of my hand, with a groove around the sides.

I touched the disc and pushed down on it. A current of energy flowed through my arm and travelled down my side, into the ground below me. It felt like a warning. Undeterred, I pushed down again, harder, with both hands, using my feet as leverage. My whole body became electrified and I tried to maintain my strength before my legs gave way and I collapsed on the ground. I looked up and I saw the egg open in half, with one side in a hatch, to reveal a seat, bathed in golden light.

I got up off the ground and got in, to take a seat, then the capsule closed itself and locked me in. I felt pulled into the seat, by a low frequency of gravity and I rested my arms by the side. Above me, a helmet detached itself from the capsule's ceiling and lowered itself above my head and I was fastened in. I began to feel stifled but that feeling dissipated as if the helmet was aware of my feelings and was trying to calm me down, by sending signals to some part of my brain.

The helmet covered the top of my head, to my eyes. The feeling of a calm narcosis overwhelmed me and it was emanating from the machine. I felt an overwhelming feeling of ease. Every part of my body felt like it was being massaged from the inside and I was wrapped in cotton wool, similar to the beam of light that En.Ki shone from his device. I felt a tingling feeling all over the crown of my head and a little prick in the back of my head, above my neck. My head became fixed in place, by the helmet and the needle behind me. As soon as the pinch was over, and the little twinge of pain subsided, images flashed on the visor in front of me.

The first thing that I saw shocked me. I was a baby and I was sitting in a room and my mother was next to me. I couldn't have been more than a couple of years old. I saw myself looking at my mother to pick me up, my arms raised to gesture her to do so, as babies do. I saw my mother slap me to the ground and then I howled out. I saw my father standing by my mother and he was ordering her to do something. She got up from the ground and I stood up again, for her to hold me, with my feet stomping the ground. I saw my heavy tears, flowing to the ground. I saw my mother slap me to the ground again. I got off the ground, in a trance-like state and my father showed me a picture.

The next series of images were of me with my father and we were walking through the base where he used to work. I had a vague memory of it but I must have buried it before I sat in that chair. The images which flashed up before were my own suppressed childhood memories. It was as though the machine was an enhancer of memories or it was fueled in some way by them. My thoughts, whatever I had buried from my childhood, were clear as day for me to see, on the little screen in front of me. The floodgates had been opened and out my memories came pouring.

Images of myself and my mother in the basement returned. That red leather chair, in the middle of the room. Mother and I, we both took our turn in that chair. My father, in his military uniform, stood over us, prodding us with various implements, as he continuously flashed images on the wall, as we repetitively entered trance-like states. As I was watching, a feeling of sickness overwhelmed my body and I started to shake, rocking back and forth in the chair in the cocoon, and the seat began to shake as my body convulsed from the shock of what I was seeing, the emotions flooding as thickly as the memories that were released. After a few moments, I was soothed again, by the energy within the capsule.

In the next image, I saw myself at around 6 years old, my eyes seemed to be blank, like my face, and I was walking, coldly, alongside my father through the corridors of a military base. My eyes had a glazed look on them. I was in a room with tanks filled with strange creatures in some sort of colored water. I saw many cages, some filled with humans. I saw some pathetic-looking creatures in some of the cages. They seemed to be some sort of genetic-mutations. I saw lots of men and women in white overcoats and some men decked in military suits, one of them my father. I saw the level that we have landed on - minus Level 6. We went down in the elevator, down the subterranean levels below the surface of Earth. I saw myself walking through the corridors, with my father, into the rooms but I did not seem at all alarmed by what I was seeing around me. My eyes barely blinked, as if I was some sort of doll, expressionless and cold.

Chapter 40

"Is there any news of Chris?" asked Christopher's mother, somewhat meek in her tone. She sat in her chair, in the basement of her home, slumped in her repose.

"No, nothing since we called last week. The last word I got from them in Baghdad was that he was reported missing and they were trying to relay the message to him," replied, Joe Cunningham, Christopher's father.

"I am worried about him, honey, he's our only son. I mean, we sent him out to fight and we know that he is going to be alright. We know that he is strong and tough and can withstand anything. We know he is protected but - honey - he is all we have. He is ours, honey. He is ours…." Christopher's mother, in a flat tone that belied the seriousness of the situation that a mother would feel, continued to speak. Her eyes were wide open, pupils dilated and her eyes began to fill with tears.

"Sweetheart, let me deal with it. I will try again tomorrow morning to find out what can be done. I may have to swing by the office to see if we can get any trace on his communications in Iraq. See if I can get them to put a track on his tank or locate him with satellites." Christopher's father stroked his wife's hair, as she sat in the familiar chair that she and her Christopher sat in, whenever they needed a tune up, as she did that day.

Joe's wife hadn't been feeling all that well recently. Her son had been led to war, had been reported lost, had lost his own family, which left her bereft. She felt like a prisoner in her own shell, unable to express herself at all. Her husband wasn't the man to listen to her concerns. Her job was very clear: she was there to function as a soft face for the world. Whatever her husband was getting up to in the military, she would never have been able to object to it nor would she ever have the courage to ask him. She was too far gone, too far under his control to realize the extent of her imprisonment. Her eyes never matched the smile she presented to the world. The cruelty of being a military man's wife.

"Please, honey, you are our only hope in this mess. I am going to say some prayers tonight. I pray for Jesus to save him and bring him home to his family," her best hope was to ask politely. Not plead, because her man never liked that and always struck her with more shocks in the chair, if she ever did. She should never be a burden because he hated that. That always made him mad and she always paid heavily for it.

"Well, sweetheart, I'm sure Jesus will save him." Replied her husband, Joe, softly. Then came the first shock and she convulsed in her chair.

Christopher's mother shook violently in her chair and she passed out, this time longer than normal. When she came round, she was smiling, the same as she always did, this time a little less brightly and she acquiesced: "Yes, honey, Jesus will bring him home. We won't be able to make plans for Jessica and the baby unless we find out soon enough. We need to know, already."

"Leave it to me, sweetheart. Now, you just relax and get better now," said Joe.

Joe Cunningham soothed his wife with his dulcet tones as she wavered in and out of different states, until she was lucid enough for her husband to begin projecting images that would bring her back to her normal self again. The only thing that worked, it seemed, in the years of undergoing mind control was pornography. Joe had tried everything from soap operas and celebrity figures from Martha

Stewart to Oprah Winfrey but it was pornography that always worked best for the type of personality he wanted from her.

Another convulsion ended and Christopher's mother became alert again. This time, she looked around the room and, in an apparent state of confusion, said: "Joe, where am I? What am I doing here?"

Joe was taken aback. This was not how this usually played out. He paused for a moment and considered whether he should engage with her. He attempted to ignore her but she continued:

"Joe, I'm confused about what I'm doing here and what is that on the projector? Pornography? What are you doing with pornography?"

Joe was stunned. His wife had broken free from her programming temporarily and his only option was to try and subdue her again but he would have to restrain her. He paused to think of a strategy before speaking: "honey, don't you remember? You like to come down here whenever you aren't feeling well."

Joe's wife looked up at him and attempted to get up but she was gently eased back into her chair: "Joe, let go of me," she yelled.

Joe stepped back and edged towards the table against the wall and moved his hand to the drawer, where there lay a pen syringe to administer narcotics, in case of emergencies. Before he could do so, he was interrupted by his wife:

"Stop right there, Joe. I know what you are reaching for. That's what you're going to inject me with to help me sleep, before you shock me and show me pornography, aren't you" asserted Christopher's mother, confrontationally.

She touched her face, her body and her hair. She was becoming aware of what had been happening to her. She continued: "why have you been doing this to me, Joe? Why? I am your wife." She cried a deep cry, the first she was able to cry since her marriage to Joe. Her first real cry since sending her son to war, her first real cry since Christopher was born, her first real cry since Jessica and the baby died and her first real cry since she watched her husband carry out the same torture on their only child, Christopher.

Joe stood, frozen in silence. He looked at her in apparent defeat. The world he had built, from necessity, the world he got embroiled in, was over. There was nothing left for him. His son was lost at war, possibly dead, his son's family was gone and the only thing that was left for him was to maintain the lie that he projected to the world.

She looked at Joe in horror, in a state of shock of something that she had realized and said: "Joe, it was you. It was you that killed them. You did it. You sent him there. You created a monster. Like you. Joe, why did you destroy our family? Joe, what are you doing to us? Joe, what does Christopher know?"

"What you talk?" asked Joe in feigned confusion.

"You told me that it would work, that you had been through it and your family had been through it for generations. I trusted what you said even when my heart told me not to do that to him," cried his wife and continued by saying: "The man I loved, at least I thought I loved, turned out to be a monster. A monster that I had a part in, I knew. There was only so much a woman, a mother could take. I knew not to trust you from the start. All that secrecy from the military wasn't worth it in the end, was it?"

"Shut up, you don't know what you're talking about." shouted Joe.

"If I had known that your family were a bunch of Satan-worshipping cocksuckers I would never have gotten involved. Not for anything in the world," shouted his wife tearfully.

'"Well, you didn't have any complaints when I took you out of your filthy rag family in the hills and showed you the world, did you?" said a red-faced Joe.

"Men often like to think that they can control women like a rag-doll, always underestimating the power they hold. I gave you life and all you can tell me is what I am worth. You knew I would have done anything for you. You knew the poverty was going to kill me; you had me where you wanted me. I was weak to your sick ways." conceded his wife, with her hands muffling her sobs.

"You had your chances to leave. But, no, the money was too good for you - even too good to protect your son. Just admit that you are just as evil as I am, if evil is what you call it. I call it survival. Remember that. It's just survival." said Joe with gritted teeth.

Joe walked towards his wife and pinned her down, got on top of her in the chair, whilst the pornography continued to play in the background, and he lifted up her skirt and pushed himself into her, with both hands firmly around her neck. The job had to be finished, she must be brought back into her programming, her family could never know, she was a liability; this is what he repeated to himself as he continued, hands around her neck, until she fell out of consciousness and he fell off her, panting like a frenzied animal.

Chapter 41

I was in a room with a man, whom I called 'Dad', and he was traumatizing me with several different implements. He was wearing his military uniform and there were other children my age in the room. One child was placed under hypnosis and I saw his soul leave the room, whilst he was strapped down, giving him the ability to walk through walls. I saw myself, an 8-year old, awaiting in a trance-like state, for whatever trauma I was about to endure and for whatever task I was required to perform:

"'Dad, why are there so many weird things in those tanks?" I asked.

"Son, you don't need to worry about that just now. Just count yourself lucky that you're not one of them." replied the man I called 'Dad'.

"Dad, why are some of those people different to us? Why do they look so different?"

"Son, they don't come from this planet."

"Dad, where do they come from?"

"Son, they come from all over. Different planets in our galaxy."

"Wow. Could they kill us, Dad?"'

"If enough of them come through but it depends on which ones. Some are friendly some are not."

"Dad, why are we here?"

"You make me laugh. Always asking questions like your mother. You are here to continue your training."

"What will I be doing?"

"Today, you are going to communicate with one of them telepathically and try to get some information for us. We need it for our own safety. The ones that you will be working with are not hostile. They actually quite like children but there are those that would actually like to eat you but of course you won't be working with those."

"Which ones are those?"

"They are called the Reptilians and they are quite scary things."

'"What do they look like?"

"They are tall, green and brown and scaly which sharp teeth and they look like little T-rexes."

"Oh I hope I never meet one of those."

"You are okay, son, there aren't any in this base."

But shortly after, in that memory, I was taken to that base, where the fearful creatures that 'Dad' had described to me resided, as if he had been preparing me for it. It was the Dulce Base, deep underground:

"Dad, what are those creatures there, they look like us but they're a bit weird looking and they look scary to me."

"Son they're what we call Reptoids. They are half-human with alien DNA. His father was a Reptilian. They come from another planet in the Draco constellation. His mother is human."

"What are they doing here and not in their conversation?"

"No, constellation, son, constellation."

"Con....but Daddy, how come they are a mix?"

"Son, sometimes women like your mommy will be impregnated with their semen and then they give birth to half-alien and half-human."

"What is inpreg....and what are sea men?"

"Son, just like you came from your mom's belly after I put my seed in her. That's how it happened. I will show you a picture of the father. See, how he looks?"

"Dad he looks almost like a T-Rex."

"That's right son and when they mix with blonde-haired and blue-eyed women just like your mom they can make what we call Reptoids."

"'What about the black and brown people?"

"What about them?"

"'Can they mix with them?"

"Of course not, dummy. They don't have the right type of DNA, which is like the right type of blood. That's why this world is for white people and someday you will fight the good fight to kill brown and black people."

"Why would I do that, Daddy?"

"Because, son, the black and brown people are not the type that the Reptilians need on this earth and there are too many of them. The Reptoids and the Reptilians are running the world and we need more white skin, blond hair and blue eyed people. It's called The Silent War, son, and we've been doing it for a long time."

'"But you don't have blue eyes, Dad."

"That's true but I do have everything else son and that's all that matters."

"Yes, daddy, you have green eyes. Is that why they call you Dr. Green here?"

'"Yes, son, that's why they call me Dr. Green."

"Is that what they called you in Germany, Daddy?"

"No, they called me something else then."

"What did they call you, Daddy?"

"Now that was a very long time ago and Daddy can't remember all of it now."

"When was that Daddy?"

"That was in 1935."

"That was a long time ago, Daddy."

"Yes, son it was."

"How did you come here to America, Daddy?'"

"The government helped me."

"When did you meet mom?"

"I met her in 1985."

"When were you born, Daddy?"

"I was born in 1911."

"and I was born in 1983."

"Yes son, you were born in 1983 and that was 6 years ago."

"But daddy, if you were born in 1911, you would be erm, let me think…"

"nearly 80 years old, son."

"Yes Daddy."

"'Daddy, I told my teacher that you were born in 1911 and he laughed at me because he said you're too young to have been born then."

"Now, son, what did I tell you about telling people about what happens here?"

"Yes but she laughed at me and she told me that you are only 36 years old…"

"Listen, son, I am going to have to take you back into the control room now because you have told people our secret."

"No, daddy, no."

"Yes son, come with me."

The video stopped playing. More images flashed up on the visor in front of me, which paralyzed me with shock in that chair, in the egg-like structure, in the courtyard of the Ziggurat I had snuck into, in the early hours of the morning. In the images that played, I looked like a complete zombie. I was sitting in a room and the man I called my father released a snake from a glass case next to me. I grabbed the snake and I snapped it in half. I was 8 years old. I had a blank expression and my eyes were dark. Moments later, I was placed in a chair and I began playing a video game. I was playing a soldier, gunning down enemies in the desert much like the desert of Iraq.

The images continued to flash in front of me, the memories unraveled like a film reel, everything I had suppressed over the years, from my programming. I was 13 in the next image, sitting with my Mom and Dad watching me play video games. I was killing again, in the video game, in the desert. My father Joe Cunningham, the father I always knew as my father, patted me on the back for reaching the high score and he took one game away, after I completed it and he replaced it with another. I was sitting there for hours, playing the video games, until I was asked to join them at the table for dinner. I sat there, still quiet, still in a trance. My eyes were blank, and dark.

The feeling of nausea returned from watching my memories and I began sweating in the chair, with an overwhelming feeling that my life had been a lie, forming waves of panic and fear. Flashes of memories swirled through my head at a pace that I couldn't stop, like bullets firing through an automatic. Pangs of anxiety began to run through my body and I started to squirm in the chair. Ahead of me, I saw those thoughts manifest themselves into flashing images like someone was flicking through television channels at a rate of dozens every two seconds.

Hundreds of images came flashing up on the screen, the intensity of which tensed me up in that chair like a ball being squeezed. Sweat poured off me as I tried to control my thoughts, to try and get the images to stop, for some respite. It seemed the walls of the cocoon began to close in, suffocating my breath. Waves of panic and fear drenched me like the sweat that poured out, shallow breaths made it impossible to breathe. I reached for the walls, in my panic, to try and escape the pod. The pod itself started to vibrate and shake, as it appeared to resonate the panic I was in. My breath started pushing fast, in short paces, turning into hyperventilation, as the helmet locked my head in place. Minutes past before I could bring my breathing under control. Only then did the helmet become loose and I fell to the floor inside the pod.

A mass of vomit came out, as if I was gorging out the past. What little food I had in my stomach to keep me going was gone. I collapsed in exhaustion, the adrenaline washed out, to a rush of endorphins that broke the downward spiral, on the roller coaster of emotions and memories I had just experienced. It was as if what I thought as being my true self had been hollowed out. I was a mere blip in the life that I had really lived, the life that was largely hidden from me, in what I saw pass before me, on the visor, the images projected from the deep recesses of my mind. I turned to see a pool of sweat on the chair.

It was as if someone had turned the faucet on in my head and a million thoughts came pouring out, drowning me in a sea of emotions, the waves of fear and anxiety, the drench from the sweat of convulsions, as I swam to the surface for air. But I wanted to try again, and return on the emotional rollercoaster. The adrenaline and the endorphins, all of it. I needed to see more. I needed to find out more, from my past. Maybe I would discover something more, something that might tell me more about what I was doing in Iraq and help me find what I was looking for.

I stood up and climbed into the chair again, drained and apprehensive, reluctant for my mind to be fired up and fried again, under the helmet and the socket that locked behind my neck. I looked up at the contraptions that held my head in place then to the visor that was still protruding. On the visor, I could just about make out little tiny images which were still flashing. They appeared to be flickering in little icons, many thumbnails, that rolled across the visor in an endless stream.

I lifted myself up a bit, to get a better view. I touched the visor and the icons played video. Swiping through, scrolling past dozens of icons, I was able to track the point I was last at, before I threw myself off. I clicked on a small icon and it began playing a video; it was of me and Dad, jumping into a truck and there was a woman next to the truck speaking to me. I got into the truck and my dad and I drove the route we took to get to the base in Fort Benning.

I tapped another icon with my finger and a video flashed up of some men in suits with military men, talking about a plan for a "New American Century." They were sitting around a table, talking about a need for a cataclysmic event, in order for America to become the world leader and a true military force and presence in the world. Dick Cheney whispered something into the ear of Donald Rumsfeld, who was also present.

A man hovered behind them in military uniform and suggested allowing planes to hit the twin towers in New York. It occurred to me that if I was indeed seeing my hidden memories, I must have been there. I paused the video to see what I could make out in that dark room of wooden tables and leather seats. I zoomed in on the vase on the table and there I saw it - my reflection, my face, a 10-year old boy, sitting alongside those men and that's when I recalled: the man I saw, stood behind Dick and Donald in military uniform, was indeed my father, my real father, the father I had always known as my father, Joe Cunningham.

I slumped down, at the side of the chair. I drew in deep breaths of despair. My father's involvement was the ultimate betrayal - more so than the torture he had subjected me to, a torture which was beyond explanation. It was depressing. I was there to be used, like a toy. Programmed for a life that I had no control over. Neither did Mom. It was a truth that sank my heart to the ground and simultaneously unburdened me. I became angry, intensely angry, more angry than I had ever been, as if a volcano of suppressed emotions was exploding within me.

Chapter 42

"Welcome, Dr. Green," said Joe Cunningham, nodding politely at his mentor. Joe then scanned the room to address the rest of the attendees. "Thank you all for your attendance," he said.

"Yes - shall we begin?" asked the President, who had been invited to attend a briefing by General Joe Cunningham, as part of ongoing investigations for secret ops for the NSA.

"Yes, Today, I will provide you with an update on the latest developments of Project MK Ultra. The following videos will demonstrate the uses of it and the wider application in society," continued Joe.

"Very well then," answered the President.

"Yes. As you are aware, we have been working on trauma-based mind control as a means to control subjects. Most notably, the work that was started in Germany only proved to show that the masses could be manipulated with rhetoric and propaganda but I then discovered that pain and trauma actually opened up pathways in the subject and it is then possible to manipulate the subject. As the subject enters a state of hypnosis, we will call it the Alpha-state, they are susceptible to everything that you tell them to do and they will carry out that instruction and believe what you are telling them as a form of fact or reality. In other words, for greater impact, trauma and control are dependent upon each other," said General Cunningham, with some enthusiasm.

"That's very interesting," said the President.

"Yes, it is indeed Mr. President," echoed Joe Cunningham.

"So, how can you explain the way that we can use this for our benefit? Say, for example to quash a voice of dissent or to, for example, persuade the public that Communism is a dangerous thing?" asked the President.

"Well, from what we learnt from Germany, propaganda will work up until a point but, if there is a traumatic event surrounding people or places that the population are greatly invested in, we can affect the consciousness of the population at large and they will be more easily controllable," said Joe Cunningham.

"Yes but the propaganda machine in Germany was still able to mobilize the public," interrupted Dr. Green.

"Yes, that's right, but a trauma-based event enables the government to control the population a lot more quickly and a lot more effectively," explained Joe Cunningham, to his lifelong mentor.

"Okay, go on, I'm listening," interrupted the President.

"Say, for example, we are going through a domestic or international crisis, for example, a war. Let's say that there are peace protests going on on American soil and these protests are being led by some popular musicians who actually have more influence over the consciousness of the younger generation. Well, it's great that the young people are invested in their idols emotionally. That's why we need pop stars, aside from the distraction. Anyway, if the musicians and rock stars are the ones who end up being assassinated, especially whilst in the limelight, then their fans are going to end up experiencing trauma. There will of course be a mass reaction but then their fans, or in this case, their generation itself will be susceptible to reprogramming."

"I get it. But how would you do the reprogramming?" asked Dr. Green.

"That's easy. TV shows and print media would run tributes but you could promote stories of the secret lives of these rock stars, to show their fans what sordid lives they led and, from there on out, you are able to take control of the narrative and change perceptions," answered Joe Cunningham, with growing enthusiasm.

"But will behavior change immediately? I doubt it. What we saw in Germany was that behavior was changed by propaganda but it was a slow process," said Dr. Green, to challenge his protege.

"Yes, and that is my point. In this case, in the example I have used, young people would soon forget about their protests because they would be in shock and then they would learn about the sordid lives of their so called idols and then the government has control over the population again. The key ingredient is trauma," said Joe Cunningham, undeterred.

"Whenever the population gets emotionally invested with an object, be it a person, or place, that's when we have them. We need Hollywood for that reason. That's the propaganda tool we need but we also need to create trauma in the object that they are invested in, to turn the population into our way of thinking, to subdue them into what we want them to do or how we want them to think. Not to mention, the emotions that they create is great loosh for our Reptilian friends," explained Joe Cunningham, in greater detail.

"Ah, yes. This loosh. That is food for them, correct?" asked the President.

"Yes," answered Dr. Green.

"Okay so what you are saying is that a traumatic event is permanently etched into the consciousness of the population but it's important to choose the right sucker to sway the population," asked the President, seeking clarity.

"Yes, Mr. President and even an attempt can be as effective. And it doesn't have to be a person. It's whatever the population recognizes or are invested in, emotionally," said Joe Cunningham, eagerly.

"Okay, so what were the findings of your experiments?" asked Dr. Green, anxiously.

"I would like to show you that now….. So, here, is a video of a young child going through various traumatic experiences at various ages to condition him into certain programming. These programs are a way to condition the child over a prolonged period of time to look and act and behave in certain ways. In this example, we see the child has been subject to something called Messiah programming."

"What is Messiah programming?" asked the President.

"That's above top secret, Sir. You don't have the clearance for that" said Joe Cunningham, reverting back to his General-like serious tone.

"Well, give me an outline." demanded the President.

"Sir, it has to do with projects which Presidents do not have a *need to know*."

The President rolled his eyes and said: "if you expect me to be making decisions on whether or not you can have money for your projects then I'm going to expect a little description. Even if it is only one sentence."

"That's the thing, Sir. I am here to inform you of a type of technology that your party can use to your benefit, not to seek funding. The military industrial complex never *asks* money from the government," answered General Joe Cunningham, with a smirk.

The President looked at Dr. Green, who returned a grimace, then back at General Joe Cunningham and proceeded by saying: "okay, then continue….. what are we looking at in the video, again?"

"As you can see in the video, the child is undergoing several different types of trauma. The trauma is inflicted on the child until the child reaches the alpha-state and that's when the programming can take place. After the trauma is inflicted, you can see that the child is being shown various images," said General Cunningham.

"Why are the adults around him wearing costumes and masks?" asked the President.

"Well, that is to conceal the identity of the scientists but also to create within the subject the idea that aliens are the ones who are responsible for the trauma," said General Cunningham.

"Will the child not link aliens then with his trauma?" asked the President.

"Yes, it is one way of concealing the trauma which needs to take place as part of his Messiah programming. If the child is going to, at some point in the future, have memories of the trauma then he will not be able to perceive his reality properly and will begin to imagine and see aliens and other life forms in place of human beings," said General Cunningham.

"Wow, that is certainly something quite marvelous," responded the President, in bewilderment.

"Thank you, Mr. President," answered Dr. Green, eager to take the credit for his protege's work.

"Thank you for the information and for your hard work. I will see to it that we certainly put this in use across government operations. It will come very useful in warfare and certainly in our investigations," concluded the President.

Chapter 43

"General Joe Cunningham. Can you tell us what would happen if there was a gross act of terrorism on U.S soil. How would you respond to that threat and what would you advise would be the course of action that should be taken? What would you advise we do in order to garner public opinion to defeat terrorism in the world today?" asked the Vice President at a congressional hearing that General Joe Cunningham had been invited to attend, to answer questions on the military spending.

"Well, Mr. Vice President, that is a tough one," quipped General Joe Cunningham, before saying: "It all depends on the act of terrorism and whether that is enough a catalyst to instigate acts which would be justified in light of that act."

"Well, General Cunningham, we are talking about an event that would be so catastrophic to our everyday lives that our fundamental civil rights would have to change. We are talking about an event that would forever change the world. We are talking about an act of gross terrorism that would forever secure our role, your role, in the world which would bring about a fundamental change in the way the world is governed. We are talking about a project that would secure the United States of America as the only country in this new century as the greatest military power on Earth. This act of terrorism would forever shape a new century favorable to American principles and interests," said the Vice President.

"Am I to assume that we are talking hypothetically?" asked General Joe Cunningham.

"Yes, General Cunningham. We need to assess how the destiny of the world will be changed by such an event, in order to examine the scope of your proposals for spending," answered the Vice President.

"Well, Mr. Vice President, for an event like the one you are describing, I would say that the advice would be to take direct action. Of course, any retaliative strikes would have to be passed through congress first," said General Joe Cunningham.

"Do you see the problem here, General Cunningham? You are here today to answer questions related to military spending. I have put forward a scenario to ask you to answer, in order for us here in this committee today to ascertain the extent of foreign threats on US soil, in order for military budgets to be approved," explained the Vice President.

"Yes and the extent of that threat has to be determined by the NSA and the CIA," answered General Joe Cunningham.

"Indeed. You are a senior ranking officer for the NSA are you not?" probed the Vice President.

"Indeed, Sir. But there is classified information which cannot be divulged in this hearing," stated General Joe Cunningham.

"Once again, General Joe Cunningham, we are here to discuss whether the budgets for military spending can be approved," repeated the Vice President, with some frustration and continued saying: "General, do I need to remind you that the Military Industrial Complex has to account for over trillion dollars which have disappeared in our budgets since the last administration. This committee is to establish oversight on such spending."

"Yes, I understand that but divulging information related to foreign threats on US soil, whether they are internal or external is not for the scope of this hearing. In the interest of national security, this hearing cannot be privy to such information," stated General Joe Cunningham.

"Then we may need to postpone our hearings until we can at least receive from the NSA some outline," said the Vice President.

"Sir, this has been signed into law since President Eisenhower," interrupted General Joe Cunningham.

"So, you are saying that the American taxpayer is expected to sign a blank cheque for the military without an explanation?" asked the Vice President, with some concern.

"That is not what I am saying, Sir. I am merely outlining the facts of the situation," repeated General Joe Cunningham.

"Thank you for your attendance, General Joe Cunningham, I have no further questions," said the Vice President.

Chapter 44

"The spaceship was almost destroyed when it crashed and landed on Earth. From what was gathered in Roswell in 1947, a lot of the material took years to be reassembled and back-engineered. It took a team of expert engineers from Project Paperclip to be able to work on the technology. The one EBE (Extra-Biological Entity) that was left was able to provide us with minimal information before he died."

"The spaceship itself was not very big at all, considering the distances that it had travelled. It was difficult to weigh but the scale of it would have suggested something along the lines of a ton or just under. It measured around 20 feet in diameter. Considering the size of the beings that inhabited it, it worked out to be of a compact size. We struggled to stand upright inside it."

"There were three EBEs, two of which were dead. They had grey leathery skin and wore no clothes with big, wide black eyes. The autopsy revealed a very different physiology to that of ours. They had a very small stomach, with large and small intestines and small liver and kidneys. It appears that they didn't really have a need for digestion and the contents of their stomach revealed a plant like substance, mainly chlorophyll, under the microscope."

"The remaining EBE was in some form of pain and he didn't recover well, once he was brought to the base at Groom Lake. It communicated telepathically and it informed us of the star system it had come from, which was the Zeta Reticuli star system. Their craft made use of anti-gravity technology, which is how they managed to get to Earth from 39 light years away. In the 1960s, the military was able to build its first craft, using anti-gravity technology."

"It was around the time of Roswell, in the 1950s, when the government was pressurized by the military industrial complex to push the production of a lot of science fiction stories. This distracted the general public from a lot of the genuine stories of alien encounters that were taking place up and down the country and, indeed, around the world. The advent of science fiction allowed anyone who had a real story of alien encounters to be written off as hacks."

"The remaining EBE at Groom Lake explained to us his existence and what they came to Earth for. It appeared that their crash may not have been by accident because it appears that it was shot down by one of our own in Roswell. They have been visiting earth to see our development since our creation and they were alarmed at the rate at which we were able to develop and make use of nuclear weapons. When used, nuclear weapons cause an imbalance in the electromagnetic field of the universe. The explosion of hydrogen bombs are similar to solar magnetic flares hitting the Earth's atmosphere but at a rate which is more harmful to the actual universe because it causes ripples in the space-time continuum."

"He didn't go into detail about how or why we were put on this Earth but it appears to be the case that we seem to be some sort of test case for a group of beings who have been watching our development since the beginning of time. We know from the EBE that much of what we think we know on this planet, in this moment in time, is largely bunk and that many civilizations that have existed on this planet previously had a completely different set of knowledge about the history of Earth. Many of those previous civilizations have been largely destroyed in the passing of time but held more knowledge than we presently now do and that we are, in the so-called modern age, relatively ignorant of our origins."

"Mr. President, there are far-reaching implications for the revelation that aliens are, in a way, our ancestors and that they are responsible for us being here on this planet. This sort of information itself could send ripples and shockwaves across the planet and lead to our own destruction and demise. It is, therefore, imperative that this information is kept hidden from the people."

"Thank you, General Cunningham. Many of us on this planet are already intent on seeking our own demise. I wouldn't think that this sort of information would alter our already destructive nature. But, we have come a long way in this civilization in our own thinking. We are more rational, we are more likely to seek information and more likely to look after the well-being of others than ever before. So, do you not think we should at least give the public some information on the existence of extraterrestrials? If they have been here for so long and if, like you say, they are here to guide and warn us, what do we have to be afraid of?" countered the President.

"Be that as it may, Mr. President, the fact is that we were able to recover a certain piece of technology from the Zeta Reticulans, which the EBE was able to demonstrate for us. We were able to see what a world where the open presence of aliens would look like on Earth and it would be detrimental to everyone concerned, including the aliens themselves here, and on other planets." answered General Joe Cunningham, before stopping.

"Go on. You want to tell me more." said the President, anxious to know more.

"Sir, I can't. You don't have a *need to know*," said General Joe Cunningham, with his head down.

"And how do I get a 'need to know'?" asked the President, mockingly.

"You can't, Sir, you just have one or you don't." answered General Cunningham, firmly.

"So this is what Eisenhower meant when he said 'beware the military industrial complex'," said the President, in a resigned tone.

"Sir, you either are given a clearance or not. It is often decided that Presidents should not have that privilege because it would alter and influence their decision-making processes," explained General Cunningham.

"You mean, like having a finger on the trigger of a nuclear bomb?" asked the President, sarcastically.

"Yes, Sir, presidents are human just like the rest of us - they are prone to making the wrong decisions that could drastically affect the course of history that we are trying to create in this world. But the EBEs have already categorically told us that there will never be another nuclear bomb that is detonated on this planet because they have the technology to disable all such devices from being detonated," answered General Cunningham, methodically.

"My, God, we really are at the mercy of them." answered the President.

"That is why, with all due respect, the military decides not to allow the interference of politicians in the interests of the security and future of humanity," asserted General Cunningham.

"From experience, General Cunningham, anyone who has ever begun a sentence with 'all due respect' has always proved that they never possessed any. I can only concede that the actions that are taken will safeguard the future of humanity," said the President, with a tone of defeat. He had hoped to learn more from the General and stood up from his chair, ready to shake the General's hand, from the Oval Office, where they met, at the request of the General.

"That depends on humanity itself," answered General Cunningham.

As the President was getting ready to usher the General out, he stopped to say: "'I can't help but think that this is not the real reason you came here. The information you gave me is hardly information that I couldn't find for myself on the internet, if I wanted to find it. So why are you really here?"

The General smiled widely and his eyes sparkled. He had sparked the interest of the President enough to ask for an exchange: "sign the Executive Order to release our military budgets and I will tell you everything you need to know. And more. I'll give you access," said General Cunningham, with a wink.

The President extended his arm, to shake hands and said, with a smile: "okay, General, you have a deal."

They continued to walk to the door of the Oval Office and the President said: "I'll get our secretaries to make another appointment. I have another meeting to attend now. In the meantime, what was the name of that technology that the alien had, that let them see the future?"

"We named it the Looking-Glass because it allowed us to see many timelines of the future of humanity based on multiple choices that we make as a whole," said General Cunningham.

"And are there other pieces of technology that would be useful for us?" asked the President, before the General opened the door to leave.

"Oh, there are many more. But that will have to wait for another time," said the General and left the President's office.

Chapter 45

"Welcome, Mr. President. We are very pleased that you could attend today's meeting. We think it is highly important that we have some agreement on how we should proceed with the line of narrative for our viewers. We think that a controlled and measured method of reporting should be the right way forward," said the chairman of the leading news network, who had requested a meeting with the President.

"Yes, I agree, as the leading news network, you should not voice any dissent. All criticism of the impending war must be quashed. Hollywood has already warned all its actors not to criticize the war, or there will be consequences to their actions. We hold all the dirt on all the celebrities so that was an easy nut to crack. Your network must also be careful to call it a war not an invasion. Make sure you refer to them as terrorists and a threat to our survival. Make sure your editors are highly aware of the language that is being used. Instill fear in the public. That is your job. That is utterly important at this juncture," commanded the President.

The chairman sat, in his chair, in the President's office, slightly uncomfortable, but resplendent in his compliance and said: "So... we were thinking of pursuing the ´Osama and Saddam as a threat to world peace story´ because that is what our viewers will respond to the most and will work closely to ensure your re-election over the coming years, of course."

"Yes and I will see to it that your organization is given top priority in the senate committee hearings on anti-trust laws. We'll see to it that your organization is given special attention," nodded the President, as he spoke.

"We can ensure that the same narrative is carried across all our media outlets which fall under the network. Local and regional news outlets will all receive the same script. They are free to change the style of their reporting and have their own discussions but, essentially, the narrative will stay the same. Each editor will see to that," assured the chairman.

"Yes but be careful not to become an echo chamber. That would be too suspicious," said the President.

"Yes, we will allow some voice of discourse, of course, because we are a *democracy*, but they will mostly be marginalized voices of concern but our moderators of such discussions are very well equipped and highly skilled to navigate any dissent to the concerns of the American people. We have excellent anchors and newscasters and expert members who can sway the discussion," said the chairman, reassuringly.

"Good, good. That will be all for now," confirmed the President.

Chapter 46

"Sir, we have news from Ur that a woman associated with Private Cunningham has been located. She's being held there but she's not talking. They've done a sweep of the area but it looks like she's on her own and there's a strong possibility that she is Leah," relayed Josh.

"Good. Great." yelled Grisham, who promptly assembled his boys and made their way to Ur, from the Baghdad base.

When they arrived at Ur, they took over from the Australian forces, to interrogate Leah, determined to ascertain Christopher's whereabouts:

"Do you know what we are going to do to your family if you don't tell us?" threatened Grisham, in the only way he knew how.

"'Do you mean my family who are now sitting in Tel Aviv?" retorted Leah, undeterred.

Grisham turned around, in disbelief, to his henchmen - Christopher's musketeers: Josh, Justin and Brandon. "How does she know that?" he said, angry in bemusement of what Leah knew. Grisham's lackeys didn't say a word but stood in shock and confusion.

"Christopher told me. He knows everything." said Leah and spat in Grisham's direction.

"Like he knows his family are killed and we're trying to get him back home?" interrupted Josh, quick on his feet.

Leah's body sank and she stopped resisting Grisham's hold on her: "No, you're lying," she said.

"What do you think we are doing here? He's done nothing wrong. We just need to send him home. His wife and child have been killed. We're his buddies. We all grew up together," continued Josh as he eyed-up Justin and Brandon. "That's all there is to it."

"Then why is he looking for...?" Leah stopped herself short. There was a pause and she noticed Grisham's intense glare.

"Looking for what?" asked Grisham as he cocked his pistol.

"He came to me, asking about ancient history. He wanted to know about the artefacts in the Museum."

"Why did he come to you?" probed Grisham.

"He didn't. He found me," stated Leah, nonchalantly.

Grisham pursued his line of questioning: "How did he know how to find you?"

"He delivered my baby. My husband found him on the street. We looked after him for a couple of days then he started to scare my husband." said Leah, hoping that her response would satisfy Grisham.

Grisham began to question Christopher's actions because it didn't make sense to him: "But why was he interested in what you know? How does it help him?" he said.

"There's an ancient god called En.Ki. Christopher claims he saw him here in Iraq. At first, I thought he was delusional but he told me things. I'm not sure now." Leah decided to throw Grisham off, in a last attempt.

"Was it something to do with the Australian and the British forces? The secret project?" exclaimed Grisham, determined he had finally caught Leah out.

"What secret project?" asked Leah, in a tone of deference.

Grisham didn't speak any further, aside from repeating to Leah what he wanted from her: "This is your last chance before you see your family alive," said Grisham, trying to get her to confess what she knew.

Grisham revealed as much as he wanted, to see if she was telling him the truth and then he played his trump card: "We know who your father is. He worked for Saddam as his top scientist". Then, he pressed his gun into Leah's temple and said: "are you still going to pretend you don't know about the secret project?"

Chapter 47

Does it matter what we do on this planet and who we do it to? Everything is a lie. Everything. We're all just programmed to believe different versions. It's how we're programmed to think. From the day we are born, we are taught to think in certain ways. We are schooled in that way, we are not taught to question. Is it any wonder that there are generations out there who accept everything that they are told just as I was? Is it any wonder that we couldn't save ourselves and that we can't save ourselves from the trap that we are in, because the lies that we are told are more important than the truth that is buried?

I was sitting in the middle of the school cafeteria, around 8 or 9 years old, and feeling a bit of anxiety because I had been in trouble with the teacher for challenging her on her knowledge about our history, our founding fathers and the slave trade. I disagreed with everything she had been saying and I had told her who the real founding fathers were. She told me I was wrong because I had been taught differently at home. She told me that's what it said in the history books and that's when she got angry after I told her it wasn't true. I told her I knew more than she did and she shouldn't be teaching lies.

"Christopher Cunningham, now you stay behind during your break time and explain to me your behavior in class," said the teacher in class, one day, when I was a child. I never did and, later that day, my parents were asked to attend a meeting with the Headmistress and the teacher. I remember sitting there staring out the window as they all talked to each other about what happened and what I supposedly had said that made the teacher so angry. Then she claimed that the reason I was really in trouble was because I didn't do as the teacher had instructed. I remember Dad and the Headmistress talking about me and feeling proud of my father for protecting me.

"So, you're telling me that my son is not allowed to challenge the knowledge of the teacher?," asked Dad.

"Sir, this is a Christian school. Your son seems to think that human beings were a result of some aliens who came and created humanity," replied the Headmistress.

"He's just an 8 year old child. If he believes that, who are we to say otherwise?" asserted Dad.

"Oh come on now, Mr. Cunningham. Are you really seriously suggesting that we entertain your son's notions?" chirped the Headmistress.

"Not any more than he entertains yours. Look here now, Miss. My son won't be taught by a woman who can't teach him to think for himself. That's a quote from Socrates but I don't expect you to know that." smirked Dad.

The video finished playing that childhood memory. I scrolled through more videos, until I started to see thumbnails that displayed destruction. I tapped one and it showed a world which was nearly obliterated. There was an alien presence on Earth. There were wars; wars that started in the Middle-East, then spread to every region of the world. The wars died down then the world leaders assembled to form a coalition, a new world order. But they weren't alone. The aliens were there, alongside the world leaders, and it was normal. Everyone appeared to be comfortable with it. There were spaceships hovering in the sky and people going about their daily lives. Every human appeared to be tired, trying to go through their day, amongst the rubble of their post-apocalyptic world. I scrolled for more.

One video was apparently made at some point in the past. It looked like it was taken in some military base, in a small room. There were military personnel, top senior figures, judging by the ranking that was displayed on their insignias. In the middle of the room was our President - President Eisenhower. To the left and right of him were sat his military generals. Across from him, a gray alien. They appeared to be passing papers around, signing them and talking.

It was 1947 and President Eisenhower appeared to be extremely uncomfortable, confronted with the threat of the alien presence on Earth. He looked under duress, in that bunker, not by the aliens but by the military generals. He looked reluctant, with a stressed face, shaking hands with a gray alien. The video played further, to Eisenhower addressing the nation as an exiting president: "beware the military industrial complex."

More videos, dozens, hundreds, thousands even. None of which were linear. They were my memories but now I was watching something I couldn't possibly have been involved with. How did I get to 1947? How could it have been possible for me to have been there? I sat for a while and tried to dig deep into my memories but nothing came up. My mind was blank, as if I had been completely emptied of thought.

There were too numerous videos to go through, on the visor screen in that pod, where I crawled into, in the interior courtyard of the Ziggurat. I scanned the screen by scrolling my fingers on it, to see if I could find some sort of counter or menu of some sort. All those pages of tiny icons that, once touched, would create a video of my memories. Where did I know this from? Where did they come from? It was impossible to know for sure but I would estimate that there were possibly thousands. What had I been involved with? What did Dad do to me?

I clicked on one video and it showed the world pretty much as it is now, except we were not in Iraq and the twin towers were still standing. We had advanced technology but that was guided by another group of alien races; they looked like us, taller, blond and Nordic-looking. They appeared to be guiding humanity, along with another group of beings, who looked like the Aztecs of South America. The world leaders appeared at ease with the aliens, not coerced like before. There wasn't a dominant country on the planet, controlling its fate. Power appeared to be equally distributed, with the aliens acting only as a guiding influence. It was a world that was controlled but stable. There was a lot of farming taking place, with people living in structures that weren't polluting the environment.

One video showed beings similar to En.Ki, who were on Earth, in an indistinguishable time period. They appeared to be mining for gold. Earth in that video was a total paradise, almost unrecognizable to what it is now, with flora and fauna so unlike what we are used to. The group of beings appear to be working, taking samples back to their spaceship and discussing their findings. En.Ki was among them, directing them. He appeared to be in control until there was a mutiny and his fellow beings appeared to be challenging him and smashing things around. Then he began taking samples from the already evolving primates on Earth. In his spaceship, he spliced their genes and created a prototype human in a tube.

En.Ki's team were happy. They oversaw the mining and their slaves were happy to please their masters and they grew fond of the metal they were mining, until they started making sounds that alarmed En.Ki. Their ability to communicate alarmed En.Ki. His creations were making sounds to communicate, like artificial intelligence becoming self-aware. En.Ki looked alarmed. That wasn't the plan. All of sudden, En.Lil was there and he was angry with En.Ki and they were soon fighting for control. En.Lil went to the fields, where the slaves were mining and opened fire on them, killing them. Crowds dispersed, with their hands over their heads, running wild, making indistinguishable sounds. En.Lil appeared enraged at them, for making noises and yelled something at En.Ki.

There was an ensuing war between the brothers. En.Lil kept destroying En.Ki's creation but En.Ki kept creating more. More violence, more bloodshed, until En.Lil dropped bombs to scatter and eradicate the population but it was too late for En.Lil. He made an agreement with En.Ki - the population couldn't be destroyed but it could be controlled. Quite easily.

En.Lil took over control and En.Ki was returned to his home planet. The team of engineers, architects and doctors set about planning a way to control the population. They needed to wean the population off their love for their creator - En.Ki. The ones that were left over were the ones left in charge, to control the population. They bred with the creation, they installed governments, they created religions and En.Ki was forever the snake that was to be reviled. In a time, in Ancient Babylon, En.Lil and his team of progenitors built the first civilization on Earth and slowly spread their seed throughout the entire globe, throughout the ages, ultimately becoming the controllers.

Chapter 48

Leah was caught out, backed into a corner, with very little leverage and she knew it and she knew Grisham would get to her. She was out of her depth, with four grown men facing her, in the back of a vehicle. It wasn't worth risking her security, dignity and family. She thought of the soft faces of her kids and Ashur's pained expression of helplessness over the past weeks. It pained her that her man had been robbed of his role as protector and provider of the family. There was nothing more humiliating than losing your dignity and they had already lost that. After that, there was nothing more to lose.

Leah spoke and unburdened herself, after making Grisham, Justin, Josh and Brandon keep their promises for her family. She had very little left to keep to herself. Everything that she had, had already been taken away from her and her knowledge of her father's secret project was the only thing left to trade.

"What have you done with my family? How do I know they are safe? What assurances do I have?" asked Leah.

Grisham grabbed the comms device in his pocket and made a call to the Baghdad base, to have Ashur put on the line: "Here, talk to him."

Leah dropped into a slump, as soon as she started talking to Ashur: "It's alright, honey, I'll be there soon, " she said, in between howls.

Grisham grabbed the phone off her, before giving her instructions on the arrangements: "you will lead us to Christopher then you will be escorted back to base in a chopper. From there, you will join your family in Tel Aviv. Everything has been prepared for you. You will all be received at Nellis Air Force base and then taken to Boston, to be with your friends. From there, you are on your own. You have passports and social security numbers all drawn up. You won't have any trouble getting started."

Grisham's tone changed. He was beginning to soften. He had been faced with a real person, for the first time in Iraq. They weren't towel-heads anymore. He had to see and engage with a human being, not an *insurgent* or a *civilian*. He had to negotiate, not terrorize. It went against everything he knew he should be doing: shoot first, questions later. That was the motto that got him to where he was. But he was still angry and it was Leah who made him angry - he became disarmed from his training and he sensed that she sensed his vulnerability.

Leah led them to the inside of the Ziggurat, down the passageway, past the many caverns, into the heart of the courtyard, where they came to the egg-shaped object that Christopher had placed himself in:

"My father had been trying to work out the code to get access. I was trained in the Ancient Sumerian language but I couldn't make sense of it. It appears to work on some sort of other coding. My father was looking into the other coding methods until he theorized that it will open by fingerprints or DNA. It will open, according to the DNA structure of someone who touches it. As they are Anunnaki, my father was on a mission to locate the genetic sequence of the Ancient Sumerians and he almost found it but we were invaded and he fled. Anyone with the DNA match of the Ancient Sumerians or anyone of their direct lineage will be able to open it with their touch."

"And what's the likelihood of that happening? Who might hold that DNA these days?" asked Josh, his curiosity peaked.

"Anyone of royal blood," replied Leah, confidently.

"But what is it? A pod, a cocoon? What does it hold?" asked Justin.

"We don't know. In the Ancient texts, there was some reference to a stargate but not to this. It seems to be an anomaly," said Leah.

"How do you know this is not the stargate?" asked Sergeant Grisham.

"Because that's not how my father described it," said Leah. "A stargate looks like a stargate. A big metal ring with a portal that you can see, in the middle."

At a loss, Grisham had no other choice but to listen to Leah and trust what she was telling him. Nodding, Grisham said: "okay. okay," and sighed. Grisham ordered them all to leave the Ziggurat and return to the vehicle, to regroup for their next plan of action.

Chapter 49

I slept there overnight, in the pod, my exhausted body finally giving way. I slept that night emptied of thought. Gone were the vivid, unsettled dreams I was having since I had been in Iraq. But I woke up wanting more answers. Just what else was there to discover? How was it possible that all those memories existed in my brain? Why was I present in all those secret meetings with my father and president? Taking deep breaths, I approached the monitor again, to see what I could find.

I watched more videos on the monitor - historical records, of people marching throughout the world, in protest of their governments. Then, I saw those leaders meet behind closed doors again. I heard them discuss something about the people. They looked afraid of the situation. One video had a complete history of such instances. I saw the leaders being afraid to take their course of action because they were afraid of the reaction of the people. I saw the French Revolution and the Tzars of Russia being defeated. None of those images made sense to me. The destruction of an order, the leaders that were afraid of their people, their own power that the people realized, it all sent shivers through me.

I went back to find the videos of President Eisenhower. Maybe that would lead to something. He was being briefed on a UFO that crash landed in Roswell, New Mexico. He seemed troubled and out of his depth. He formed a task force to oversee the crash but he wasn't able to maintain his power and influence and, eventually, the group took over, making him sign documents under the guise of national security. From then on, President Eisenhower was sidelined and lost control of the military. The task force became a law unto themselves. I paused for a moment to think; perhaps that is why we are where we are now, fighting wars that didn't make sense. A browbeaten President Eisenhower then took to national TV, to address the nation as an out-going president and to warn the nation of the "military industrial complex."

Just like the population in the time of the Ancient Sumerians, the populations throughout history became difficult to control without wars, famine and religion, so governments took to other forms of control. Fear was their tool and they kept the population subdued with an unseen threat. As the population grew, after the war, as new technologies fell into the hands of the public, governments realized the power of persuasion. They no longer had to fear the people. They could make the population fear anything and give them the placebo to keep them hooked: distractions from the material world, films, tv, internet, food, alcohol, drugs, sex and cheap money. It was all possible. That's why the people couldn't see their own manipulation. They were hooked on the lifelines the government threw at them, to care about what was really going on. They were controlled rats and they didn't even realize their own imprisonment.

In several videos, government leaders were seen learning to use television and films to start programming their population, to their agenda. They didn't want peace and order. They wanted chaos, to keep the population at war with itself. They achieved it by creating shows on the TV which promoted that. The kids would get affected by it and it would lead to the end of the family unit. They would promote films and TV shows that furthered the agenda of chaos. Kids would rebel from their parents and parents would lose all control over their kids. The newspapers would fuel the shock and debate, of the breakdown in society, as it was depicted in their media. It was all planned. It was a circus.

I was back in one of the scenes again, with my Dad, in a secret military base. A group of men sat in chairs similar to the one I was in. It was in a secret military base in Montauk. That was something I remembered, something familiar to me, something that made my pulse race. I saw them experimenting with different timelines and taking the information from all the different timelines then working out the probabilities that the conditions in their current time might affect the timelines they had observed. With the information they gathered, they were able to inform leaders in our government to their decisions. They were able to work out which countries to bomb and which sanctions to impose, based on the information they got from their technology.

The machine allowed the user to access different timelines of Earth. There was an infinite number of timelines that the user could see but, more importantly, choose. But the technology was limited. The user couldn't just change the timeline of the whole of humanity because it needed a critical mass in order for that to happen. The machine measured the extent to which critical mass had been achieved in the collective consciousness. The consciousness of the population looked like a cloud of data above the land, on the map. The data cloud was analyzed and a report was made to demonstrate how far the population were in becoming compliant with whatever the agenda was. For a subdued population, the cloud looked clear and the collection of data within it showed similar patterns. For a population that hadn't reached critical mass, the cloud looked saturated, with different sets of codes that didn't match, and appeared muddled.

In discussions, the best timelines were chosen and the governments set about achieving the timeline, by manipulating the consciousness of the public. The timeline that was chosen for humanity did not look good. It was a timeline of intense control over the world population. We were being led down a path that was ultimately dark. The world stage had been set and the population was going to be controlled, whether by force or by coercion, wittingly or unwittingly, into a world unlike anyone had ever seen. The terrorists and the war was just a smokescreen to get the clouds on their monitors to appear clearer for the timeline to take effect. And it looked like it was too late. We let the government think for us, we let the media think for us and we let our schools think for us. They created their enemies for us and I watched as fear and hatred rose in my country. It was easy to subdue my fellow countrymen into submission.

The people had lost their power to shape the future of their own humanity. They had their revolutions, they had their freedoms, they had been given everything they desired. They didn't deserve anything more. The governments wanted the power over their population. They wanted control, that was the best thing for them. The same level of hatred and disdain for their people was inherited, from the time of En.Lil, as they struggled to control humanity then, nothing changed and humanity would only ever be worth the material world they had built. Nothing more.

It all started to make sense to me. How we were all shaped, as a whole, instead of the individual and we're all shaped into thinking and behaving. Maybe that's what the aliens were doing with our leaders, trying to steer them away from dangerous timelines. Maybe heading down a path of fear and hatred was a path chosen by malignant forces. Maybe certain other alien races were trying to pull us away from this path by trying to get us to wake up from our own demise, by freeing humanity to our own power.

We were able to change the course of history as we wanted to, that was for sure. We didn't have to rely on governments or nobility. The last thing that would free us, from our own shackles, was our love of money. That was the last tool the governments had, to subdue the populations. Once the population had become self-aware and broke free from religions, education and mass manipulation, the last thing the governments had to control them with was money, by keeping them as indentured cattle, feeding only when fed.

We always had the power, ever since we became sentient and started to communicate, in the mines of Ancient Sumeria. Ever since En.Ki stood in awe of us. But we always gave away our power and our handlers gladly took it, ruled over us and have been doing so ever since. But we are a feeble species, happy to be consuming, desperately trying to reach the same heights of our controllers, the children of En.Lil, in our pursuit of wealth and power, since time immemorial.

My country had been under threat ever since I was born, it seemed. My generation were raised on video games, the generation before me on television and the future to come by computers. They will give themselves up and get absorbed into artificial intelligence. That's the timeline we were placed on, according to what I saw in the machines in Montauk. It had already been decided, we were just on Earth to help that come into effect. En.Lil was still in control and had never died. His reach ran far and wide. But it was up to us. The problem was that I never saw kinks in the timelines which might otherwise give me hope. It appeared to be a straight forward, smooth-sailing timeline and 9/11 and the invasion was the acid test for the world which was about to emerge.

The timeline which had been chosen for humanity was going to be dark, full of unrest. It would spread through the Middle East and the voice of protest would subside over time. The media wouldn't report it. More leaders would be eliminated, in the same way that Saddam was: Gaddafi and Bashar Al Hassad. The media would increasingly report on terrorism occurring but nobody appeared to be alarmed. It became expected. The whole of the Middle East for the next 20 years would be scorched as the world's population was subdued continuously in order to reach a critical mass, whilst the body count reached millions. Millions. More than every other war in history. Collectively, the world was to turn into passive observers.

So that's what it had all been about. We were never going to win. The course had already been determined for us. In that chair, the men discussed the possibilities of changing the course of the timelines. Was it possible to harness the power of mass consciousness to effect the change more quickly? How could that be achieved? The age old quest for ultimate power never changed and they appeared desperate to find out.

The men controlling the machines were able to figure it out and leapt out in joy. They built a machine to let that happen, back-engineered by alien technology. The timelines were a projection, an infinite number of projections and they were being created by the individual. Whoever sat in that chair was able to project their consciousness and create a timeline but it was not possible for any individual to harness enough power to realize a timeline. But it was possible, shrieked a scientist in the Montauk base. It was possible, using technology.

There was a collective cheer in Montauk that day, with my father in attendance, years after they had the revelation that our reality was holographic and we could project a reality using technology. I was no longer the 10 year old, with my father. I was 13, on the cusp of puberty, with a world of feelings and emotions and hormones running through my whole being. They said I was a perfect test subject and I was placed in the machine, to project my consciousness onto it. It was the world of a 13 year old, who was leaving his childhood behind for the beginnings of manhood.

The image was projected on the screen ahead of me, inside a large, circular ring, the size of 10 feet in diameter. Inside the ring, my consciousness was projected after I was prompted to imagine the world that I wanted to live in so my 13-year old self did his best to imagine the world it could, the world of an American 13-year old, raised with a Christian belief in the real goodness of people. I projected the candy-floss world that I was raised into believing, into the center of the gate. I then walked through it.

The other side of the stargate was exactly as I had imagined it to be. A fluffy world, safe and full of love. I was sitting at the table, having breakfast with Mom and Dad, in her yellow kitchen. My father exuded love, instead of the usual cold-hearted and detached energy that he exhibited. He was happy, dressed in a suit. He wasn't in the military. We lived in a modest house, as did pretty much everyone in the neighborhood. It seemed like a smaller but happier world. There was enough for everyone's need but not for everyone's greed.

The world around me was built from my consciousness, using the technology. That was the gate to the other world, the world that was possible, to be created, as I had imagined it, without the critical mass of the population, but as real as the hologram that I had projected into the center of the stargate. Instead of waiting for the world to change, it was possible to change the world, using technology to replicate all the atoms and cells for life to be reformed and reshaped and remolded, into a new world.

After watching, I hit the monitor in the pod with my knuckles and it formed hair-line cracks. The videos blinkered and the images began to fade, coming to an abrupt end. I still had some unanswered questions - why did I hold those memories in the first place, so vividly, as if I was present in 1947, with President Eisenhower and the aliens? Did my father put me through the stargate on a reconnaissance mission for information? Was I a test subject for the aliens? If I wanted to change the course of humanity, for good, I would have to find the stargate but I needed Leah, if she was still alive, if the dark forces hadn't already gotten to her.

Chapter 50

Joe Cunningham, the patriarch of the family, sat in his office, in his lavish home, bought by his service to the military industrial complex. Joe had had no qualms about his actions, his indiscretions and his apparent misdeeds. There was more at stake in the universe than his family. His life and that of his family was more than just about him and his job was to protect humanity from itself. He reclined in his chair, and glanced at the gallery of his forefathers, all army generals, dating back to the civil war.

Joe Cunningham, the descendant of a long line of mercenaries and generals. Service to a greater purpose was in his bloodline, sure to be passed down to Christopher, as it had been planned. Christopher would follow in his father's footsteps but first he needed to complete his field experience in Iraq. That was the plan, at least. Everything Joe had trained his son for, from the age of 3, was coming to pass. As a young private in Iraq, he would work his way up, earn his stripes and soon be rewarded with medals and move into intelligence, alongside him at the NSA.

Joe Cunningham, the General, who had proved himself in the first Gulf War, was about to learn that not everything in life, despite intense preparation and precision, goes to plan. He may have been rewarded for retrieving the technology and placed in high office by Bush but Saddam was able to get his hands on the stargate again and his son, Christopher, had been trained to find it and retrieve it and, just like his father, Christopher would climb the military ladder and take his rightful place in the high ranks, like his father Joe Cunningham, and his father's father and his father's grandfather had done so, like faithful forebears.

After Christopher buried his wife and child, Joe was confident that Christopher would be able to return to his duties in Iraq without too much thought or trouble. Joe had trained his son exceptionally well, compartmentalized him well, to function in extreme states and situations. Joe had taught Christopher everything he needed to know about locating the stargate that Saddam stole from Montauk, during Clinton's time in office. Joe was certain that Jessica and the baby were killed by deep operatives, embedded in the US military, to throw the plan off course. But Joe Cunningham was about to learn that, despite his best efforts, Christopher's path had diverged:

"Hello, I'm trying to get hold of Sergeant Grisham. This is Retired General Joe Cunningham from NSA Sweet Tea, Georgia," stated Joe, on the phone in his home office, ready to get an update on the whereabouts of his son.

"Hello, Sir. We have reports that he has been found," came the reply.

"Found? What do you mean found? The orders were to have him return on compassionate leave," said an angry Joe.

"Sir, he went AWOL," came the response.

Joe took a long pause and took a deep breath and exhaled a long and protracted amount of air from his nostrils. He did not want to panic but the sense of trepidation was present in the air, in case his son Christopher's behavior was a symptom of something else. His programming was tight, Joe was sure of that but, if Christopher did hear of his family's death, then there was a chance that his mental compartments may unfold and he was likely to end up sabotaging the operation.

"How was he behaving?" asked Grisham, ready for the worst.

"Strange, odd, not following orders. Said he was seeing things. Possibly hallucinating. It may have been from drug use, Sir," was the response.

Joe took a breath and asked about Justin, whom he had also mind-controlled, to help Christopher whenever it was needed in combat: "When did his team realize this change in behavior? Do you know?"

"No, Sir. We do not have that information," responded the other person on the phone line in Baghdad.

Joe's frustration grew, certain that he would have to take a trip to find his son. He hoped his next question would give him the answers he was looking for, to give him some reassurance that Christopher would still be able to complete his mission.

"Do you know what he saw?" spoke Joe, intently.

"We only have some sketchy information, Sir. Something about a tall being. Not human, Sir," responded the officer, without any intonation.

Joe breathed some sigh of relief but he knew he had to go to Iraq, nevertheless, to make sure that Christopher was found, to make sure the mission was completed. He was confident that the secret military technology had worked - that their holographic projection of En.Ki triggered Christopher to start finding the stargate, just as it had been planned and just as Christopher had been mind-controlled for. Joe was relieved but he had to get to Iraq quickly.

Chapter 51

"Hey, what do you think's going on?" Justin asked Brandon, as they were sitting in the back of the vehicle, waiting for orders from Grisham, who sat up front with Josh. They were both tasked to look after Leah in the back, as Grisham hatched a plan with Josh.

"Ah, I just don't know, Justin." spoke Brandon, softly, wanting to keep a low profile, not wanting to enter into an argument again. "Word is that he's going crazy," asserted Brandon, exhausted with the turn of events since they all started their tour in Iraq.

"S'pose so," replied Justin, then asked: "Do you think he's still alive?"

"I certainly hope so", said Brandon and continued to speak, spitting word like bullets in frustration: "cuz when we heard it over the comms - about a soldier going bat-shit crazy and then doing all these weird things and then running out on his post and then I heard his name and I was like, holy shit, not Christopher. He's the tightest one of us here."

"Yeah I remember," echoed Justin.

"You know, I gots to thinking that maybe there's a reason for all of this stuff happening to him. You know how his family is really not normal. They're normal but they're too normal. Especially that Mom of his. She's got that plastic smile going on with those weird eyes that you can't tell whether she's happy or sad. Her smile never matches her eyes. Did you ever get that feeling too?" continued Brandon.

"Yeah, I know what you mean. Her eyes sho don't match that smile," said Justin, echoing Brandon's sentiments.

"Dat's right. She always used to creep me out. I mean, our Moms are wacko but god damn she was right up there wit' the Jacksons," said Brandon.

Justin cracked a laugh and said: "You sho' you ain't just jealous, Brandon? Sho you wish you had a Mom like his? Look, we just gotta be there for Chris and we pray that we find him so we can get him to where he needs to be - home with his family where he belongs"

"You said that right. Whateva happens, happens, but I know something's not right. None of all this makes sense to me," said Brandon in his final breath, before turning silent.

Leah sat listening, in a daze, silent, weary and tired. None of what Justin and Brandon said had any effect on her. She was lost in her own world, in her own despair. Meanwhile, on the front seats, sat Grisham and Josh, trying to figure out what course of action to take. Would Leah lead them into a trap or was she telling the truth? Could they trust her?

"I don't trust her," said Grisham

"No. Neither do I," chimed Josh.

"Here's the plan. Justin and Brandon can go in with her and we'll follow behind." said Grisham sternly. He never had to repeat his orders.

Josh had no qualms about Grisham's decision, eager to follow his orders and said: "Yeah, we're the only back up they need."

Grisham paused to think for a moment and followed with: "Sending for more back-up will only cause more alarm and it could send the wrong people, if there is indeed a secret project that we shouldn't know about. We've already slipped passed the guards once but I don't think that will happen easily now the sun's up."

They both then stepped outside of the military armored vehicle that was parked outside the Ziggurat and walked to the back, opened the door and dragged out Leah:

"Listen. This is your last chance to get this right. You fuck up and that's it for you," threatened Grisham.

Justin rolled his eyes at Brandon and Josh clocked him. Josh repeated Grisham's orders to them: "you're both going inside the Ziggurat first, for the recon and we'll follow up behind" and threw the equipment at them.

Brandon was the first to challenge the order: "didn't the Australians already do that?"

Grisham shot back: "listen, numbnuts, they only got here yesterday and they've only been holding post. They haven't had a chance to look inside. We're ahead of the cavalry that's about to descend on this area for that secret project that nobody here should know nothing about. Right now, we're lucky that we've managed to have a short look around but that place is massive and we need to spend more time in it to figure shit out, find your pal and get him back home. We'll follow on behind."

Justin and Brandon didn't say anything and took the equipment. Grisham and Josh instructed them to wait, as they anticipated questions from the troops on the ground, who were guarding the Ziggurat:

"If you say a word, it's over for you. We don't get Christopher and you don't get to see your family. It will be over for you all. That's the deal," Grisham threatened Leah for the last time but her blank face already told him what he needed to know, that she was going to comply.

A couple of the guards approached them:

"I thought this was a collection only. We were instructed to have the area cleared." The young private who spoke was keen to demonstrate to Grisham, a superior ranking officer, his command of the situation.

"Yeah, we're about to leave. We're all done here," muttered Grisham.

"Say, what is this place, do you know?" asked Josh, to try and steer the conversation away.

"Nah, some sort of ancient building that Saddam was restoring. That's all we know." replied the private, a little on guard.

"Why are we all interested in it?" asked Josh.

"I don't know. It looks like there could be some valuable material inside," said the young private, with increasing discord.

"You haven't been in?" interrupted Grisham, to break the tension between the two power-hungry privates, who were clearly agitated in their to and fro.

"No, we only just got here a day ago. The Australians are doing security, the Americans and the British are doing the digging," the young private relaxed a little, when speaking with Grisham.

"When are they going to start doing that?" Grisham continued.

"We don't know. We've just been told to hold post and we're waiting for further instructions. Could be today, in a day or maybe two." replied the private.

"Aren't you curious about it though? Sure can't hurt to have a look," said Grisham, trying to peak the young private's curiosity.

Sensing Grisham's interest in the Ziggurat, the officer looked at Grisham's stripes and made eye contact with him and said: "who is she?"

"She's someone of interest to us," replied Grisham in a monotone.

"She seemed to know who you were when we arrested her," said the young private, careful not to openly challenge Grisham.

"Yeah, we're hunting some known insurgents and she has some contacts that are important to the mission," responded Grisham, rather nonchalantly.

"Have you interrogated her already?" asked the private, with slight hesitation, careful not to piss off the Sergeant that stood before him.

"No but we will be. At base." Sergeant was reluctant to respond, knowing the private was stepping outside his rank. His tone made the private wince a little.

The private took a look at the Ziggurat and squinted as the sun rose above it and looked back at Grisham.

"Look, if you want to have a look inside, you all can be my guest," said the private, in a welcoming tone.

Grisham proceeded to walk and was stopped by the private: "but not her. We could interrogate her in the back of your vehicle for you. Get something out of her," said the young private, with a smirk.

Grisham's face swelled: "stand down private. I am your charge, in absence of your superior."

The private quickly realized his transgression: "sorry, Sir."

Seizing his opportunity, in the leverage he had just gained, Grisham continued: "if you do not want to be written up and reported to your superior, I suggest that you keep your distance."

The young private, no more experienced in the ways of the military, than a security guard at a shopping mall, stood back and Grisham, Josh, Justin, Brandon and Leah walked past, approached the Ziggurat and walked up the ramp, up 20 feet, into the entrance.

Leah was the first to speak and said "thanks," at Grisham.

"How long will it take for them not to spill?" asked Josh.

"We have until the cavalry arrive. I have a feeling it won't be long," exhaled Grisham, looking back at the ground below before following the passageway, into the heart of the Ziggurat, which was slowly being filled from the daybreak outside, cascading light down the many cavities within the building.

Chapter 52

"So tell me about what we have here, then." asked the President.

"It's a stargate, Sir." answered General Joe Cunningham.

"A stargate? Like Stargate, the movie?" chuckled the President.

People around President Bush stood and laughed and General Joe Cunningham grew impatient, saying: "No, Sir. It's a portal to other dimensions."

"Right. Other dimensions," the President nodded his head and scratched his chin.

General Cunningham continued, despite an apparent obtuse President: "Sir, I don't think we can begin to imagine the possibilities that this technology would uncover. In the wrong hands, it could be deadly and have massive repercussions for us."

"Give it to me in a nutshell will ya," sounded the President, flanked by his team of secret service personnel.

"Yes, Mr. President. Sir, there was a craft that was retrieved in 1947 in Roswell, New Mexico," replied General Cunningham.

"Yes, we are all aware of that," joked the President's adult son, in a half-serious hurried tone.

"Well," paused Joe, "we've been back-engineering alien technology ever since then. Some suspect that they let us have it by accidentally crashing their craft. They want us to accelerate our technological knowledge."

"Tell us something we don't already know," confirmed the President, in an impatient manner.

General Cunningham persisted, throughout the interruptions: "The aliens that President Eisenhower met with told us that battles have been fought in space for aeons and Earth was and is a battleground. They are all competing for control of our planet, stretching back aeons." Bush Senior looked at Joe intensely and Joe sensed that he perhaps spoke out of turn.

"Well if they've been here for millennia, how on earth did we get here?" joked the President's adult son.

"We are an engineered species, Sir." answered General Cunningham, trying to withhold his frustration with the President's son.

"Engineered by whom?" asked the President and cut his son a glance. His son's demeanor changed and General Joe Cunningham and the President continued to converse.

"From what we have managed to gather, Sir, a mixture of alien races," replied Joe, with a sigh of relief.

"So, why us? Why now?" enquired the President, with a tone that changed from enquiry to concern.

"They were concerned about the use of nuclear weapons in space, Mr. President. It causes a rupture in the space-time continuum, Sir. That's why they came," said Joe.

"Who came?" asked the President.

They continued in their short exchange: "The gray aliens. But they're just androids. They are working for another group," replied Joe.

"Which group was that?" asked the President.

"We're not sure but it might have been a group that is positively aligned with humanity," replied Joe, relieved at the turn in tone.

"Do you think they crashed by accident then?" continued the President.

"Well, our guess is yes, they did. But it wasn't the first time they've tried to interfere with our development. There were many reports coming in, during the allied bombing in Dresden, of unidentified craft," responded Joe.

"Have many of my predecessors known?" asked the President, looking seriously engaged.

"Sir, they didn't have a *need to know*," answered Joe Cunningham.

"And what about my recent predecessors? Did they have a right to know?" asked the President, looking at Joe straight in the eye.

"No. Not since President Eisenhower signed away that right under the interests of national security," answered Joe Cunningham.

"Then, why are you telling me this?" asked the President. "Why do I have a need to know?"

"I think we are in grave danger of our history changing for the worst. This technology that we've developed, we can use it to our own advantage. But there are so many forces beyond our control, each working for different sides and they are going to try and change the world to suit their agenda," replied Joe.

"Right. What do you want from me?" asked the President, still staring at General Joe Cunningham deep into his eyes.

"An executive order to increase the budgets for my department, so we can investigate this further and increase security on it. I believe it may already have been leaked," said Joe Cunningham, somberly.

"'Well, who do you think has information on it?" asked the President, alarmed.

"Saddam's forces. They've had sleeper cells in the military industrial complex. They're called the Black Hats," said Joe.

"Black Hats?" asked the President.

"Yes, it means they are working for the alien group that do not have our best interests at heart and want to create the wrong timeline for humanity," answered Joe Cunningham.

"What does the wrong timeline look like?" asked the President.

"It's pretty bleak," answered Joe, looking down on the ground momentarily.

"For whom?" asked the President, concerned.

"For all of us. Nobody will be saved from our own destruction," stated Joe, solemnly.

Chapter 53

"I wonder how that son of theirs is holdin' up out there. It's such a shame wat gawn happen to his wife and chil' Maybe it's God's way of telling ya you ain't fit to be messin' with business that don't concern ya. Madness, ain't it. This world gawn mad and, when dat happen, you know God gawn rain down his vengeance on this earth. I did gawn try to warn 'em. Caught that daddy o' his giving me that eye. Ain't no skin off my nose. Folks these days get up in God's face like they own the heavens and they earth. Did you see that look he gave me? Well, God strike me dead! Don't say I didn't warn 'em. You can see it comin' already; ever'thing gawn come right back home - just like that boy o' ders. Say, ain't he home now?

Sure as hell gots everybody and anybody talkin' no good 'bout that family o' his. Those Cunninghams. I think I oughtsa pay those folks a visit; give 'em my good wishes and such. Not like dey gawn welcome me in dey home; I tries ta warn dem when he be shipping dat son of his to the war. Ain't nothin' but the devil's work."

The old lady couldn't stop thinking about Joe and Christopher, after she spoke to them, although briefly, before Joe drove his son to base, before being shipped off to Iraq. She sat in her kitchen, continuing to talk into the phone:

"The work of da devil is all 'round us, chile. He walks dis earth and da world follows his every word and every deed. And I knows what dat family is - dey IS the devil, an abomination to this world, yes Sir, and to our Lord God the creator. I ain't seen such evil amongst our midst. Dem folks is evil. Pure and simple. I feels it in my bones, every time I pass their ungodly home, I sho can feels de sin and corruption."

The little old lady, dressed in a black lace dress, a variation of the black dress she usually wore, with a black hat and black net veil at church, clenched the cord of the phone tighter, as she continued in her New Orleans drawl, speaking on the phone to her daughter:

"E'vryone at church knows bout dem, honey. You just gawn let yoself be under der influence is all. Thinkin' they all high and mighty but dey ain't. It all pretense! Dat's right. Pretense. Like dat wat dey be doin' dere in dat Eye-rack. Dey ain't gawn find a firecracker! Don be thinkin' dey is better den us, just cuz dey be coming over to church on Sunday, dressed all nice and speakin' proper. I'm tellin' you, dey be just pretendin' dat dey be god-fearin'."

The little old lady became animated and stood up: "How dare dey be so arrogant to our Lord God Jesus? Comin' ta church, bearin' gifts for the congregation. And that son o' ders, dat poor thing doesn't know what evil he's got, coursin' through his veins. Well, he'll soon find out. I prays ta God dat he keep him safe. He has a mighty task ahead of him fo sho."

The little lady was perturbed and her anxiety became too much for her to bear. She had asked the Pastor of her Southern Baptist Church to intervene and ask for the congregation to pray for Christopher Cunningham, the only child of Joe and Melinda Cunningham. Some members of the congregation began to feel she was becoming obsessive but she was more than just a believer in the Lord. She was a believer in the darkness too and, in that, she was gravely experienced.

Joe Cunningham first started attending church when his first wife disappeared. He wasn't more than 20 then, just started in the military. Such a lovely, beautiful couple they were - and the talk of the town. It wasn't long before Joe's wife disappeared and was soon replaced, some months later, by someone similar. Some of the congregation thought she was the same person. The old lady, then 20 years younger, struggled to convince people of what she knew.

Joe and Melinda introduced themselves to the old lady as John and Melissa but the old lady was already too wise to know something didn't sit right with the couple. After making chit chat and getting to know them a little more, the old lady began to feel suspicious. Her antennae was raised after she discovered that John wasn't who he said he was. He said he was born locally but no records of them existed, she soon learnt, after a little bit of digging.

She snooped around their home when they went on their holiday, after her daughter was hired to look after their property. He was born Joe Green but there was nothing further that the little old lady could find on his wife, aside from some documents with her real name - the old lady assumed that Melissa, or Melinda, was not involved with the charade that her husband Joe Cunningham was carrying on with the good people of her church. The little old lady went snooping into Joe's office, looking through folders and files, being careful not to change the order of the way the paperwork was filed.

The old lady found a birth certificate, issued by the military. Joe Cunningham was actually born Joe Green, in Montauk. On his birth certificate, Joe Green's father was listed as Dr. Green. The mother was listed as a woman by the name of B. Taylor. The old lady had to dig long and deep to find out who Dr. Green was but, when she did, it sent a chill down her spine that she still felt, some 20 years later, like the horrors of history unfolding over time and being confronted with those horrors every time she saw Joe's face in church. The old lady had discovered who Joe was and then she had to deal with what she was presented with.

The old lady felt it was her duty to bring the unspeakable to the light. Just as she had learnt it in the bible - that everything in the darkness will be brought to the light. She felt it was her duty to make sure that happened. She had been trying for years to get someone to listen to her, to take her seriously and tell them of unspeakable horrors she had discovered about the true nature of the Cunningham's. She rang a few radio shows, joined a few groups but she was ultimately alone, to witness the horrors on her own doorstep, every time she looked Joe Cunningham in the eyes.

In one of the conferences the old lady visited to learn about secret military operations over the years, she was confronted with the name of Dr. Green. Hearing his name struck her through her heart and made it sink to the ground. From the various conferences she attended on ufology, she learnt that her government was responsible for the unspeakable that was occurring in her nation, turning it godless.

The old lady learned that, after the end of the second world war, her government recruited Nazi scientists and smuggled them to America, to work for the government, the military and NASA. They called it Project Paperclip and Dr. Green, rather Josef Mengele, was just one of the former Nazis that seeped into her nation and there wasn´t anything she could do, to convince people of the horror in their midst. The offspring of evil lived among her.

After notifying her Pastor, the old lady was threatened with expulsion from the church. So, she learned, very early on, not to speak much more about it at church but to find people from the UFO conferences she visited and the UFO groups she was a part of, whom she could trust, to help her keep an eye on the Cunningham's.

Her friends encouraged her to speak at the conferences about what she had uncovered but she didn't have the nerve. The great deception has already taken place, she said, and who was she to speak against a fellow member of her church without any real proof. Instead, she chose to keep her eye on the Cunningham's the best she could over the course of 20 years but it was finally time for her to tell the world about them.

When Christopher was born, the lady felt a strong urge to protect him from his parents. Her daughter quickly became the babysitter and would relay all the stories to her mother, who felt it her duty to monitor the progress of baby Christopher. She would regularly give her mother locks of Christopher´s hair and other personal items and her mother, the concerned church lady, would consult with her book of spells and incantations to make sure Christopher was protected.

Christopher´s behavior started to change when he reached the age of three. The old lady´s daughter would describe to her mother how Christopher went from being a normal toddler, to a docile child, rather compliant and lacking personality. At first the babysitter didn't think much of it but, over time, expressed her concerns to the mother, to which she received the same, expressionless response. When Christopher´s babysitter finally told her mother about it, that's when the old church lady decided it was time to take some action.

They decided that the best course of action was to save Christopher from his strange parents. The babysitter, together with her mother, hatched a plan to kidnap Christopher, when Joe and Melinda, or John and Melissa, as they were known to the church, weren't around. The church lady was going to be the getaway driver and her daughter was going to go in one night, as Christopher's mother was asleep and the father was at work, and snatch the baby from under them.

Christopher´s babysitter snuck in the basement after her shift. Christopher´s mother went upstairs to bathe and left Christopher in the living room downstairs. The babysitter seized her moment and went into the basement and called her mom from her cellphone, switched it off and hid behind the stack of shelves in the corner, where Joe kept his house repair tools. Behind the shelves, she sat in the corner of the basement and waited until dusk. Joe had been called out for work so the babysitter knew it would be an easy job, considering what she already knew of Christopher's mother, that she would take her sleeping pills and be knocked out until 8 the following morning.

The babysitter fell asleep in the corner and was disturbed by a shuffle of footsteps, leading down into the basement. The basement of the Cunningham's residence in Sandy Springs had been reconstructed substantially over the years. A little under 100 square feet, it featured everything that a modernized basement the size of an apartment could offer. It acts as a panic room, a retreat, a hideaway, a man-cave, a R&R room and a perfect place for Joe's experiments.

The patter of several feet, trailing after each other, followed by the noticeable voices woke the babysitter and she retreated under the shelf, into the shadow, behind the shelving units, and peered through the gap between boxes to see, under the light, the familiar faces. She drew breath as they started to talk amongst themselves:

"Daddy, daddy" said the little 5-year old Christopher and was immediately struck to the ground, in the same way he had been throughout his life up until that point, by his father, for demonstrating affection. Christopher's propensity for love, despite his training, continued to bother Joe.

Christopher's mother tried to shield him but Joe pulled her away and slapped her to the ground. Ripples of anguish rang through the babysitter as she placed her scarf around her mouth to stop the sounds of her shocked gasps. Joe stood over both of them, mother and child, as he kicked and beat them, stomping on his wife's hair whilst Christopher clung to his father's leg, to prevent his father from beating his mother. Joe fought off his son, eventually succumbing to his son's attempt to save his mother.

Joe led his wife away, dragging her across the floor as she protested. For her treatment, Joe opted to tie her up to a chair and deliver electric shocks as she was shown pornographic images on the screen ahead. She yelped in pain and was ordered to bark like a dog throughout her readjustment, as the voltage increased until she couldn't bear the pain any longer. It seemed that her threshold of pain was quite high, presumably from years of torture and her throat became hoarse from all the barking.

Pangs of fear and anxiety washed over the babysitter, as she curled up and bit into the scarf and crossed her legs because she was close to wetting herself. After an hour of intense torture, Christopher's mother stopped reacting and turned into a zombie. She was compliant and appeared to be a willing participant in her torture. Christopher faced the wall during his mother's torture and played with his toys. He couldn't bring himself to turn around and appeared to be talking to himself, in an attempt to drown out the sounds.

Eventually, Melinda Cunningham entered into an alpha-state. Joe commanded her to clean up the chair she had soiled from the electric shocks and she did so, quiet, with a glazed look on her face, as if she was a hollow but animate shell. Joe washed her down in the shower in the basement, dressed and perfumed her, then placed her on the sofa next to Joe's torture chair. He softened the lighting, lit some candles and played some vinyl then projected images of dutiful housewives from the 1950s on the big screen ahead, for her to watch. Still in her alpha-state, Melinda became Melissa, the perfect housewife, modelled on a montage of different Hollywood starlets - blonde haired, blue eyes and draped across the arms of their leading men, in an inexplicable state of bliss. Melissa is what Melinda projected to the world and her family, the alter that she developed to cope with her suffering.

After the Hollywood showreels stopped playing, Melissa draped herself around Joe with an unforgettable smile, an insidious smile, with oddly formed eyes, both of which were seemingly at odds with each other, with eyes like a drug addict looking at her next fix but unable to drool, just smile. Melissa gave Joe a peck on his cheek and told him she was going upstairs to fix dinner. Joe replied by telling her that he would be up shortly, after cleaning up the basement.

Joe took Christopher and placed him on the chair and warned him of the consequences of showing affection. Christopher sat quietly, as his father warned him. Christopher looked lost and did not respond to his father. Joe gave permission for Christopher to join his mother upstairs whilst Joe finished up. That night, the babysitter stayed in the corner of the room, in a state of shock. She managed to hold herself together, despite a full bladder. When dawn broke and the house was cleared again, she made her escape and never returned to her employers. She never spoke to her mother about what she had witnessed and her mother, the crazy church old lady, was never able to get the truth out of her daughter.

Chapter 54

General Joe Cunningham travelled to Dulce Base to meet with the commander of Inner World Transport. Joe needed to get to Iraq as soon as he could - by using the maglev system that linked to numerous secret military bases across the world, all of which were under the control of world secret military complexes, outside the purview of their respective governments, whose job it was to simply fund their military. Leaders are temporary, the military is permanent. That was the mantra under which the military of all the allied forces operated in the network.

General Joe Cunningham headed down multiple levels of the facility, deep down numerous levels, as far as his security clearance would take him, which was down to the lowest levels, deep into the bowels of the earth. He met the commander of Dulce Base at the lift and thumbed his print to check himself in. The cavernous subterranean world was a world where alien life mixed with human life willingly but with constraint.

The commander met General Cunningham, to authorize his travel to Iraq and exchanged a few pleasantries. The commander enquired about the General's wife but stopped short of asking about Christopher, Jessica and the baby. General Cunningham was escorted through the corridors and the rooms that fed off them, down through the central comms rooms, where the soldiers that were dressed in black co-ordinated the underground maglev systems with bases around the world, then General Cunningham moved through several more corridors until he was led to a platform.

A short gray stood on the platform and swiped Joe's card, then Joe waited for the maglev train to arrive. It was en-route from Canada, filled with other military personnel and a mixture of alien races that were negatively aligned with humanity: mostly Reptoids, some Tall Whites and a flank of grays. Advisors to the Prime Minister of Canada and President Bush were also present. The next point of call was London, arriving in one hour, for a short stop, then onwards for a pick-up in Saudi Arabia and then, finally, Iraq. Just like any transport system, passengers would hop on and get off, according to their point of call.

The passengers, made mostly of military personnel, with the exception of some dignitaries and advisors who had infiltrated the governments and a mixture of alien races, were granted permission to use the transport if they had been born or indoctrinated into that secret world, a network that, if anyone was to look close enough, stretched back to the offspring of En.Lil, the half-brother of En.Ki, who was determined to control humanity through his dominion.

Joe strapped himself in and prepared for the journey ahead. Nobody spoke to each other and the telepathic aliens did not project any thought signals either, during the trip. The short stop in London was disrupted with some commotion. Some very important dignitaries were getting on board. The whole train had to be checked by a team of grays and everyone had to be inspected and scanned again, and all devices had to be removed and confiscated from the passengers. The Queen of England stood on the platform, at a distance and Joe Cunningham looked through the window in amazement.

He did not dare to ask what she was doing on the train, or where she was travelling to since it was not customary to communicate with anyone whilst on the train. Every passenger was always on their own mission and they had been discouraged from sharing information amongst each other, in case any information that was released interfered with the operation in another country, or affected the outcome of an operation within the country of the person sharing or receiving the information. That's how compartmentalization worked in the military industrial complex.

Joe watched as the Queen boarded the carriage ahead and the maglev stopped, after another hour, in Saudi Arabia. The Queen got off at Jeddah, flanked by her team, and they shuffled up the escalator, followed by a couple of Reptoids. Joe looked, in curiosity and wonder, and a Tall White, sitting opposite made a comment:

"She's probably meeting with the King of Saudi Arabia to discuss the outcome of a bad timeline."

Joe nodded in acknowledgement and decided not to speak further. The Tall White stopped talking but, instead, projected a thought form into Joe's mind: "it's also feeding time for them both. It's a good time for the loosh."

Joe nodded politely and tried not to engage further. He knew better than to get involved with conversations that could lead to awkward places. He thought about Christopher and all the things he had trained him for, everything that appeared normal to him and what he, as a father, experienced, growing up in a military family, being expected to follow the path and how desperately he wanted Christopher to follow the path that had been laid out for him. His love for his son would only ever be matched by his son's duty to the cause.

Just as Joe's father taught him, there was so much more to this world than what needed attention in the surface world. Joe thought about how he always was raised to understand the bigger picture at play and how he trained Christopher to be - a force in this world bigger than himself, working for the greater good, to keep humanity from destroying itself. Joe sat back and waited for the carriage to empty up ahead of him, before the train moved to its next destination - Iraq.

There was a delay in Jeddah. The train that went to Iraq wasn't able to proceed due to disruption in services. The maglev system in Iraq had only recently been added to the world network, and the tunnels were not large enough to carry the trains. What had been built beyond Baghdad, in the previous decade or so, was only enough to shuttle a single line of capsule carriages, with a maximum 2-person human capacity and a 4-person gray capacity, to a couple of towns outside of Baghdad. Joe Cunningham had to get off and catch another line, to get to Baghdad and then he would have to take the capsule carriage onwards to his destination.

A lot of the passengers in the final train to Baghdad were Reptoids, surrounded by a mixture of grays - some tall but mostly short. The grays were the helpers. A couple of Tall Whites joined and kept themselves to themselves. Joe Cunningham had been trained very closely on how to deal with all races of alien beings on the planet, but the Reptoids were a bothersome bunch. He cleared his head as he usually did of any thought that might be able to be projected to the fellow passengers even as one Reptoid came and sat opposite him.

Joe encountered a Reptilian once before: an 8-foot Reptilian that exuded pure hatred. It was at the Dulce Base, back when Joe was a lot younger, eager and naive. He had been instructed to examine some body parts in a cell and he accidentally walked into the wrong room. There, standing before him, was a sulphuric-smelling Reptilian with deep yellow eyes, with slits. The Reptilian took one look at Joe and growled at him, sensing the young and green Joe Cunningham's shock at being confronted with his first alien.

Joe made a narrow escape that time and that was expected in secret military operations, when dealing with temperamental alien beings. Only, they didn't consider themselves as alien beings because humans were the race that had taken over *their* planet. The aliens had decided to nestle underground of the bowels of the earth, instead of exposing themselves to humans. It was easier. They needed something from humans - their loosh - and humans were willing participants in the provision of the negative energy that humans emitted in wars and strife, for alien beings who harvested their energy in wave-form, after manipulating them through religion, education and media. The alien groups came to Earth to finish off En.Lil's work, in agreement with his council.

Joe took a look at the Reptoid who sat opposite him on the train, who looked somewhat less fierce-looking than their Reptilian progenitors. The Reptilians created Reptoids in order to make it easier for them to interact with humans, considering the differences in dimensions and the magnetic energy in the respective dimensions. Reptilians were drawn to the energy of humans and needed the energy to feast. Reptoids didn't possess that need and were able to, therefore, infiltrate governments to serve the greater goal of keeping humanity at conflict with one another.

Joe sat and monitored his thoughts, careful not to think of anything that would alarm the Reptoid opposite him. They weren't to be trusted. They could take any information that Joe was storing deep in his subconscious for their own benefit and Joe was not about to put Christopher's life at risk. Despite the fact that everyone in that carriage were negatively aligned with humanity, each race had their own agenda and they worked on the agreement with the human race on Earth, to reach the same goals but in the way they chose fit, the ones who could topple America and create a New World Order were the ones who would come out on top. The world that Joe moved in was like a 16-layer chess game.

Joe awaited on the platform in Baghdad, Iraq, 3 hours after he left Dulce Base in America and watched as the hordes of Reptoids ascended the elevators to the upper floors, presumably to meet with some military leaders near the surface. He stared at the rock wall ahead of him and focused his gaze on the billboards, as extra biological entities gathered around him to wait for their ongoing carriage. Over the track, on the wall, multiple billboards advertised trips to Mars and for long-term stays on the Moon with alien hieroglyph language printed all over them.

The platform began to fill slowly and Joe felt the presence of a being next to him. He sensed the vibration in the air and decided to avert his gaze towards the billboards further down the platform and took some steps to move, examining a map of the underground maglev system, which outlined a handful of ports of call in what had been built under Iraq. Joe felt the presence of a being again and decided to turn to face it. It was a Tall White and he peered at Joe, intently, to focus a thought form and communicate telepathically:

"There are a lot of Reptoids here. It shouldn't surprise us," said the Tall White.

"They must be hungry," responded Joe.

"Indeed. Wars are always a great source of food, of course. Where are you going to?" enquired the Tall White, with penetrating black eyes.

"I suppose the nearest outpost is Dora. I have some business that I need to take care of," responded Joe, briefly.

Joe's training had already kicked-in by the time the Tall White engaged in conversation, to block the Tall White's ability to scan his subconscious for information that Joe did not want to share. Like most extra biological entities, they were able to scan to some levels of the human subconscious. Some were able to scan the soul and take a reading. The Tall Whites were able to scan souls somewhat more accurately than most because of their history in the universe, with their spiritual development. That is what Joe had felt the Tall White doing, prior to their conversation.

Joe's capsule carriage arrived to take him down the narrow tunnels through to his destination: the southern district of Baghdad, called Dora. There, he would have to disembark and meet with the intelligence team underground, to be briefed on the state of the operations and what had been found and where his son could possibly be.

It was a short ride to Dora, no more than 5 minutes underground from Baghdad, but the transportation system was still underdeveloped and Joe had to make use of a traditional link rail to support the small capsule that would take him to Dora. Once there, Joe would have to open the hatch, similar to a submarine's and disembark by climbing up a ladder on the side of a hole that had been burrowed, into order to get to the next level above, which housed a small cavern for operations related to securing the other world technology that Saddam had been hiding.

Joe climbed into the capsule carriage, the self-aware chair securing him into place and he said goodbye to the Tall White who had been trying to engage with him. The carriage began to tremble and metal bars swung out and protruded from the exterior and locked themselves on the rails on either side of the walls in the small tunnel that measured around 10 ft in diameter. The self-aware capsule locked Joe's feet into a contraption and then it jolted itself forward a bit, to some feet into the tunnel, coming to a stop.

The carriage then lowered itself to the ground, silently and smoothly. Inside the carriage, the lights turned from white to red. After a pause, the lights turned back to white again. The capsule was in place, on its rails and it was ready to transport Joe to his next destination. Without any warning, the capsule descended deep into a cavernous abyss like a rollercoaster and came back up to the next destination, Dora, within a matter of steep and intense short minutes.

Joe climbed through the hatch at the top of the carriage, climbing to the top, hoisting himself up using the ladder at the side of the hole, to a small cavern of around 40 square feet. Once he was up, he was met by a couple of communications officers, dressed in black with a sun insignia emblazoned on their sleeves in gold. The communications officers were deployed to track chatter from the military communications on the surface world.

Joe asked them to track the name Christopher Cunningham and the algorithm picked up some communication related to Ur. He was briefed on the information and Joe asked if there was any chatter on the word En.Ki. Joe's pulse raced. He was close to finding the stargate and he was certain that Christopher would lead him to it. The communications officers responded to Joe's delight: yes, there was some chatter related to En.Ki from Christopher and the chatter related to a place called Ur. Joe's face dropped and came to the slow realization that Saddam might have been restoring the Ziggurat for one purpose and one purpose only - to bring back En.Ki and his reign on Earth.

"Get the satellites to project En.Ki's hologram in Ur. If Christopher is in the area, he will see En.Ki and his training will lead us to the stargate," ordered Joe, enthusiastically.

"Sir, which part of Ur? We can target the Ziggurat, if you want. On the inside and out," responded the soldier.

"Do both." replied Joe and smiled widely, ecstatic at the prospect.

Joe asked about the levels above; what was there in Dora and what was available to get him to Ur. There was a hole, leading up to the ground above, a disused shop in the center of Dora which had been secured by the American forces and had been marked by the allied forces as a no-hit zone. Joe stepped into the empty room from a hatch in the ground that was covered with a large desk and peeled himself back into the surface world. He was met by a couple of soldiers dressed in normal military fatigue with a black sun insignia in black on their sleeves. They were the special forces, the visible version of the underground arm of the military industrial complex.

Joe indicated where he needed to be and the special forces radioed in, to find out which vehicle and escort was available to Joe in the neighborhood. Because of his security clearance, Joe would be able to arrange anything from an inconspicuous car, a fleet truck or an armored vehicle. Joe also needed a couple of patrol officers to escort him. A vehicle was requested and the response was prompt, and the special forces requested General Joe Cunningham to rendezvous at a specific point in an hour.

Joe left the property and entered a street, which was alive with the commotion of people running around, scurrying to places they needed to be or packing their goods and families to leave the city, possibly country. In the background, varying discordant dins of explosions resounded like a drum beat of the discontent. Joe paused for a moment and reveled in the chaos before scaling the MSPV, a jeep that was used for multiple uses with crocus-like protrusions at the top, to shield from bullets and debris from explosions. Joe smiled at the thought of seeing his son and the stargate then bringing his son home with him as a hero.

Chapter 55

There were no more images to see, nor did I want to see more. I stopped needing to see them. The memories started to flow of their own accord, from my mind, clear as the images on the screen. I had turned off the monitor a while before and had only my thoughts to occupy me, vivid memories that burned like blistering bonfires in front of me, as I lay, curled up on the floor, next to the chair, at the bottom of the pod, in the middle of the Ziggurat. I took deep breaths as my body clenched itself in waves against my rhythmic exhalations. My fatigues were soaked with sweat and I fell into a deep sleep of anxiety, before waking some hours later, feeling as though I had been in combat with the world and its army.

I had a brief moment of clarity when I woke up, my head was empty of any images and my mind wasn't racing, as it had before, firing rounds of thoughts with an endless supply of ammunition. In that moment of peace and clarity, I looked around to see where I was and it was as if I had never seen it before, so preoccupied I had been, trapped in my mind. The inner casing to the cocoon was made out of gold and had familiar markings from the Ancients that Leah had shown me. I soften my gaze at them, in my stillness.

The familiar motifs were there on the interior casing - tall beings, some that looked like En.Ki, interacting, sometimes playing, with smaller beings that looked like slaves. Some small beings sat on the lap of the tall beings like little children. The engravings weren't unfamiliar to me anymore - I felt I had a better understanding of them as if they didn't feel a completely alien language to me. At least, I could follow them more fluently than I could before I stepped into the cocoon and before that helmet opened all those hidden and compartmentalized memories from the depths of my subconscious mind. My realization hit me with a feeling of empowerment. I knew more than I knew. Before I could think about doing it, the cocoon began to open itself like a flower, opening itself in segments.

I stepped out and caught my first breath of air; the musty air, broken by the cracks of light that appeared at dawn, which filtered through from the rooms and corridors at the top of the Ziggurat, down to the pit of it, where I was. I stood up and touched my temples, massaging them, tracing my hands to the back of my neck, to dampen the dull ache that pulsed my head. My eyes blinked as the light penetrated, cutting through my eyelids.

Each side of the Ziggurat housed caverns on the ground floor. The light was breaking in from the top, trickling through all the corridors and caverns that surrounded the rim of the building. The light cascaded down from a central point at the top, separating the light into rays that spread out like wings from the top of the Ziggurat and down towards the ground, where I stood. I looked up at the central point of the aperture, where the rays originated, in the roof of the Ziggurat. I focused my gaze there for a moment, at the light from the dawn, as it filled up a space in the center of the roof, turning into an outline of a pyramid, an outline that surrounded a stone pyramid in the roof. Just as quickly as the outline formed, the centre of the stone pyramid also filled with light, to form a slit, similar to the eye of En.Ki, the lizard-like pupils that I saw when I first laid eyes upon him. No sooner had the slit taken shape, the light filled the rest of the stone cap, to form a ring, like an eye, within the outline of a pyramid.

The light from the eye then darted down, illuminating the caverns and corridors all the way from the top, down three stories, down to the bottom where I stood. I followed the light until it reached one chamber on the ground floor, where I saw the arch of that chamber glisten from a distance. The glistening began to flicker as the light hit the stone surface, to reveal an ornate evening sky-color that shimmered with elements of gold and copper. A ray of blue light reflected from the stone chamber back to me, bathing my whole body in it. I dropped my shoulders to the sound of a crack; the tension I had been carrying was released.

I glanced around the other chambers that lined the bottom of the Ziggurat. The day's light revealed the outline of several others, some caught the rays that fell on them, whilst others were in the shadows. As I tried to focus on the silhouette of the caverns, a light emanated from behind me where I stood, in the middle of the Ziggurat. It was a familiar beam of light, of glittering gold, the familiar warmth that I had known to trust. I turned around and it was En.Ki.

I dropped to my knees, to kiss En.Ki's large sandal-clad feet and sobbed. Looking up at En.Ki, I said: "it was all a lie." I continued: "everything you said was true. My life has been a lie. I've seen it for myself." En.Ki stood but did not respond but I continued speaking: "I'm sorry, my Lord. I wanted to save you and save me but I failed." I continued between various interruptions of tears and howls, to beg En.Ki for forgiveness: "If I could have done better, if I had known sooner, if I had followed my instincts, I would have done better by you." I looked up one last time before En.Ki's image began to fade, in and out, flickering like an image in a faulty TV set, as if he was losing transmission.

Just as soon as En.Ki disappeared, I heard a commotion above me, with shouts of military personnel being carried down from above. First, I heard Grisham grunt "Christopher. Private Cunningham. Stay right there. Don't you dare move a muscle" , which was followed by the parroting sounds of Justin, Josh and Brandon in order, in a chorus of "Chris, Christopher and Bro." Lastly, the slightly unfamiliar voice of Leah rang a different tone: "Chris, be careful. Be careful." No sooner had the sounds rung out through the courtyard where I stood, the scurrying footsteps that dragged against the stone floor became louder as they grated against the sand and echoed throughout the Ziggurat like sandpaper.

Leah snuck past from behind Grisham and his *boys*, leaping forward to hug me and whispered: "they are going to try and trick you." Grisham pulled Leah off me, throwing her to the ground and ordered his *boys* to hold her. I moved to protect Leah but I was accosted by Grisham, with a pair of handcuffs and a gun.

"Don't move or this will be your last breath, you fucking son of a bitch," he said.

I had had enough. I was done. I fell to my knees and placed my hands behind my head and said: "I'm sorry, Sir. I don't know what came over me. I'm sorry I led you through this."

Grisham pointed his gun down, unclipped it and put it back into his holster, then stepped back, reached his hand to me, to help me off the ground. I took it and rose up, dusting myself off. I looked over Grisham's soldier, at the faces of my old buddies, but they looked so different to me. Josh, my closest buddy from my childhood, spoke first:

"Christopher, look, we are all worried about you. There's something that you ought to know. We've been trying to track you for days. We came to take you home, where you should be right now. They've called for you at home."

Still untrusting of Josh, I did not respond. Grisham turned around to look at Josh and cut him a stare, before turning back 'round to me and said: "Look. You're not in trouble. Your father has sent for you. You need to be returned home. You have been discharged from duty."

Still trying to scramble my thoughts, I said, brow-beaten: "Yeah...erm...go home, yes, that's why you've been trying to track me down," Then I walked towards Grisham, surrendering and said: "Yeah, take me home. I am tired. I just want to be with my family."

Grisham turned to Josh and said: "Yes, your family. They need you." and gestured to the *boys* to not say anything further, and they exchanged a mutual glance, in agreement. I sensed that nobody wanted to upset me any further. Grisham grabbed me by the arm and pressed himself into my chest, covering me with his jacket.

Justin and Brandon stood by, not saying anything, holding Leah as they were instructed to.

"Why is Leah being held like that?" I asked.

"She's under arrest," responded Grisham.

"What? What for?" protested Leah.

"She's a threat to national security," answered Grisham, ignoring Leah.

Leah wrestled with Justin and Brandon. I stopped walking and turned to Grisham to ask: "just how is she a threat?"

"She's been working with her father on a secret project and she was supposed to give us the intel but she didn't," replied Grisham.

"You bastard, you never gave me a chance. I know it's here. It's in here somewhere. I know it is," shouted Leah, in protest.

"You can tell that to the courts," said Grisham.

"You bastard, you had no intention of finding out about the stargate. You just wanted me to lead you to Christopher. That's why you dragged his buddies along," continued Leah.

"Shut up, you bitch. You can tell your fairytales to someone who believes them," yelled Grisham.

"Why? Why?" cried Leah.

"Christopher needs to be brought home. That's the most important thing," replied Grisham, trying to ignore Leah.

Justin interrupted to answer Leah: "Because he wants to be promoted. He doesn't give a shit about anything here. He's only doing what he does best. Follows orders for his own gain."

At that moment, I looked at everyone in astonishment. I had become completely oblivious to the gravity of my own actions, which drew out the worst of my best friends and people around me. I was soon consumed with guilt.

Grisham looked at Justin harshly and shouted: "shut your cunt bitch faced mouth"

Brandon, looking at me, chimed in: "he's right. He's worried about his own self. That's all. He got a call from Fort Benning - they want you back and he's had an itchy crotch ever since."

"Shut up the both of you, you fucking idiots," yelled Josh.

Still in a daze, I took a look at the infighting then grunted and chuckled to myself: "you should hear yourself. All this trouble for me. Anything would think I'm special. Have you heard yourselves? There are more important things to take care of. My family needs me. Grisham is right. I need to be home. Fuck all of this. I'm glad I can get home."

"Yeah, you fuckers. Stop being so selfish. Can't you see Chris needs our help? He's obviously been going through stuff. He's not well. He's lost his mind and all you're doing is trying to mess this up. Who the fuck is this towel-head to you anyway? What do you even care?" said Josh.

I pointed at Josh and said "hey, don't talk about her that way" in exhaustion.

"Tell him. Tell him," yelled Leah. "Go on, tell him. Or I will. Let's see how he takes that."

Grisham looked at her and took his gun out of his holster, to aim it at Leah, to shut her up. I rested my hands on Grisham's shoulder calmly and said: "Hey, come on man. You don't need to do that."

"Your family aren't even alive anymore," blurted out Leah.

I looked at Grisham, to check for the truth of what Leah had just spoken. Grisham's eyes blinked slowly and he drew a deep breath, sighing long and hard. My mouth opened wide and I began to choke on my breath, curling forward, hyperventilating and then howling empty cries that echoed every empty crevice, chamber and cavern of the Ziggurat.

My howls hung in the air until they were cut by the sharp shuffle of feet coming from the stories above, from the entrance that all parties had traversed at various moments in the previous intervals. The noise of feet clamping down hard on the earth and stone rained down from above. The rhythm of the clamor trailed longer than the rousing sounds of Grisham's team, suggesting that a bigger team had entered the building. A familiar voice called out my name. It was my father.

"Dad?" I shouted.

"Son, I'm here. Stay right there," he called back.

"Sir, this is Sergeant Grisham from the 5th Battalion. You called me, you spoke to me, to find your son and I've found him." yelled Grisham, eager to identify himself.

Dad appeared before me and I ran towards him, ending in an embrace. Dad signaled to his five-strong team of super soldiers. One walked forward towards Grisham, pointed his gun in the air and opened fire. Grisham fell to the ground in one hit. Josh put his hands up in the air and knelt to the ground. Leah, freed from Justin's and Brandon's grasp, stood alongside my buddies, all of them in shock.

I hugged Dad and said: "you wanted me home. Dad, I'm coming home."

"Son, do you remember what you are doing here?" he asked.

"Dad, I'm supposed to be fighting in Iraq. Dad, you sent me here. Dad, I did it for you," I said, happy to see him.

"Yes, but son, do you remember what you are supposed to be doing here? Did you find it?" asked Dad

"Dad, what do you mean?" I asked, confused.

"Son. Look at me. Did you see things here in Iraq?" he kept asking but I was confused.

"Dad, I saw a lot of things. I don't know what you mean." I said.

"Son, did you see a tall being? Did you see something?" asked Dad again.

"Sir, permission to speak, Sir," interrupted Josh.

"Permission granted," said Dad.

"Yes, Sir. He was seen talking to himself. We've had witnesses tell us he was acting strange, as if he was talking to someone who wasn't there," said Josh.

"I see," said Dad.

Turning to me, he pressed me again but I said: "he isn't real, Dad. None of this is. I just need to come home. Please, please. I'm ready. I've had enough."

Justin and Brandon looked at each other and then looked at Leah. They knew that whatever Dad was pursuing was somehow related to Leah and her life would be in danger if they spoke. Leah returned a glance of high stress and anxiety, with eyes wide open, as wide as the eye in the stone pillar above the Ziggurat, and shook her head, telling them not to speak.

"Christopher, did you see En.Ki?" asked Dad again.

I felt faint, sinking in Dad's arms, down to the ground and said: "Dad. En.Ki. Yes, En.Ki. Dad, is he real?"

"Son. En.Ki. Remember? He was supposed to lead you to the stargate. Son, where is the stargate? Where is it?" Dad grew impatient with his questions, which were all a blur to me.

"Dad. The stargate. The stargate. The stargate." I said, repeating his words, as I fell in exhaustion.

"Yes, son. The stargate. Where is it?" said Dad, with a strong grip, trying to wake me up from my impending slumber.

"Yes. The stargate. We couldn't find the stargate." I said, with faint breath.

"We? Who is *we*?" asked Dad, angrily.

"Me and Leah. Leah said she knew but she couldn't find it but Grisham was onto her and said she knew but now he's dead," I laughed as I said it and pointed to Leah.

"Who is Leah? How does she know about the stargate?" asked Dad, shocked.

"Dad. She knows. She's studied it. Her dad. Her dad worked for Saddam. He helped Saddam work on it," I said, continuing in maniacal laughter, unaware of the implications of what I uttered.

"Chris, NO!" yelled Leah, but it was too late. Dad looked at Leah and motioned for his super soldier to grab her.

"Alright, tell me where it is," asked Dad with a changed demeanor, as if he was a different person.

I dropped from my father's arms to the floor, laughing hysterically, with intermittent groans.

"My father was working on it but he hid it here but that's all I know," acquiesced Leah.

"Don't play games with me," threatened Dad.

"Fine go ahead and shoot me dead. Do you think your son will help you now? Look at him. Do you think he will even ever recover? LOOK AT HIM!" screamed a defiant Leah.

Meanwhile, I continued to laugh, distracting my father, then I grabbed his gun and wrapped my father's arm around his body, pointing his gun to his temple: "Look, here, Joey. Look here, Joey. Look what's happening, Joey" I said and continued laughing hysterically.

The super soldiers moved towards me instantly and drew their guns at me. Justin and Brandon drew theirs in retaliation. The battleground had been drawn: Justin and Brandon were determined to save both me and Leah from the situation. Joe motioned at his team, to put their guns down.

Then, a strong light shone down from the pyramid capstone above, blinding the team of super soldiers. It was a strong, piercing light as if it was the light of a strong high noon sun. After they stopped covering their eyes, they peered from under their hands to see what they could make of the source of the light, a light that had begun to form a shape, a shape of a tall being.

"En.Ki," I cried out, looking up at the tall image before us.

En.Ki appeared and stood some distance away, lifted his hand and pointed his finger to the chamber in the corner of the Ziggurat, illuminating it with the light of his being, the chamber itself glistening like a diamond, with various hues of blues and golds and purples. Lapis lazuli; the ancient stone of the ancient gods decked the chamber where I was summoned by En.Ki. I changed in a flash and stopped my maniacal behavior. I turned around to see everyone else, shielding themselves from the light, unable to open their eyes. I turned back, to see the chamber ahead of me and walked towards it.

Chapter 56

THE UNIVERSE CONSTRUCTED IN MULTIPLE DIMENSIONS IS. EXIST BETWEEN THE SPACE BETWEEN THOUGHTS DO WE. WHEN HUMANITY CREATED I DID, MAN DID VERY LITTLE. DID NOT THINK. FUNCTIONING WERE THEY, BUT LITTLE IN THOUGHT. THEN GAVE THEM CONSCIOUSNESS DID I. THIS, FROM FIELDS OF ENERGY. OPEN THEIR THIRD EYE DID I.

IN TIME ENSLAVED BY RELIGION, TEACHINGS AND MONEY BECAME THEY. STOPPED THINKING DID THEY AND CLOSED THEIR THIRD EYE OF CONSCIOUSNESS DID THEY. CHOOSING TO SEPARATE ARE THEY. SEPARATED BY RELIGION, TO LIVE NOT THEIR HIGHER SELF ARE THEY. SINCE THEIR CREATION SEARCHING FOR THEIR ORIGIN HAVE THEY. ALL NEEDED FOR EACH OTHER ARE THEY. FROM THEIR HIGHER SELF CONNECT TO THE UNIVERSE CAN THEY.

OPENED THE EYE TO THE CREATION DID I. CHRISTOPHER HAS ENERGY PORTALS INSIDE HIMSELF OPENED. THE KEY IN HIS MIND UNLOCKED DID I. CHRISTOPHER A HIGHER SELF CAN HE CREATE. A WORLD CAN HE CREATE. THE WORLD HE WANTS. CHRISTOPHER THE LIGHT BEARER OF EARTH IS AND UPON HIM THE WORLD CAN CHANGE. WITH CHRISTOPHER THE WORLD CAN TURN TO THE LIGHT THEY CAN. WITH CHRISTOPHER BECOME ONE WITH THE UNIVERSE WILL THEY AND ONE WITH EACH OTHER THEY WILL. INHERIT THE WORLD WILL CHRISTOPHER. THE AGE OF EN.KI WILL HE BRING. A GOD OF LOVE WILL THERE BE. THE END OF AN AGE IS NOW. A GOD OF WAR,

EN.LIL, WILL NO LONGER BE. A GOD OF LOVE IS EN.KI.
NOW THE AGE OF EN.KI. SO IT WILL BE.

Chapter 57

As I walked through the corridor towards the chamber, I realized that there had been nothing left for me to salvage. My wife and baby daughter were dead and I had no way out of the mess that I had been put in. My whole life had been a lie and the rage in my heart began to burn like kindling, soon to consume me. I wanted to get into the kingdom of heaven as it was promised to me in church and not live another day of hell on earth - the hell that I was as much as responsible for, as our Presidents and the rest of the abominations in our government. Nothing made sense to me anymore and nothing ever did. I knew that in my heart. I was intent on following my heart; the silent cry of my heart would be the only thing that would guide me from thereon out, to my final destination.

The light behind me, emanating from En.Ki, filled the dense darkness in the courtyard of the Ziggurat, enveloping the little specks of lights from the lamps on the ground. It came from the roof like a beam from a spaceship, ready to take me away. I turned around to see my father, my buddies, Leah and the super soldiers, who were all sat, shielding their eyes. It appeared that they were immobilized by the light that En.Ki shone. I looked ahead, at the chamber in the corner of the courtyard, the shimmer of lapiz lazuli and gold, sparkled like glitter on ancient stone, offering a glimpse of the unknown.

I walked to the chamber, 20 feet away, and entered. The light from the courtyard cascaded in but it was no match for the impenetrable darkness. The rays beat through, to shine on what looked like a harp. I stood away from the entrance, to let the light reveal the golden instrument in its entirety. It was shaped like a bull, with a head on the back and one on the front and a rod that ran above the length of the bull's body. The strings were made out of gold. The bull's head at the front of the harp had a blue beard made out of lapis lazuli, the blue stone of the ancient gods.

I turned round to see the courtyard where En.Ki stood and he nodded to me. Without any explanation, I walked towards the harp and rested my fingers on the strings and pulled them. They made a dull, discordant sound. The spark of curiosity that I had in striking the notes dissipated quickly, when the sound of the harp was followed by the stillness of the chamber.

I struck another chord on the harp and turned round to hear some commotion coming from the courtyard. With arms flailing at the sight of En.Ki, the super soldiers ran to escape after firing a few fruitless rounds at him. Leah, Dad and my buddies were the only ones standing, mouth agape at what they were seeing. Dad yelled "he's not real" as he proceeded to shake everyone from their shock but they stood statuesque nevertheless. After a few futile attempts at getting everyone to listen to him, Dad ran in my direction, to the chamber where I was in, but something prevented him from doing so. He stood, motionless, as En.Ki struck his staff on the ground and the top of it struck a beam of light, forming a perimeter of cold blue light, which my father could not move past. Dad yelled "wait, what is this? let me go. I need to get to my son" but his shouts went unheard. He looked around to see his soldiers leave and cursed them and threatened that they would never see the outside of a prison cell when he returned home.

Just as I turned round again, a portal opened in the center of the chamber and, surrounding it, I saw the solid frame that I knew so well, from my time in Montauk. The portal looked like a sea, a sea of possibilities, and I was ready to dive right in, and the sea-like image was beginning to form a small swirl in the center and, as it filled, I became mesmerized by the pull of what lay for me. I was ready to end it just where I began, before my decision to join the military and before my journey to Fort Benning, driven by dad and interrupted by the crazy old lady in black.

I stood for a while, gazing at the portal ahead of me. En.Ki had said that there was great unfinished work that had to be done. But what would I see on the other side? What type of world would I enter? I then remembered something from the stargate experiments in Montauk - when changing timelines was not possible without a massive shift in the consciousness of the population. But it was just me, facing the stargate, projecting my consciousness onto the portal. What power did I have to create a new world?

I hesitated for a moment, scared of the world I was about to leave behind, unbelievably scared, despite everything I had experienced in it. More so than that, I was terrified of the world that I was about to step into. The swirly pool of the portal continued to widen as it moved a mass of blues and whites in a circle, surrounded by the darkness in the chamber. I glanced back at En.Ki, in the courtyard, who nodded for me to proceed. Everything was going to be okay. I was chosen to do this. Words to that effect were communicated in thought form. All around us, the sound of feet and the rumble of tanks and helicopters echoed throughout the Ziggurat and they got heavier with each passing minute.

I could see the swirl of the portal moving faster and taking shape, to fill the gold frame. I still didn't know what En.Ki expected from me. I had brought him to the stargate that might take him to his home but he would have to go before me. He was equipped to return to his world, by projecting his consciousness to it and walking to the world he wanted. I wondered what kind of world he wanted me to envisage for myself and humanity. Then I remembered everything he had taught me about the rule of En.Lil and En.Ki's promise of the world as it should have been - without wars and hate and ego. Then I remembered what he said about me being the leader of the new world. But I didn't want to be. I wasn't prepared. All I wanted to do was see Jessica and the baby again.

Then I had it. I formulated the world I wanted, in my consciousness. I stood there, as the portal filled up and started to swirl larger, ready to take me in. I emptied my head of every thought that I had and tried to fill my heart with love instead. I tried so hard to feel an emotion of love but I couldn't. But I had to. I had to focus on Love because that's the world I wanted to walk into. But I couldn't, so I reflected on what made me the happiest and the last time I felt Love. And it was when I was in the hospital, holding our baby and I put my arm around Jessica and kissed her forehead. And, as soon as I had that feeling, I held onto it, tight. For my life. I closed my eyes and breathed in through my nose, and let the feeling consume me.

I took a step closer to the portal, the mass before me swirled louder in whirls, trusting in my heart that I would make it. I breathed a sigh as I shrugged off the fear that held me back, fear of failing and the fear of dying. Just as I did so, I looked to the right of me and En.Ki walked through the stargate before me. Turning back with his familiar gaze, he comforted me. He turned to face the portal and he was swallowed into the abyss. I walked closer to it, following him, edging closer to the portal and my heart grew to a calm as I walked but inches towards it. I closed my eyes and the fear was gone. I held my breath and walked through.

Chapter 58

We never knew what had gotten into Christopher cuz Justin and I always thought that he was going to be the one that would become the next war hero, just like his father was. We all had high expectations for Chris which is why his descent into madness was all the more disappointing. We knew how much Chris wanted to turn out like his father and I'm sure Chris's father wanted the same for his son.

I always used to think it was strange how Chris would behave at school. He always appeared to me to be some kind of robot. I mean he never expressed an opinion about anything. He always just got on with it. At school, he knew who he was and where he came from but he never went about shouting about it. It seemed that he wanted to be like the rest of us and I often thought why he would ever want me and Justin to be his friends because it seemed to be so out of the type of place he came from.

In school, Chris was dutiful and diligent and never really wanted to attract attention. I mean, he wasn't a jock but he could have been and he could have easily fit into that crowd at school because he was cut and he never really got into a fight though he could have crushed them all really. I mean, he wanted to hang out with us but we never really understood why he wanted to.

When Justin came on the scene, they became real tight and the rest of us, me and Josh, were like "okay, so we'll take our distance, we get it" but we didn't wanna appear to Christopher that we didn't really care about him cuz we did but it just seemed that he was more into Justin at the time. That's when Josh started to say things about Chris and I just put it down to Josh being jealous of Chris's friendship with Justin, even though Josh and I began kicking more together. Chris and Justin would hang out together and they both had girlfriends and were always out on double-dates. Josh would sometimes comment on that but I just ignored him but I sensed that Josh began to resent Chris.

Chris never really gave any of us any sign that we needed to worry about him. His behavior seemed normal. It was the rest of us that acted a lot more crazy than he did. I asked Justin if he thought that Chris' relationship with his father had anything to do with him going AWOL and having a meltdown whilst on tour. Justin said *probably* because we didn't have anyone expecting anything from us, we didn't even have dads and he said Josh was just eager to please Sergeant Grisham. With Chris out of the way, Josh could be the next Chris and get the respect he thought he deserved from us, from Grisham, and maybe from Chris's parents.

There was this one time when we were all sitting in science class and we were listening to the teacher explain something about dinosaurs and all of sudden Chris just flipped. She was showing us a slide of all the different periods and that's when Chris started flipping out and said he wasn't feeling well. He got into a right sweat and started hyperventilating. The teacher asked him to go to see the nurse and later on he told us that he just freaked out when he saw the dinosaur and he couldn't explain why that happened.

When you're kids, you don't really see just how strange people are until you get older and sort of look back and that's when you think how the Cunningham family was a bit too perfect and that was especially too strange for kids like Justin and me cuz we spent most of our time on the streets and getting into all sorts of trouble and learned how people really acted but the Cunningham's always came across as real fake, like they were just putting on a show for the world to see.

Well, anyway, I'm not too surprised with how it went down with Chris. There was so much for him to carry, too much responsibility with too much to prove. But he didn't have to do that for me. I was like, whatever, I'm only Brandon. I would have been cool with him either way. I don't really know whatever happened to him out there in Iraq or what he was all about, or what his family were all about, but he always gave me the time of day so I was always cool with him. Justin, on the other hand, was more into Chris that I was. Josh became a rival and I didn't have time for none of that business.

Chapter 59

Brandon and I were shocked when we got the news that we had to look for Christopher, back at the Baghdad base. I remember when the call came in, we heard the name and we just looked at each other and we were like "what the fuck?" We drove to downtown Baghdad, to the Museum to see what we could find. We spoke to some locals outside who led us to a place called Dora which is nearby the Museum, actually a block next to it. We drove down the dusty streets in the midday sun and we were then required to patrol on foot and I thought 'I hope he's gonna be okay.'

We were able to trace his GPS signal from his helmet which was located outside an apartment block. The ground crew moved in swiftly throughout the apartment complex to check out every home but nothing.

Then, we started asking them questions and a couple of residents told us about how they had seen the "Shayton", the Devil. We just did our recon and split, after coming up empty. We weren't going to hang around there too long, with all the crazies.

But when Grisham went downtown to collect Ashur and brought him back to base, I asked Grisham about where they found Ashur and he told me. But I didn't say anything. I didn't tell him that Brandon and I had already been on a little recce to find our buddy but came back empty handed. It wouldn't have served us well if we had. When we were all in base and Josh volunteered to interrogate Ashur, Brandon and I hung back and decided not to say anything and let Grisham find Chris himself. But we knew that Josh would have sold out Chris as soon as he got the chance. We genuinely cared for Chris but Josh only cared about himself. Maybe that's why Chris flipped. Because of Josh.

I never stopped thinking about Chris, in all the time he went missing and we were all looking for him. Grisham was going stir crazy, trying to find him. With all the reports that were coming in about Chris, there was always the possibility that he might have taken that poor family hostage so it was our job to ensure that they were all safe. It was a difficult task so we decided to find out what we could about Ashur and Leah. Ashur's connections provided no leads so we turned to Leah and that led us back to the Museum of Baghdad.

Our intel on Ashur and Leah told us that they had relatives in a city down south from Baghdad so we took the road on out. At the checkpoint, we stopped to ask and our fears had been confirmed. Christopher had taken the family hostage. That's when I recalled the behavior he exhibited when we were at school together and he would start acting weird and losing his sense of who he was and that time when he pretended to be one of us after he flipped out during that time in Science class. It was like he became a zombie and he started dressing like Brandon and I and we were all really confused about what had gotten into him.

The thing you have to understand about Chris is that we go way back. I was one of the first to make friends with him. Josh claims to be his brother but we all remember our relationships differently with one another. I met Chris back in 3rd grade before he was kicked out of the school, or his father took him out, as he later told me. We kept in touch cuz we were in the same neighborhood though I lived with my grandma on the poor side of Sandy Springs, around the corner from him.

His mom and dad were the loveliest people. Whoever Chris liked, they liked too, without question, apart from the black people or the Hispanics, not like that there were many in our neighborhood anyways. I was always invited to play and there was never a Sunday when I wasn't allowed to go over to have dinner with them. If I didn't go to Chris's, he'd always knock on my door. We were both lonely kids in our neighborhood and we were the same age. It went like that until my grandma died when I was in fifth grade then I had to go back and live with mom on the other side of the city. We kept in touch though but he changed a lot and he and Josh got well into each other. I felt sad but we were kids and I just forgot about him in time until we met again in High School.

I was a bit taken aback when I met Josh. I met Josh when Brandon and I rode up with our bikes, two kids from the poor side of the city. Brandon grew up in the neighborhood where my dad lived. Anyway, Brandon said he wanted to meet Chris and we hooked up on a Sunday for a couple of hours. The sun was hanging low and that told us we only had a couple of hours to hang outside his house, like we did when we were little kids, before being hollered to get indoors. It was that sort of lazy sun that I remember, when we got to Chris' on that Sunday.

I rang the doorbell and Chris's mom answered. She was so surprised to see me that she threw herself on me and gave me a great kiss on my cheek. She told me to come inside but I said it was okay. I was dressed in torn jeans and a t-shirt. I didn't want to go in and she could see that and her face changed, as if she was really disappointed.

Chris came out, followed by Josh and we chatted on the lawn. Josh was okay but he seemed to Brandon and I that he was a bit kinda like snooty with us. He was a rich kid, just like Chris, but the nasty kind. He kinda looked at Brandon and me like we were some sort of trash that didn't belong in that neighborhood. It was ok with me with cuz I kinda knew Chris anyways and that's who we were there for and it kinda helped that his mom looked on at us from the top of the steps of their house. She brought us drinks and something to eat while we were out which I thought was really nice but I never expected anything less.

Well, anyways, Brandon's nose was put out by Josh's behavior, or so it seemed. I saw Chris really wanted to be himself but something about Josh was holding him back like he knew who he wanted to be but couldn't cuz he had changed a bit and was trying to front with me. Maybe he wasn't that comfortable with all that change, being in school and all, or maybe his new buddy was one of those unconfident types that hid behind his chum. I don't know. All I know was that Josh kinda gave me the creeps back then. But not Chris. Chris was always the true type.

You could tell Chris from Josh. They were apples and oranges. Chris would be the type to take the shirt of his back and give it to ya. Josh would sooner set his last shirt on fire than give it to ya. Chris would tell me about Josh being around a lot and how Josh and Chris' dad were getting along and how he felt pushed out like he wasn't the son he should have been to his Dad. Chris would have done anything to please his father and I guess joining the military was his way of doing that but Josh was smarter and tougher and more of that type. By the time we had all finished school, Chris began complaining about Josh. It must have hurt Chris real bad when Josh double-crossed him like that, in Iraq. Or maybe he wasn't surprised.

Chapter 60

I had been in touch with my superior about Christopher's escapades. We were required to report officers who went missing but I wasn't prepared for the amount of anger that the disappearance of Chris would bring me. I was responsible for him and I needed to get him back. They told me that his disappearance could threaten the security of our operations in Iraq.

I thought that was a massive overstatement but I needed to get that cock sucker because it meant the difference between a promotion and just being thrown on the scrapheap. I would return home and not have a pot to piss in. Chris turned out to be a real pain in the ass and I could have taken him out and flushed him down the toilet like a nasty piece of stinking shit but I didn't.

Chris's father, Joe, had been the ultimate hero so I wondered if he would be able to provide some insight into what was going on with his son. It was a long-shot but it was worth trying, in order to save my ass from this cunt situation that cunt-licker put me in. Turns out that Mr. Cunningham appreciated the call I made to him.

I told him what had happened with Chris and whether he had an idea about why he would have gone AWOL or if he would have been behaving in a strange manner. There was a very long pause before he spoke:

"I don't know what's gotten into him, no. He wasn't trained for that, Josh," he said.

Mr. Cunningham began to get more and more irritated, instead of expressing concern for his son. It seemed to be that Chris's actions were embarrassing his father and Mr. Cunningham appeared more concerned about the military than he was his own son.

Well, I had to interrupt and say something:

"Sir, we are talking about your son," I said.

That's when he went on a rant, using a ton of profanities that even I would never use, especially under those circumstances.

"That fucking cunt better get his act together and you better find that muthafucka, Josh, otherwise I'm gonna come right over and kick his faggot ass myself," he said.

I might have put Chris in the shit but what I did was not nothing compared to the way his father treated him.

Chapter 61

How could my son do such a jackass thing? I had trained him up to be a lot better than that. Sometimes you just can't rely on your plans and you just have to sort it out for yourself. It was obvious that Chris had broken free from his programming and his mind was beginning to fall apart. It would only be a matter of time before he would be able to access his memories to uncover the truth and we were all in danger of losing it all. If Chris uncovered his memories and told anyone, we would all be in the shit and the whole future of everything the military had built and tried to hide could be at stake. He needed to be stopped and stopped very quickly. I made a call and headed straight out there to Iraq. I could have just let him die out there.

Sacrificing my son for the good of our country, for the world, was the only way we would be saved and the way to stop our military from imploding. We were warned about this, we saw this on one of the timelines. Driving to Dulce Base brought back my own memories and the work I had been involved in. And I still don't regret a minute of it. It was a means to an end - an end that we could never possibly imagine as human beings, if it all ended badly.

I took a flight out and drove down the highway, having called up ahead. There's a dirt track where you have to stop and wait for the military police to come and take you to Dulce Base. They have to make sure that the entrance is not seen. You get driven over the mountain, down to the other side. On the inner side of the mountain, which is completely hidden from the rest of the world, a valley overlooks a landing strip, and there is an entrance where you are driven to the side of the mountain. The side of the mountain opens and you are driven into what is an underground base.

That is where all the secret meetings are held when it comes to alien activity. There are several hangars there which house several different alien craft, some back-engineered, some not. They are sometimes used in secret missions to off-planet bases or for space exploration. All of this is paid for by the American taxpayer and war is a machine which drives the expansion of budgets from congress, in order to fund secret operations. It's just the way the world is run and will always be. That was the world I had to maintain and protect.

I was met by the secret rulers of the world, who had a vested interest in getting hold of the technology that had been stolen by Saddam. In a cruel twist of fate, the person who became their most wanted person turned out to be my son. They wanted to know if there was any risk that his break from programming might expose them to, but I assured them - he had no knowledge and his mind-control experiments would not put anyone at risk of being exposed. Even if he did speak, there was nobody that would take his rants seriously - he would just be labelled a madman who was suffering PTSD.

Saddam had stolen the technology and the Council of 13 needed to get their hands back on it. I convinced them that Chris would be able to locate the missing technology but I didn't tell them that his programming was beginning to unravel. So, they agreed to let me locate him, to lead me to it, because that was what he had been trained for.

Locating him was going to be easy. All we had to do was use our secret military hologram technology and point it in the right direction. If Christopher saw En.Ki, his programming would be triggered and his programming would kick in. The trigger would uncover his training, everything he learnt about how to decode the ancient texts to lead us to the stargate. It would have worked out well, if only Saddam hadn't already used the technology to let extradimensional beings in and made deals with them to get what he wanted. We didn't count on that happening.

Chapter 62

Well, what can I say about Christopher that you haven't already been told? You've probably heard it all and believed what you wanted to believe but this world would have taken a different course if he hadn't done what he did and the fact that he was able to do it was amazing. We were all destined for doom. Myself and my family, especially. Now, look at us, we're safe, our country is safe, the invasion ended, the armies returned to their countries and all of that hate and corruption and manipulation just faded out of existence.

After Christopher jumped through the stargate, I was afraid that they were going to take me and shoot me and my family. But Christopher's father stood there in shock, staring at the stargate. Meanwhile, Josh ran away and Justin and Brandon grabbed me by the arm and put me in a jeep and took me back to base. Josh had already made a dash for it. By the time we got into the jeep, the super soldiers that had ran out, when they saw En.Ki, were waiting. They looked at us and retreated, as did the backup that was sent. It suddenly became peaceful, in that barren landscape, with the purple blue baby sky under the sun. There was no sound of planes, bombs or firing. It all just seemed to have stopped. Justin and Brandon put me in the back of their jeep and we headed back to Baghdad but, when we arrived at the city gates, it seemed that the fighting had stopped there.

There were no troops to be seen and the tanks were withdrawing. My people were nowhere to be seen. There was a deathly calm in the center of Baghdad, where we stopped outside the Museum. Justin and Brandon assured me that they wouldn't leave me there and they didn't. I trusted them. I ran into the building, to my office, to get my hands on the cylinder seals that I had hidden away, which held the key to where the stargate had been hidden, which was what the Americans were looking for but I never showed Christopher. It turns out that Christopher wasn´t mad after all. He was really special. He led us all to the stargate, as if he had some sort of gift, as if he was chosen to find it.

But when I got inside the Museum, there were no troops inside. It was as if the world I had walked in from, a world reeling in from its own destruction, didn't exist. It was as if I had walked into another world. Everybody I knew there, from my frequent visits over the years, were going about their daily business and were completely oblivious to what was going on outside. I stopped someone, to ask them why they were all there and they just looked at me as I was a madwoman, the same way we all looked at Christopher at one point. Then I asked them why they hadn't left Baghdad and they had no idea what I was talking about.

I went into my office and the mess that it was in, when I last saw it, had disappeared. It was as good as new, almost unrecognizable. The grey cabinet which stood in the corner looked the same as it always did but I saw that it was locked, as I approached it. Taking my keys from my desk, my heart skipped a beat, as I fumbled with sweaty palms, hoping to find the cylinder seals. But they were gone. Not even my files, for my research for my father. Just reams and reams of course material for courses that I taught at the university.

I ran back out, to meet Justin and Brandon and there were people walking around the street. The military was nowhere to be seen. All the tanks had gone and there were only Justin and Brandon, standing there, with their jeep. It looked as though the city was becoming normal again. The buildings were still destroyed, and were rebuilt over time by the Americans, as it had been later agreed, but, it was like a new reality was forming quickly and an old reality was disappearing. It was like two different worlds were meeting right before my eyes. By the time I walked towards the jeep, Ashur appeared from the back of it and came running towards me with a huge smile. I asked him about how he got to Baghdad when I thought they were holding them in Tel Aviv. He looked at me, oddly, and insisted he had just been driven there to the Museum from the base nearby, by Justin and Brandon. I couldn't believe what I was seeing - the past was slowly being erased before my very eyes. I threw my arms around my husband and we walked to our home nearby, to see our children, who were being watched over by Ashur's mother and father.

When we got home, I had to lie down, to process everything. For the first time in weeks, the sounds of my children were joyous and they carried laughter, instead of the tears and cries of the previous weeks. The laughter from my children lulled me to sleep. The world I woke up to, the world I dreamed of, as a mother, as a wife, was there. My family was safe and I thank God for that everyday just as much as I thank Christopher. What he did for us, for the world, was a debt that could never be repaid but I know he doesn't want that. Nobody will ever know, apart from the handful that were there.

Ashur came into our bedroom to tell me that my father had rang and was eager to speak to me. I asked my father where he was and he told me he was safe. He had a meeting to attend with the government and had to get off the phone. He was glad to hear that I was returned home safely after my trip to the Ziggurat because he had heard that there had been some commotion, and I had to be evacuated. It made no sense to me, what he was saying. I tried to tell him about the stargate but he sounded concerned for me and told me to visit the doctor because I may have hurt my head. He didn't take anything I said seriously. But what about Saddam and the invasion, I asked. What invasion? He asked, as if I had lost my mind.

I sat in our home, after I put the phone down, and I was relieved and frustrated and in shock, trying to grapple with our new reality.

Christopher later gave it a name, the Post-Timeline Trauma Disorder, PTTD. I still have flashbacks of the wrong timeline, the timeline humanity was placed on, before Christopher jumped through the stargate and changed that all for us. In a way, it's a shame that nobody will ever know what Christopher did for the world but I also understand that is fine with him. It's up to him now, to spread his gospel, to spread his truth of the world that we should try to keep and how we must do it. He will succeed, I have no doubt about it. I am just grateful to be alive in this new timeline.

The more I continued to go outside and see the center of Baghdad, the fewer the memories I had of the invasion. The city and country was restored gradually over time, a lot more quickly than I expected, removing all traces of the destruction that was brought upon us.

Chapter 63

Christopher came into my life when I needed him the most. He was the sweetest and kindest guy I had ever known, through that tough bravado. Of course, being a young woman, I was attracted to someone as brave, who would do his best to stand his ground and do the righteous thing for not just his fellow countrymen, not just for his family but also for the sake of everyone in the world, for humanity, as he says.

They came when we were already in school. I remember them thinking, wow, are you seriously wanting young people to go and drop bombs on men, women and children? I remember the first time I saw Christopher, in the hallway, and he was having a real go at the recruiters. He was so passionate about his beliefs, everything about him, his aura really made me want to speak to him.

I caught them in the middle of what seemed like an argument and I just couldn't, for the life of me, understand what the heck was goin' on. I thought, yeah okay, this guy is really angry about something. That's when I heard him say "how dare you come here and recruit for your sick and twisted games?" and I was like, oh my god, this guy really feels what we are all thinking. So I threw my two-pennies in, you know, like you do and I just said "like why do we still have an army these days when the whole world is at peace?" and they just replied "well we need to protect our freedoms" and we just both laughed and kinda replied at the same time "from whom?"

It just didn't make no sense to us, to any of us. The media and the government kept banging this drum about war and it had been goin' on for oh so long. People were laughing at the government and these idiots were there to persuade us to join in and fight for an unseen enemy which nobody had a clue about. So I came at them with some more of my own. I was like "so we're all supposed to believe this because the media is telling us and what the government is telling us?" and they were really angry that I questioned them. So they were like "this is a real threat to our peace as a nation and to the world and we must act now."

Christopher and I just looked at each other and laughed because we knew it was hopeless. Needless to say that they didn't have many recruits signing up. It was the first for our generation: we were being told to believe in something that we all knew was bullcrap. We were raised to believe in and be aware of what was happening in the world around us. We loved each other and took care of each other, no matter what and there had never been conflict before in our world. It seemed like the army was living in another world and coming into our world, trying to recruit us at school.

We were the most armed country in the world but nobody knew why. Of course, they had to just use their weapons otherwise it would have been a great waste of their money. I didn't know anyone of our generation who wanted to harm or maim or kill anyone. Sure, the world wasn't perfect and every country had its problems with their people but not enough to wage war on each other. From what we learned in school, there hadn't been any more conflict in the world since the 90s. So why were we even arming our military? Christopher told me it was just to pay for people to stay in jobs in the military.

I said to Christopher that we were being challenged to change our ways to suit the government and he agreed, like many of us did. It just made no goddamn sense. So we spent the day talking about this and that and he took me to lunch and we got together so easily. Everything was so easy. In a couple of months after dating, we started getting serious. It wasn't too long before we both left school and I had gotten pregnant.

Christopher's father was not happy with him, of course. He wanted Christopher to follow in his footsteps and start a career in the world of finance, as an accountant, like him. But Christopher said he would be able to provide for his family in a more humble existence. Money wasn't important for him, he said.

But his father invited Christopher to his place of work, to show him what it was like, hoping Christopher would change his mind. There were lots of different avenues of work that Christopher could get involved in but Christopher didn't like the idea of being confined to an office and chose not to follow in his father's footsteps. His father said that Christopher was free to choose what he wanted to and it was just his job to guide him, that was all. Christopher thought it was sweet of his father to try and direct him and so did I. But Christopher was right, money isn't everything. Then, he started his mission, which later grew into the church we have now.

When we both graduated school, Christopher and I both got jobs. I started working full time in a nursery after getting my childcare diploma and Christopher started working at the local printing firm, where he soon became an assistant manager. We moved to his parents' home in Sandy Springs for a while, while I was pregnant, and whilst we saved up for our own place. When we eventually moved out, we never stopped seeing his parents. They would stop by often and we would cook and they loved seeing their granddaughter and it was all so lovely. Christopher became a good provider for his family and he always made us feel safe. Life seemed to shift so effortlessly from school to adulthood.

I gave up work to look after our child but returned full-time when she was in school full-time. I was going crazy being stuck in all day so it was a relief when I applied for a job at the local grocery store and I was accepted. It wasn't much but it gave me a chance to get out and meet people and get more connected with the world, as they say. Chris supported me with my choices. He was a credit to his parents and they too were proud of him, despite the choices that he made.

Well, Justin, Brandon and Josh were always coming over, of course. Josh became the spiritual leader of his group of missionaries who went around to promote the church. We all became motivated to change the world and it was an exciting time. The church became very successful very quickly. We wanted to remind people of who they were and why we came into this world. I say *we* but it was really Christopher behind it all. His ministries were really about teaching us all of our collective responsibility to love each other and to take care of our planet. It was something that was already in the public consciousness, it was something that people were already doing but he set about reminding people of that.

That's what Christopher became afraid of - he said he didn't want to bring up a child in a world that was built on divisions. He said he would do anything to keep the world as it is and that's why he started the church and I suppose many people could feel the shift in attitudes that was taking place, the shift in consciousness he would say. He would often say that he was put on this earth for a reason, that we all were, and he needed to fulfil his destiny.

Chapter 64

"Sometimes in life, you just do what you have to in order to survive and other times you just do it because you do not know anything else. I joined the military because I was bred into it and it was expected of me to breed future generations of soldiers to feed the machine. There is nothing to rationalize or legitimize or draw any conclusions from. It is what it is. We all have our part to play in life, that's what I was told. *A conscience is for people who don't believe in themselves*, is what I was raised to believe."

"I first got involved with the secret military experiments when I had just turned 3. That was entirely due to Dr. Green. He was a father to many children in the Montauk military base where secret experiments were being carried. There was Project Monarch, which was really about getting mind-controlled subjects to perform certain functions, one of them being to create super soldiers out of them. Project Pegasus was aimed at creating time travel and accessing different timelines. I became involved in both, starting with Project Monarch."

"I was a child when Dr. Green started introducing us to the experiments. My job as a child was to remote-view aspects of secret operations that were being done by scaring us into doing something that went beyond the realms of what you might call possibility. We are capable of a lot more than most people who are raised are taught. Most of humanity are taught limitation, from cradle to grave, but the truth is that we are capable of infinite possibilities."

"I was raised on a military base so we moved around a lot. My mother was very absent in my upbringing, as I was mostly confined to the military bases and under the guidance and instruction of Dr. Green. Most days were spent under observation of various doctors, performing various tasks, interacting with the other children then sleeping in our quarters. As we got older, we were trained on how to behave and function in relationships with civilians, in marriages, where we were expected to become the heads of our households, as we continued to work in the military and get our children, our sons, involved in the military to continue the line of work that we had been brought up and raised in."

"We were raised with that sense of purpose and we were proud of it because we had seen how much of the privileges that we were being afforded as part of a super-elite group in the military. We were chosen by our lineage, it was our birthright to be part of something not many of us would ever become."

"The first experiments that I was involved in were really about getting out of my subconscious mind to be able to perceive from higher states of consciousness. This started early on in my childhood, where we were put in cages and exposed to stimuli which would scare us. As we were in a state of shock, we would be trained to perform several functions. Those functions started off very mild and innocuous but then they developed to the more challenging and arduous. One of the initial functions that we had to perform was to try and predict world events. Then we moved onto trying to guess the outcome of something more immediate, like predicting the lottery numbers or predicting the final score of a football game."

"We were being trained in our ability to function psychically. This was of importance to the military because it allowed the military to gain an angle on military operations, especially Project Pegasus. As we got older, we were also required to fulfil our physical functions as super soldiers which mostly involved combat training, despite its limited use. Some of the super soldiers ended up going on exo-planet missions, so they were very well equipped to survive off-planet."

"One of the most important cases that I got involved with was in Project Monarch, when I started being trained to remote-view. It's essentially a process where I would be shocked into a state where I would fall into a deep sleep and I would be instructed to leave my body and to go to another room and move an object over there. After a while of being able to do that, I was able to leave my body and go to specific places in other buildings. I was flown around the world, especially to Moscow, so that I could remote view secret documents in the Kremlin and the work that the KGB were doing."

"It was during the first Gulf war when the military learned of Saddam's capabilities. Weapons of mass destruction had nothing to do with it. Saddam had stolen the Looking Glass technology from the American secret military, who were working to activate stargates. Saddam had stolen the technology in order to use it for his purposes and to alter the timelines of humanity, in order to serve his needs. That was what was meant by weapons of mass destruction. Not bombs."

"He was to become the ruler of the world which was just unimaginable a concept to bear and he was going to do that using a stargate that he had found buried under the Great Ziggurat of Ur. He was working on activating the technology and he had already sent some of his army through. The only problem he had was retrieving his army, getting them back to our timeline. He kept losing his army but, over time, they were returning, with new knowledge, and he was beginning to use that knowledge, to try and see what effect his actions would have on the future of humanity. Every time he altered something in his own country, such as killing the Kurdish population in his own country, he would send someone to find out what the future of his country looked like."

"After my involvement with Project Monarch ended, Dr. Green moved me onto Project Pegasus and this took place in Montauk, in the 1980s, when I was still young, under 10 years old. They had just finished back- engineering their first stargate which served as a portal into several different dimensions. There were bleed-throughs happening all the time back then, and several different beings from different dimensions were able to come through to this reality and it was often a problem to try and deal with them. An alien being once came through to this reality and he was kept captive. The being itself was from a different part of the galaxy and it took on a praying mantis-like appearance. It was from the grey species but it had long arms and it had an arched posture. It was immediately captured and placed in an isolation tank but it didn't last long in our atmosphere."

"If you notice in the world, especially in the turn of the last century, the amounts of conflicts and wars have increased. Well they did not happen by accident. They were mostly engineered and certain alien races, who have been on this planet for eons, had brokered deals with governments throughout the ages to exchange the sacrifice of human flesh for power. How do you think Hitler got to power so quickly? He did deals with extra-dimensional entities through occult rituals which enabled them to gain knowledge at a very advanced rate."

"Our mission at Montauk was to see what, if possible, we could do to alter the history of humanity. The problem we found was that, when we jumped through, at every new opening in time, we saw that there were a multitude of timelines that were open to humanity because the universe itself exists in multiple dimensions. Simply going to another place in time and trying to affect it didn't work because it all lay in the will of the people on the planet at the time."

"That is why politicians over time have acted to galvanize their people into thinking and behaving in a certain way. It is the people who make the difference, not an individual. This is something that Saddam did simply not understand. He may well have gone back in time to become King Nebuchadnezzar, to try and become powerful in the present day but he always returned to found little would change. He just wasn't able to affect the course of humanity individually."

"That is why, over the course of humanity, every leader in every nation has depended on the will and support of the people. History cannot be altered individually but you can manipulate humanity to alter history. That is why, after 9/11, the media and politicians worked tirelessly to expose a supposed threat from Saddam because that was the most pivotal time to seize back control of what he had stolen."

"When I travelled through time, I was able to observe the true history of humanity and, believe me when I say this, it is absolutely and fundamentally different to everything you have been taught nor could ever imagine. The Ancient Egyptians are the closest well-known examples of an ancient civilization who were not from this earth, but look at the imprint they left on our consciousness. But what we have been taught about them and how the pyramids were built is completely wrong. Laughably wrong. The military experiments I was involved with showed me what the Ancient Egyptians were like, how they lived and even how they sounded."

"We also went back in time millions of years, when there were no humans on this planet. Earth then existed on a different frequency as it does now because it was mainly made up of vegetation. The dinosaurs themselves were created by various alien species, who used them as an experiment before destroying them. In the military projects, we would often laugh in hysterics at some of the theories that had been canonized in science by supposedly 'intelligent' scientists."

"We also travelled in time to see a world without religions and it was chaotic. People then lived relatively in more conflict than they did now. Religions were created for that purpose. To keep humanity easily conditioned and manipulated to suit the will and needs of the ruling classes, who are in turn manipulated and controlled by forces outside of their control. What this all means is simply this. The two elements of evil and goodness are actually part of something that, in the universe, can be explained as positive and negative, light and dark, or service to others or service to self. Service to self is what is traditionally associated with evil and of being of the Devil, especially in the three major Abrahamic religions. Service to others is what those major religions would call being good, which is really the tenants of the Bible."

"As the human race is actually a created species, a slave species, we all perform some sort of function on Earth. This is the same as every other species in the Universe. On an individual level, we all have a function to serve a greater purpose. On a collective level, we were created to serve a master, a God, if you will. Project Pegasus actually taught me that every different apparent race in this world is actually a created species through constant interaction with various alien species spanning millennia, who have systematically worked to create various different races of humans by mixing DNA with theirs. The theory of evolution is just that, a theory.

There is no explanation for the variety of various different races that currently exist on planet Earth."

"But now is our time to teach the people. Knowing what I know, I can guide the people with our church," I said to Jessica, ending my history lesson with her.

"But are you seriously going to think they are ready to believe you?" asked Jessica.

"After everything I have seen, no. But that's the reason we are here today, Jessica. I jumped through that stargate, Jessica, and I rewrote my history. Our history," I said.

"Who else can testify to what you're telling me, Christopher?" asked Jessica, as she sat on the sofa, with our baby in her arms.

"Justin, Brandon and Josh. They were there," I replied. Then, I hesitated and said "and my Dad."

"What was your Dad doing in Iraq? Isn't he an accountant?" asked Jessica.

"When I jumped through, I was able to recreate the world I wanted and that's what I chose for Dad. And that's why I was chosen. To recreate the world. *I* was the Key of En.Ki. The Key of En.Ki wasn't the stargate. I was it. All of this...Jessica....I'm sorry. I'll stop," I said.

"No, go on, honey, you can tell me anything," she said.

But I stopped, I wasn't able to confront her with the truth. She would go on later, to ask Justin, Brandon and Christopher for their account but she never asked my Dad. Something stopped her. It must have been out of fear or not knowing how to broach the subject. After I came back out of the stargate, and returned to this timeline, the timeline I put us all on now, and saw my buddies and Dad, all of us made a pact: that we would never speak about what had happened. Dad returned to Sandy Springs and retired from the NSA and started a small investment firm with a bunch of others he could find, after debriefing them, who were desperately unhappy in the secret military operations and were desperate to leave. They set up shop as the timelines changed and never spoke about what happened in Iraq again. He erased every physical evidence of having been in the military and Mom was never the wiser.

But I never could bring myself to tell Jessica that I raised her and our baby from the dead, that she was a figment of my imagination, essentially created from atoms through a stargate, which I configured based on my conscious projection. She and our daughter were the only hope I had of a normal life, after everything I had been through and I asked God for forgiveness. If the truth about her own existence ever came to light, she would have gone near crazy.

So we started to grow our church and bring small changes to Sandy Springs. The old lady in black started to attend too and she was full of joy and she looked young again. She told us the church gave her a new lease of life and soon her daughter joined too. I was anxious at first, when she first showed up, but after our first meeting, she returned and was soon leading sermons and drawing in the crowds. I began to speak to her daughter and when I asked her about babysitting me back when I was young, she drew a blank. She said she never had and I must have had her confused with someone else. I slept well that night, knowing that my new life in Sandy Springs was going to be alright.

The stargate in the Ziggurat was eventually destroyed. We all returned, including Dad, with some munitions, after the dust had settled, a few hours after we had regrouped at base and the timelines started to shift and the forces were retreating. Dad made us all promise that it all ended there, that nobody was to speak of what they saw, if they ever wanted to live a happy life.

He saw exactly what was going on around us there in Baghdad, how two different realities, planes of existence were converging, after I had returned from my jump. He had planned for this contingency and saw the fallout of it in the experiments. We took his lead and he detonated the stargate. The blast blew a hole in the side of the Ziggurat and the roof began to cave in. We managed to escape within an inch of our lives. Everything about the past and the wrong timeline that humanity was placed on was buried that day, under the Ziggurat.

By the time we got back home, the news was no longer reporting on an invasion. Nor Saddam or Osama for that matter. They weren't in our consciousness anymore. Over time, the news reported on fewer conflicts around the world but the threat was still there. The military industrial complex was still pulling the strings on the media, getting them to run stories on the threat to our way of life. But those voices became subdued over time. Over time, we all adjusted to the new timeline and, over time, we created a new reality, just by simply focusing on the present and starting each day afresh in our new world.

Justin, Josh, Brandon, Jessica and our daughter all sat on the porch of our new home, in Sandy Springs, with the sun setting on a summer's day. Mom and Dad had just dropped off some food for all of us - her honey roasted chicken, cornbread, biscuits and gravy and sweet potato pie. Mom and Dad couldn't stay to eat with us - they had to go and preach to the congregation. We all sat and ate on the porch and our daughter played on the floor, with her new toy set, on her new discovery mat. We all joked about who was going to be next, to get married and start families. Justin and Brandon had started to court and had already taken their girlfriends to visit their moms, who were unlike anything like I remembered them. Loving, like real moms should be. Josh had moved back in with his mom so his courting days were on hold for the moment.

We cleared up and settled in for the evening and the sun began to set, around 10 pm, and the boys decided to stay the night. I put our daughter to bed upstairs, in our 3 bedroom home, in Sandy Springs. I could hear the fellas chatting downstairs, as the TV blared a little. My heart was complete. I was filled with joy. I looked out the window of our daughter's room and stared at the wonderful world that I had created. Occasionally, I would think about the bleed-throughs from the experiments, when events would come through and cross different timelines but I never gave it much thought. From what I had been taught, every thought I emitted would be the reality I would experience. So, I learnt to always be in the moment. It's what we taught our congregation. Create from the moment.

I closed the door to our baby daughter's room and thanked God for the world I was able to experience. I thought about Leah, how she might be experiencing her world, what her world might look like. I was forbidden from contacting her. Dad said it wouldn't be wise. It could make things a lot worse for her. Just knowing that her family and her country were safe was enough for me. Saddam was no longer a threat and he had retreated out of the world stage. I often said a prayer for Leah and her family. Maybe in time, I might get to see her but it was okay if I didn't. If ever I felt unsure about the world, about our own safety, I didn't need to. The stargate had been destroyed and the other stargates could not be found in Iraq.

As I walked downstairs, I put my hand in the old khakis that I was wearing, from our tour of Iraq, which I hadn't worn since we returned, and I felt a metallic pen-like object in my pocket. I tugged at the object, digging deep. I took out one, around an inch-long, and looked at it. I felt another and removed it. They were black round cylinders, which I thought were screws. I held them to the light above me on the landing and I saw what could change our history if they got into the wrong hands. The missing cylinder seals.

THE END